After leaving school at 15, Desmond  doing short-term jobs in various citie Devon General bus company as a c Paignton, Brixham, Newton Abbott a

Two years later he left Devon a Company as a conductor, working on c ̲ ̲ ̲es qualified as a driver and spent a number of years up in the cab. This was during the period of the colour bar, when the bus company was refusing to hire black or Asian workers, and the subsequent black boycott of the buses. Des saw the gradual disappearance of open-back buses, the introduction of front-entrance buses, the first black and Asian crews, and the first one-man operated services.

He later worked for the Ribble bus company in the North West, and Western Scottish, running from Carlisle up to Glasgow.

After leaving the buses, Des spent ten years working on various RAF stations supplying spare parts to front line aircraft. He then moved to Whitehaven to work with mentally and physically disabled young-sters, before returning to Bristol and spending fifteen years working with troubled teenagers.

Des ended his working life as part of the Visitor Services Team at Bristol Museum and Art Gallery. He has been married for forty-five years and has two children and three grandchildren.

BRING
ON THE
BLACKS

DESMOND WARD

SilverWood

Published in 2017 by SilverWood Books

SilverWood Books Ltd
14 Small Street, Bristol, BS1 1DE, United Kingdom
www.silverwoodbooks.co.uk

ISBN 978-1-78132-593-3 (paperback)
ISBN 978-1-78132-594-0 (ebook)

British Library Cataloguing in Publication Data
A CIP catalogue record for this book is available from the British Library

Page design and typesetting by SilverWood Books
Printed on responsibly sourced paper

INTRODUCTION

For those who do not know it, Bristol is a city of some half a million inhabitants, situated not far from the sea in the south-west of England. Cleaved in half by the great gorge of the River Avon, the city has always been economically and culturally among the most important of the nation.

The River Avon, straddled by Brunel's great Suspension Bridge, leads downstream to the Atlantic Ocean and upstream to the city, and it is here in the old docks that tall sailing ships once moored, preparing for long voyages to distant lands.

But today's pleasant and peaceful ambience of the docks hides a brutal and shameful past. Between the seventeenth and nineteenth centuries over two thousand ships left Bristol to make the journey to Africa, from where, with a 'cargo' of captured black Africans, who were chained in the fetid darkness of the holds, the ships would sail onwards across the Atlantic. As many as 500,000 slaves endured these overcrowded, unhealthy and harsh conditions. Those who survived the voyages were sold into brutal slavery in America.

That was in the past, but this story starts in the balmy autumnal days of 1962 when black men and women were still being ill-treated and discriminated against.

CHAPTER 1

The city lay calm that morning. Even the feral foxes which roamed the gardens and squares of that ancient part of the city were silent. Down on the river basin, not a boat stirred.

Dabber, sitting alone in his dingy bedsit in the very early hours of that autumn morning, did not feel easy. His mind was troubled as he thought how easily his youthful innocence was being stripped away in his new job, where he found himself working with men and women who thought it all right to bawl narrow-minded and prejudiced opinions without regard to the hurt they might cause. They were only a few, these bigoted men and women, among the large workforce, but Dabber had to work with them every day and at times he found their words intolerable.

The worst of them was Ratso. That was not his real name, of course; just a nickname his workmates had given him because of his sallow, narrow face. Ratso had a never-ending supply of nasty remarks about anything and everything, but especially about black people.

Anyone with any conscience would surely challenge bigots like Ratso, Dabber thought. He was young and new and not sure if he would have the courage, but he had decided that today was the day that he was going to speak out.

While Dabber sat brooding, downstairs in her basement flat, the landlady of that house of cheap bedsitters, middle-aged Mrs Amy Racks, was sitting slouched in her armchair, her chin on her chest and her eyes half-closed. Beside her on a dilapidated wooden table stood a half-empty bottle of sherry and a grimy glass.

The dull tick of a 1930s-style clock on the mantelpiece seemed to mock her as it ticked its interminable hours away. From time to time Mrs Racks stirred, groped for the bottle and took a swig, before reaching sideways and fumbling the bottle back onto the table. Her head drooped.

Dabber, still upstairs, was due on duty for his shift at 5am. It was already 4.15, but he had not even started to dress.

Downstairs, Mrs Racks sat snoozing for several more minutes with her head on her chest before she slowly came to and gazed blankly around. She rose unsteadily to her feet, wobbled across the threadbare carpet to the window and pulled aside the ragged net curtain. The slimy-green brick wall filling her view seemed to press in on her like some claustrophobic nightmare.

After a short time she stumbled back to her armchair, slumped down and reached for the sherry bottle again.

Upstairs, Dabber, still deep in thought, suddenly came to with a jerk and looked at the clock. Then he was out of the armchair fast and dragging on his uniform. He hurried to the cracked mirror, slapped some gel onto his jet-black hair, dragged a comb through it and carefully slicked it back in the latest style. His sharp dark eyes scanned around quickly to ensure he had not forgotten anything. He took a last look in the mirror and then within minutes of leaving the armchair he was out of the door and racing along the cold, empty street as fast as his twenty-year-old legs could carry him. His depot at Winterstoke Road was over a mile from his bedsitter and he could not afford to be late.

So with his bus conductor's coat flapping and his cash bag flying, Dabber raced down steep Granby Hill, across the narrow wooden footbridges of the basin, and rushed on again round the back of the great tobacco bonds whose ugly russet warehouses reached up several storeys high. Dabber grabbed a breather there and gazed up at the twin reinforced, super-protected edifices. They were stacked full of tobacco destined for the huge Wills factories, where machines raced and thundered day and night, spitting out two thousand cigarettes a minute. Dabber often wondered how much tobacco had once come into the city's warehouses as a result of the brutal treatment of slaves on the plantations of America and the Caribbean many years before.

In those days a lot of Bristol families had accumulated great wealth through profits they had made from dealings in slavery-produced sugar and tobacco.

The young bus conductor took a last glance up at the warehouses and then it was a final dash across the dark Greville Smyth Park to the depot.

When Dabber rushed into the signing-on room it was already noisy and hectic as crews rushed around, busy with all the things that were necessary before their buses went on the road: conductors talking, jostling, grabbing ticket machines, filling in waybills and checking change money; while drivers stood around harrying their conductors, checking duty cards, routes and running times. The foreman, Quade, was there as usual, standing importantly, pot-bellied and red-faced, behind the counter with his pencil and rubber and his big sheets showing duty numbers, bus numbers and times. Quade pored over and nurtured his sheet like a mother with a newborn baby, his eyes flicking constantly to the wall where a big round-faced clock ticked remorselessly. The foreman's one aim in life was to get those buses out on time. He looked at Dabber when the conductor rushed in.

"Second six," Dabber said, and Quade carefully and meticulously ticked the 'conductor box' on his big sheet against the entries for the crew of the second number six bus.

"Your driver's Ratso – he's already here," said Quade. "I got a driver and conductor for once. I'll be able to get that second six out on the road today. Couldn't get the bugger out yesterday – no crew."

"Yeah," said Dabber, "everybody's fed up with all these buses off. The buses that do run get stacked out with extra passengers and they get all the complaints from people that's been waiting."

"I know all that and there ain't nothing I can do about it," Quade said. He swept his hand over his sheet. "Look at this – two buses off the road already, and it ain't even five o'clock. I mean, it don't bear looking at. There just isn't enough staff."

"I don't know why they don't take on black drivers and conductors," said Dabber. "There's plenty want a job on the buses."

"The company won't hire them. That's the management for you," said Quade. "*They* put this colour bar on. We just got to put up with it."

"It would make it easier for everybody if the colour bar was dropped," said Dabber. "Why don't they just take black people on? I mean, what's wrong with 'em?"

He pulled his conductor's box for the second six bus out of the rack and went to the counter at the back of the room.

Ratso, who had been loitering about and listening, sidled up to Dabber and said in a whiny voice, "What the hell you want blacks on the job for, you stupid bugger? Get them on the job they'll be all over the goddamn place. Job'll be knackered."

"It wouldn't bother me," said Dabber.

"You ain't been on the job five minutes and you think you know it all," said Ratso.

"How long I been on the job has got nothing to do with it. I'm just saying I got no objection if blacks come on the job," said Dabber.

"You don't know what you're talking about, mate," said Ratso. "You got no idea about blacks."

Dabber dragged his fingers through his black, well-greased hair and gave him an easy smile. "Yeah, well, it wouldn't bother me if they came on the job," he said.

"It's attitudes like that don't help the situation," said Ratso. "I'm your driver today and I don't want you coming out with a load of your namby-pamby stuff."

"I'm entitled to my opinion. Everybody's entitled to an opinion, aren't they?" said Dabber.

"Just hurry the hell up with that waybill, will ya? We're gonna be down the pan," said Ratso. He grabbed the duty card and marched, furious-faced, out of the door, leaving Dabber scrambling to collect his box and waybill and rush after him.

Open-backed double-decker 8028 was there among dozens of other buses in the darkness of the garage. Ratso started the engine, switched on the lights and they were off with a jerk, all lit up like a fairground ride, with rising revs shaking every panel and an explosion of crackles from the exhaust as Ratso, in his temper, wrenched the gear lever this way and that, trying to whip the double-decker to go faster.

The bus was rocking and swaying so much that Dabber's pen was all over the place as he struggled to put the starting figures down on his waybill. He slung his Setright ticket machine over his shoulder, checked there was an adequate ticket roll in it, adjusted his cash bag and then the first passengers were piling on, irate and grumbling because the bus was late, and if they were late into work they would lose pay. At each stop, *slam*, Ratso hit the brakes hard and more passengers piled on; *bang*, up into second gear and yet more passengers, with Dabber staggering about the aisle as he tried to collect fares. *Bang*, into third and they were almost full; *bang* again, up into top, a short period of turbo-like acceleration and then *slam*, Ratso hit the brakes again and it was into another stop.

It was pell-mell then all the way into the city centre. There were crowds at all the stops, and then near the Salvation Army hostel a man, slightly the worse with drink, pulled himself with difficulty onto the platform. He was all ragged and grimy and as he tried to orient himself he gazed at Dabber with bleary, watery eyes. He tried to pull himself up the stairs, but the effort was too much and he slid back to the platform again, calloused hands sliding down the rails.

On the platform, he wobbled about and went, "Whhrrraag, aaahrrgh," from deep down in his throat, and then he suddenly pushed his filthy, unshaven face within an inch of Dabber's with a fug of alcoholic breath which caused the conductor to reel back. The drunk tried then to get into the lower deck. He grasped the sides of the entrance for dear life with both hands and one foot pawed the air like a pantomime horse while he tried to locate the step.

Dabber gave him a push up and the ragged fellow banged and ricocheted drunkenly from seat to seat, looking for a vacant one. Every so often he anxiously checked the big brown bottle in the pocket of his tattered old coat, scared to death that all the banging about might crack it and his treasured scrumpy might seep away down his piss-stained trousers.

The people sitting down were all shifting about, spreading out and gazing fixedly out of the windows so as not to catch his eye, and some of the workers, anxious to get to their workplaces to make their big pay packets, were shouting, "What the hell? Drunk at this time of the morning! Get 'im off, conductor."

Ratso, up in the cab, was looking back, furious at the delay. Dabber gave him the double starting bell fast and the driver's head flew round once more to face the bleak Cheltenham Road ahead. At the same time he banged back the stick and his boot crushed the gas pedal to the floor.

The clutch pedal slammed up, the bus took off with a jerk, and the old drunk staggered and then collapsed in a dirty, smelly heap onto a well-dressed woman who squealed, "Oh, my goodness."

All the weary, downtrodden workers thought it was funny because she was posh, and they went, "Hah-hah-hah, heh-heh," but she glared at them and they looked away quickly.

Ratso was crouched over the wheel, pulling the gear stick furiously this way and that, trying to make up time and no doubt cursing the stops and the waiting passengers and the whole damn setup. Through the glass partition behind the driver's cab, Dabber could just see Ratso's left arm moving, whacking the gear lever in all directions. Dabber made sure that he was fast on the bell with the starting signals, so that by the time the bus reached the terminus, the load was light, they were back on time and the driver had recovered his composure.

By this time the drunken passenger was sprawled over a seat, dead to the world, so Dabber and Ratso carried him off and laid him on a patch of grassland.

Ratso growled, "Bloody disgusting, the state he's in. Just leave the bastard there." But Dabber was concerned for the man, so pulled him up and arranged him sitting up with his back against a wall so that he was as comfortable as possible. He put the man's bottle on the ground beside him, where he would see it when he woke up and be happy that he hadn't lost it.

Ratso was watching with a scowl on his face. "More of your bloody namby-pamby stuff," he said. "Your trouble, mate, is you're too much of a do-gooder. You think a drunk bugger like that is gonna thank you for helping him? Or them goddamn blacks you're so keen on, f'r instance.

The frigging country's gonna be full o' blacks if the likes of you get their way."

Dabber did not reply.

And then it was back down the Gloucester Road with Ratso's driving reflecting his fury at the sludge of traffic slowing their progress in the peak of the rush hour. The bus was packed out and Dabber took fares, whirled the dials of his ticket machine and whipped tickets off fast. They ran out to Hartcliffe then, with the route quieter, but coming back in it was approaching 8.30: school time and office worker time. It was rowdy and noisy then on the upper deck, with school kids shouting and messing around, but on the bottom deck it was a lot quieter, the passengers pensive or reading newspapers. Dabber and Ratso ran the bus into Old Market smack on time to hand over to a new crew and then they headed down into the busmen's canteen in Carey's Lane for a spot of breakfast.

The canteen was crowded with drivers and conductors, and what a subterranean hellhole it was. The canteen was reached by descending a flight of steps, which over the years had worn down to strange topographic shapes under the feet of countless busmen and women. Then you had to pass the stinking toilet, and beyond that was the canteen, a squalid, windowless room with ageing wooden tables and chairs.

Long-bladed fans dangled from the brown ceiling, turning and rocking incessantly. The walls, nicotine-yellow with age and tobacco smoke, oozed a film of dirty moisture. Little black flies flitted everywhere. And all around, in this depressing basement, men and women – the bus crews – were eating, drinking, talking, thinking, arguing; the flotsam and jetsam of the working world. There were young ones: eager, keen and fresh; and older ones: washed-up, knackered and almost finished as human beings, but all living and working to serve the travelling public of the city of Bristol.

Dabber's driver, Ratso, went over to join a card school while Dabber sat down with his plate of fry-up with a group of drivers and conductors from various depots at the next table.

One driver, a ruddy-faced character with sideburns, was saying,

"I been stacked out all morning, man – running with a bus off in front, passengers moaning...I mean, this shortage of staff, how long's it gonna go on?"

"It'll go on as long as the colour bar's on," said Dabber. "Why don't the company want black people or Asians on the job? Anybody know?"

"Why don't they want blacks? It's because they don't want 'em. That's the reason, pure and simple," said a driver with a bony, almost bald skull.

"Yeah, but why? That's what I can't work out," said Dabber.

"They'd drag the job down, mate," said Skully, his bony head glistening and a sullen look on his face.

"How would they drag the job down?" said Dabber.

"They wouldn't do the job right. They'd lower the tone of it," said Skully.

"How would black people lower the tone of the job?" said Dabber.

"Well, they'd be down 'ere talking a load of gibberish," said Skully. "And the passengers, they ain't going to like it, taking change and tickets from black hands."

"It wouldn't bother the passengers," said Dabber. "People would just want a bus running, even with a black conductor or driver, rather than a bus that's off the road."

Ratso, from his card game at an adjoining table, leaned over and said to Dabber, "I told you before about coming out with a load of namby-pamby stuff. When are you gonna get it into your stupid head that nobody wants them blacks on the buses?"

"It wouldn't bother me," Dabber said, "an' it might happen sooner than you think. There's a few of 'em been talking about starting a boy-cott, refusing to ride on the buses."

"Refusing to ride on the buses? Well, that'll suit me. The less I see of them blacks the better," said Ratso.

"Black people are as good as anybody," said Dabber. "Nobody with any decency in them could object to black people."

"What you wanna do, mate," said Ratso, "is go off to Africa or wherever and live with 'em in the jungle. You'd be happy then, I suppose."

13

"None of them that want a job on the buses live in Africa or in the jungle," said Dabber. "You just look at black people and judge them by the colour of their skin, but they're ordinary human beings, just like us."

"But they ain't British, are they?" said Ratso with a sneer.

"Of course they're British," said Dabber. "Most of 'em were born here and they've lived here all their lives. There's been black people in Bristol for hundreds of years."

"You don't know what you're talking about," said Ratso.

There was an awkward silence then, before it was time for Dabber and his driver to head out into the tumultuous streets again to take over another bus for the second half of the shift. It was quieter then, the rush hour being over, but Ratso's driving was full of jerky acceleration and harsh braking as if the thought of the possibility of black staff coming on the job was still playing on his mind. However, passengers were few and Dabber had time to think about his girlfriend, eighteen-year-old Melody with her long legs and her auburn hair, whose behaviour recently had become so mysterious and troublesome.

At one in the afternoon when his shift finished Dabber slung his takings into the safe in the bus office on Carey's Lane and then hurried across the road to the White Hart. The pub was almost empty: there was just Tubs, the tubby and cheery-faced landlord, polishing glasses, and sitting on a stool up at the counter, Melody.

Dabber looked at her, entranced as he always was by her soft cheeks, even white teeth and long, immaculately brushed auburn hair. A coquettish and alluring demeanour combined with her deep brown eyes gave her a mysterious aura, as if there was something about her which she was not yet ready to reveal. Her low-cut cotton blouse and short skirt revealed that she had caught the last of the summer's sun on the tops of her breasts and her legs.

As Dabber entered, the barman said, "Come on, Dabber. Where you been? She's been waiting ten minutes for you."

"Yeah, where you been, you bugger?" said Melody.

"Hey, I've been slaving away since five o'clock this morning, sweat pouring off me. I'm here now, so just get the drinks up quick. The usual. I'm desperate for a bit of alcohol," said Dabber. He grabbed Melody playfully, swung her round and kissed her.

He carried the drinks over to a table at the back of the pub. When they had settled, he said, "So what's new?"

"Nothing," Melody replied.

"How long you been in?"

"About ten minutes," said Melody, "but if you'd been any longer I wouldn't have been here." She lit a cigarette and slowly blew smoke. "I don't like sitting around in pubs by myself."

"We've just got finished," said Dabber. "Crowds, traffic jams, buses off, passengers moaning. You wouldn't believe the complaints I've had."

"Just the usual stuff, then," said Melody.

They each took a drink. Dabber lit a cigarette for her and one for himself.

"Well," he said, "what you been up to?"

"Nothing much," she said.

"You go out last night?"

"No, stayed in."

"Oh, I thought you might have gone out, seeing as it was a decent night," Dabber said.

"No, just stayed in." Melody took a quick drink and looked away.

They sat in silence for a minute or two.

Dabber said, "It's just, I thought I saw you out. I was on late shift on the sixes and I thought I saw you on the pavement down Bedminster with somebody – a lad."

She looked away again. "No," she said.

There was a long silence.

Dabber said, "Well, forget it anyway. Must have been someone else I saw."

"Yeah, must have been," Melody said.

They both drank silently for a time and Dabber put his arm around her and pulled her close. He was deep in thought when Melody's voice startled him.

"Hey, dreamer, I'm here, remember. If you don't want to talk to me I might as well bloody go."

Dabber came out of his reverie quickly.

"What we going to do now, then?" he said.

"Oh, just mooch around a bit, like we usually do," she said.

They finished up their drinks, went over the road to the Spring Chicken café and fooled about on the pinball machine. Then they took a bus up Whiteladies Road, strolled about on the Downs and looked over the sea walls at the brown river far beneath.

Dabber looked at her and said, "You know, I love you and all that, Melody, but you seem worried and sad sometimes. What's up?"

She didn't reply, just stood silently gazing out over the river.

CHAPTER 2

A good number of the black residents of Bristol, led by a young, intelligent and eloquent black man, had started to boycott the buses while the bus company was still refusing to hire black and Asian workers. The boycott had been running for some time now, and in a house of multiple occupancy in the St Pauls area of Bristol, a group of West Indians was meeting. At first there had been a lot of angry, wild talk, but now the young black man was speaking.

"My friends, now, we all know why we are here," he said. "The Bristol Omnibus Company is still refusing to hire non-white workers, and they have remained stubborn in the face of the boycott which we have started against them. Not a single black or Asian person has yet been hired to work as a driver or conductor. For some time now we black and Asian people have refused to ride on the buses. We must continue our boycott. We will not give the company our money while this dispute continues."

One of the gathered assemblage, a well-built Jamaican man, spoke up: "Those are fine words you speak, my friend, but there are many other ways in which we black people face difficulty in this city. We face insults from white people in the street and in the shops and pubs. It has been like this for many years. Have we made any progress? Are things any better now than ten years ago? I do not think so."

Another member of the audience struggled to his feet. "I am an old man now and I agree with you that we face insults every day," he said. "Do we start boycotts against all who insult us? I think not. One thing at a time is the best way. Many of us here today have African ancestry – we have the heritage of our African forebears in our blood. I remember when the great Freedom Charter was adopted at the Congress of the People in South Africa in 1955. It promised so much, but it is still not being fully implemented." He paused and then went on, "After all this time our people in South Africa *still* struggle, but they will never give up. What I say to you, my friends, is that they are our blood brothers and sisters. Our forebears were black men and women who were cruelly taken as slaves from their native land all those hundred years and more ago. Black men and women and children were made slaves by the white man. We try to forgive him, but still every day the white man never stops trying to get his heel on our neck, not only in Africa, but America and even here in Bristol.

"You ask what it is we must do – we must be patient and all the time struggle." The old man sat down.

Another member of the audience shouted, "Yeah, we know all about struggle – we struggle every day we live, but all we get is, 'You ain't welcome here, you can't go in there, this job not for you, that job not for you, this house ain't for you, blacks not wanted here, no vacancy for blacks, no vacancies, no vacancies.'"

"We all know about that stuff," another young man shouted, "but tell us about the charter, man. I've heard about that South African Charter. Tell us what it's all about."

"Don't rush me, boy," the old man said, struggling to his feet again. "I got to think. My old brain don't work as fast as it used to."

The young man who had first spoken said, "Please take your time, my friend. I too would like to hear about the Freedom Charter. It is some time since I first read it and it would be of great interest to have my memory jogged. Please go ahead."

The elderly Jamaican took a sip of water, thought for several seconds and then went on. "All of us here, my friends, know about apartheid in South Africa. In that country four million white people have got their feet on the necks of twenty million black people. Now those proud black African people, they started a movement to try to free themselves from the heel of the white man. They just had enough of being downtrodden and oppressed, so the leaders met in 1955, 26th June 1955, my memory tells me, and they made the great Freedom Charter."

The old man took another drink from the glass in front of him. "Course, I not got the charter memorised every word. I do not carry a copy around in my pocket," he said, to some chuckles from the audience, "but I can give you some main points, as my old memory remembers them. First, it demands equal rights for all people, whatever colour they be. It say that black people been robbed of their peace of mind by injustice and inequality and it call on all citizens to live like brothers and get on well together."

The speaker paused and took another drink from his glass. He wiped his lips with a pocket handkerchief and then continued. "The charter also say everybody, black or white, should be free to take any job."

An agitated young man in the audience jumped up and shouted, "Yes, that is exactly what we campaigning about now – to take any job we like. We got as much right to jobs on the buses as any white person. What else the charter say?"

The old man chuckled. "You think I am some sort of memory man? You is taxing my old brain now. One of the main things the charter says is that discrimination because you is black is a crime. No one should go about preaching hatred against another person just because they have different colour skin or have different faith or different culture. The charter also say there should be law against insults to anyone just because they is different."

"That charter sounds real good to me," someone in the audience called out. "What else it say?"

The elderly speaker chuckled again. "I cannot think what else it says. My memory is gone."

The young person who had first spoken rose to his feet again. "Thank you for telling us about the Freedom Charter, my friend. What I want to say to you is we all have to strive to improve things, just like our brothers in South Africa and many other places are striving. The bus boycott is our first tactic here in Bristol, but what we need to do is to push our case against the bus company a little harder, and I am suggesting that a march in addition to our boycott would bring our campaign into greater public view."

One of the audience, a tall, powerfully built man in his late twenties or early thirties, rose to his feet and shouted, "Marching about is not going to do much good. We got to do something more. We got to strike a blow."

The young speaker at the front said, "I hope you are not thinking about violence. Violence is not the way forward. You might think, do us black people not have enough reason for violence? Yes, possibly we do. But we must learn from the great campaigner, Mahatma Gandhi. He used a non-violent approach—"

The young speaker was interrupted by the powerfully built man, who, half-rising out of his seat and gesturing into the air, cried furiously, "Why you bring up that man? Why you bring up that Gandhi?"

"Why? Why ever not?" responded the young speaker.

"You not know that man was a racist? You not know that Gandhi say that Indians superior to black men in culture? He called us Kaffirs. You not know that?"

The young speaker was stunned into silence for several seconds, and then he went on, "No, I certainly did not know that. If what you say is true then it is new knowledge for me and I will be very grateful that you have enlightened me. However, it was his policy of *Satyagraha*, or passive resistance in order to achieve his aims, which gained him worldwide respect. Gandhi knew that violence would solve nothing. We must not go down that road."

"What? So we just march about and hope that the bus company changes its mind? Man, I tell you that could take twenty years," the muscly man shouted.

"What I am suggesting is that we push our case with marches and speeches in addition to the boycott. We must continue to push our case verbally at every opportunity, but always without violence. Let us do that and see what effect it has."

"And what if it doesn't work? What are we going to do then?" the muscly man called again.

The young speaker replied quietly, "When being reasonable finds no response, then we must find different techniques, but always non-violent techniques. We must use every opportunity to state our case and to push our position, but we must always keep our dignity. The most powerful weapon we have is dignity."

CHAPTER 3

Early shifts! They started between four and five in the morning and long before ordinary workers were stumbling from their beds, the depot was like a human anthill: dozens of drivers and conductors signing on, rushing around, grabbing ticket boxes, scanning duty sheets, talking, shouting, arguing and then out to the great wide garage to find their buses; cab doors slamming, engines blasting, exhausts belching, and the air thick with stinking fumes.

And if a man was more than a few minutes late, then his bus and his day's work would most likely be gone. That's how it was for the 'dippers', the staff who had missed their shift. Their buses would most likely be gone: given to a scheduled spare. No work and no pay then for the man who had dipped. He had the choice of hanging around to see if he could scrounge someone else's duty, or sloping off home again. Those dippers who chose to stay could sit around in the depot canteen sipping horrible lukewarm tea from the vending machine until, if they were lucky, the tannoy would crackle, a name would blare and one of the spares would grunt, "Yeah, that's me. I got a shift," and head out to take on a bus.

The handful of conductors or drivers who were left without any offers of work would then be told to go up to Old Market or the Centre and hang around as unpaid spares in the canteens there.

One morning in the grimy Old Market canteen, a young conductor nicknamed Greasy, who had missed his own shift, was hanging around hoping for some work. Greasy's heavyset face was usually blank, his jaw hanging open, as if his brain was vaguely trying to conjure up something remotely resembling a thought. When he did utter anything it was usually some fanciful ideas about the young women he continually tried to chat up on his bus. At that moment his gormless gaze was directed towards a heavily built, middle-aged and busty conductress who was munching a bacon sandwich at the next table.

"Blimey," he muttered to himself.

The conductress had seen him staring and she scowled to herself. Her peroxide off-blonde hair was piled high in a beehive style, her plump arms were bare, her eyes were tired and her breasts lay heavy inside her half-open blouse. A short, tight skirt strained to cover the tops of her beefy thighs.

"You don't want to go looking at her," said a nearby driver to Greasy. "That's Diamond Lil. She's a tough cow. She'll give you a whack no trouble if you don't watch yourself. They say she nearly gave a passenger a whack round the head last year when she got some cheek from them. I 'eard the depot superintendent called her into the office once to give her a bollocking about her attitude and she threatened to give him a smack round the head as well if he didn't shut up."

"She can't object to somebody looking at her," said Greasy.

"Yeah, but not looking hard like you're looking, mate. I mean, you're staring. She ain't gonna like that."

"I can look at who I want," said Greasy.

"Yeah, but you wanna be careful who you're looking at. Looking at people can lead to big trouble."

"There's no law against looking, is there? Nobody's gonna stop me looking," said Greasy petulantly, and in defiance of the advice he had been given, he recommenced staring, almost leering, at Diamond Lil.

Just then Diamond Lil was racked by a long, rasping coughing session, during which she did not bother to cover her mouth. She slapped the table at the intensity of the coughing attack. When she had recovered she wiped the bacon grease from her mouth with the back of her hand, glared round, took a deep drag of a cigarette, then stood up and casually smoothed herself down. She sauntered over and smacked Greasy round the ear, after which she wandered out in a relaxed manner without a backward glance.

"Blimey," said Greasy, looking after her and rubbing his ear in shock, "what'd she do that for? What the hell did she do that for?"

Nearby busmen were snorting with laughter. One said, "You asked for that, mate. You got away lightly. If you'd been a black in them slave days you'd have been whipped to hell for staring at a white woman."

One lunchtime, a slender young undergraduate with bright, dark eyes and long, wavy brunette hair was preparing to address a gathering of other students in the refectory of Bristol University. She stood there calmly surveying the audience, took her time, then moved forward and raised her hand to quieten the assembled students.

"Good to see you all," she began. "Thank you for coming." She paused slightly. "That was quite a shindig last night, wasn't it? It was up there with the most memorable we've had and I see some of you are still drinking. You have a lot of stamina. Before I go on I'd better introduce myself properly. Most of you will have seen me around. My name is Amaryllis. I'm a third-year student. In my time here I've been on many drinking sessions and enjoyed every one of them, but there is a time in every student's life when he or she must put drinking and shindigs aside, for a time at any rate, and contemplate some of the greater problems which afflict our world today."

She paused again and then went on, "Now I want to talk to you today about the bus company colour bar here in our city. I am sure you all know that the Bristol Omnibus Company is refusing to hire black drivers or conductors. Now, why should us students be concerned or interested in that, you might ask? Well, principally, it is blatant discrimination and also a matter of conscience – we students should be concerned about any case of unfair discrimination." Amaryllis waited a moment while she looked over her audience. "Another reason, which I shall explain more fully shortly," she went on, "concerns the history of the two buildings next door to this refectory: the City Museum and the Wills Memorial Building."

Amaryllis wiped her brow and flicked back her hair, before looking at her audience again. "Now, both those buildings were built as a result of the marvellous philanthropy of the Wills tobacco family – in fact if you have ever looked up you might have noticed the wording engraved in large letters on the front of the museum building. I will tell you what it says: 'The Gift of Sir William Henry Wills, Bart. To his fellow citizens, 1904.' Bear that wording in mind, because it has relevance to the point I am leading up to.

"And then the second building I mentioned, the Wills Memorial Building, which we all know so well. The tall edifice where some of us have lectures and sit our dreaded exams."

She paused a moment and then went on, "Now why on earth are those buildings of relevance to the colour bar imposed by the Bristol Omnibus Company, you might ask? Well, each of those two buildings was given to the city as a result of the generosity of the Wills tobacco family, and it cannot be denied that both of the buildings have been of great cultural and educational benefit to this city, and particularly to us students. But the Wills family were among the foremost beneficiaries of the tobacco trade, and what I want to ask is, did the Wills family at any time profit from slave-produced tobacco? I do not know – I certainly hope not. But when we look up at these buildings and remember the Wills family's great philanthropy I suggest that we should also remember the slaves who for over a hundred years worked and died under brutal conditions on the tobacco plantations."

Amaryllis paused, took a drink and went on. "Now you will all know, I'm sure, that Bristol today has several large tobacco factories. In fact the tobacco trade has always been of crucial importance in the economic growth of this city. It has not, unfortunately, always been a benign trade, though, because, as I have said, for nigh on two hundred years the tobacco which came to this city was produced by the labour of black slaves on the plantations of the Caribbean and America. Bristol played a major part in this trade: hundreds of thousands of black men, women and children were kidnapped from Africa and taken across the Atlantic on Bristol ships to be sold into slavery. No less than two thousand voyages were made by Bristol ships in this foul trade, and many families in this city became very wealthy on the profits."

Amaryllis paused and looked over her audience, but seeing only interested faces, went on. "Now, 150 years after the slave trade ended, and in this very city which houses the great tobacco factories, black people are being mistreated once again. True, they are not slaves, but one Bristol company is denying them a basic human right – the right to employment. That company runs the huge bus fleet of this city – I am referring to the Bristol Omnibus Company. They are openly operating a colour bar and are refusing to hire black or Asian crews."

"That is absolutely disgraceful," shouted a slim student with a ponytail.

Amaryllis paused, took a drink and then said, "Yes, if you want confirmation you only need to notice that not one of the thousands of buses which pass this university has a black driver or conductor – not one. And that is the reason: the bus company will not hire them. Even though the company is desperately short of workers for its buses there is not a single Asian, African or West Indian driver or conductor. The company will only employ white people as crew."

"Then we must do something! We must support the black people," shouted the ponytailed student, and several other students shouted loud, angry support.

"Yes, I absolutely agree with you," said Amaryllis. "Now Zorbo here, who I'm sure a lot of you already know, is giving me support in this campaign. He is now going to say a few words." She motioned to a student of dark-hued countenance beside her.

He stepped forward, paused a moment and then said, "I also am a third-year student and am very pleased that so many of you have turned out today. Students have never liked injustice and have always fought against discrimination. You might say that what has happened in the past cannot be altered, and I agree with you: you cannot alter history. But we can still strive to alter what is happening today. We can help to make sure that black people in our city today are treated in as decent and respectful a way as every other citizen."

Zorbo paused again, and then continued. "How can we do that? Well, Amaryllis and I have a suggestion. Some of our black citizens have already started a campaign against the bus company. Their campaign takes the form of a boycott of the buses. Black people are simply refusing to travel on them, and they are thus depriving the bus company of much-needed revenue.

"The boycott has been organised and is being led by a young black man. He is intelligent, diplomatic and very eloquent. As I have said, his campaign is going well and what I am suggesting is that we join that campaign and also refuse to ride on the buses."

A tousle-haired student jumped to his feet and shouted, "I certainly agree. If what you have described is true, then it is discrimination of the vilest kind and we must certainly do something. I, for one, will not travel on the buses until the bus company introduces a fair and just employment policy."

Amaryllis now stepped forward. "Thank you for your support," she said. "I am sure that most if not all of our students will feel likewise. Zorbo and I decided to call this meeting to see what support there might be among us for this campaign. The fact that so many of you have turned up answers that question."

Zorbo stepped forward again. He took a swig from a bottle of beer and then went on, "Now, just to confirm, are we all agreed then that we join the campaign that the black men and women have already started and refuse to ride on the buses?"

"Yes," came a roar.

Amaryllis came to the fore again. "I will suggest to you what else we should do," she cried. "We must march, we must shout. We must carry banners and picket the bus company." She paused and shouted, "Are we all agreed on that?"

"Yes, yes!" Another great roar was her reply.

"Then let us start now. Let us start by marching down Park Street," called out Amaryllis.

At that most of the students jumped up, filed quickly out of the building into the chill November air and off they went: a powerful, determined, if somewhat ragtag army, marching and swaying down Park Street, some staggering slightly, waving wine and beer bottles, with Amaryllis and Zorbo leading the way, both punching the air.

The students were chanting, "*Ita vero...ita vero...*boycott the buses...*ita vero.*"

The shouts and sight of the students, all bursting with energy, all looking determined on that chilly day, caused people on the pavements to make way for them and mutter, "Good heavens. What on earth are those students up to now? What's that they are chanting, that *eeta* something?"

"They're just showing off with a bit of Latin," an earnest-looking old gentleman murmured. "I think it means 'yes'."

Other people just gazed silently, and a few curious ones, including a drunk with a bottle in his hand, started to trail along behind.

Passing the Horn and Trumpet pub and its smaller neighbour, the Drawbridge, a lot of students looked wistfully at the bleak doors, which were closed for the legally enforced afternoon period of abstinence. Over the entrance of the Horn and Trumpet was a carving of a Native American, his headdress represented by tobacco leaves. The figure was a copy of a sculpture from the paddle steamer *Demerara*, a name synonymous with the British sugar colony where, in 1823, harsh and cruel treatment led to a violent revolt among its twelve thousand slaves.

A few of the students marching in the procession paused for a moment and gazed up at the carving and, who knows, they may have been pondering upon the sad history it represented.

The marchers halted under the clock at the bus company's Centre offices. Immediately Amaryllis turned to face the crowd, held up her hand, waited patiently for silence and then launched into a speech.

"Friends, students, thank you for coming. Lots of people in this city sometimes think that us students do nothing else but hang around, drinking and having parties. Well, we do a little bit of that, I must admit."

There was a ripple of laughter and some hostile comments from the crowd.

Amaryllis continued, "But aside from the parties, we have a serious side – we have a desire to see justice done when decent members of the human race are being unfairly treated." She paused again and then went on, "The reason we are marching today is not for a students' cause – it is because the screws of apartheid are being turned here in this city. In this city, which I am sure we all love, our coloured citizens are suffering many indignities. Among other things they are being denied jobs on the buses merely because of the colour of their skin."

Then Zorbo stepped forward and gestured high into the air.

"Fellow citizens," he called, "we are at least a hundred strong, maybe more. As my fellow, or should I say sister, student has just said, we, the students of Bristol University, will support the black men and women of this city, our fellow citizens, and show the Bristol Omnibus Company what an obnoxious thing its employment policy is."

Amaryllis came to the front again. "The way to hit the bus company is through their daily takings. We, the students, will refuse to ride on the buses. We earnestly hope that the people of Bristol will join us in supporting the boycott which the black people have started."

"You're a fruity little piece," shouted a drunk who was staggering about waving his bottle.

"Let us reiterate what we are here for," Amaryllis continued, ignoring the drunk. "We are here to fight alongside the downtrodden and those who are suffering vile social injustice."

The old wino, who was now sitting slumped against a wall, waved his bottle and slurred, "Vile sosh injus…"

Amaryllis continued, "I want you to listen again now to my fellow student, Zorbo." She gestured to him and he jumped to the front, stood authoritatively and waited for silence.

"Black people are human beings just like everyone else," he shouted. "Everyone has a right to a decent existence, whatever their colour or background or qualities. Many black people would like a job on the buses, but the Bristol Omnibus Company will not give them jobs. Without employment no man has a chance of a decent existence."

"The bastards won't give me a job either," yelled the drunk. He slumped sideways and gazed blankly at the wall.

Zorbo waited a moment and then went on, "Is there any sense of fairness inside us, or are we just hollow shells of human beings? Are we without feelings, without any sense of right or wrong, and without souls? Are we so bereft of humanity that we are no more use on the face of the earth than a barren piece of rock?"

"Barren piece of rock, whey-hey," slurred the drunk, waking up again. He took a slug from his bottle, slid onto his back and stared with vacant wide eyes at the great universe above.

"We are getting nowhere, thanks to these imbecilic interruptions," pronounced Amaryllis. "I propose that we go elsewhere to continue our discussions."

"The Horn and Trumpet has just opened," a student shouted.

"Horn and Trumpet, Horn and Trumpet," other students shouted.

"I'm banned from the effing Horny Trumpet, whey-hey," shouted the drunk, wobbling about and attempting to get up, but he was knocked flat as a great cheering mass of students rushed towards the open doors of the pub.

CHAPTER 4

The football season was well underway and every match day the football specials roared out of the depot to the suburbs to pick up the fans and get them to the game.

Football specials were popular with the crews: it was easy money and as soon as the fans had been delivered to the ground and the empty buses had been parked up in Duckmoor Road the crews were given free entry to the match and a seat on a bench alongside the touchline. Dabber had worked an early shift and was delighted when he saw that he was scheduled for after-duty overtime on a football special. He nipped back to his room for a bite to eat and a quick wash beforehand, and made sure that he was out again in plenty of time. He strolled leisurely down the steep Georgian terrace of Granby Hill, and despite his determination not to be late he could scarce forbear to stop a moment outside Number 54. Dabber had once been lucky enough to see a famous 1822 panoramic watercolour of Granby Hill by Lieutenant Colonel William Booth. The lieutenant colonel's truly magnificent painting not only showed Number 54, but swept downhill to depict the Cumberland Basin and the Floating Harbour.

As Dabber stood outside Number 54, gazing down the hill at the basin and river, he grew pensive and thought of the many Bristol ships, laden with trinkets, which for over a hundred years had passed through the basin and gone on down the river to the Atlantic, and then on to the west coast of Africa. There the trinkets and other shoddy goods would be exchanged for slaves, who would be packed excruciatingly tightly into the holds and shipped across the ocean to face cruel lives on tobacco and sugar plantations.

It had been a sad, sad period in the lively history of a great city.

All at once Dabber woke from his reveries, glanced at his watch, muttered, "Oh my God," and then was racing off over the wooden footbridges of the basin, around the great tobacco warehouse, up the metal staircase and through the park, with the crowds already milling through the turnstiles at the City ground as he ran past to the depot.

He was teamed up with Driver Lepiniere, a strange, agitated character with manic eyes. Lepiniere was muttering and striding about as Dabber barged breathlessly through the doors.

"Where the hell you been? Know what time it is?" Lepiniere said, following the conductor all over the room. "We're down the pan, man. We're gonna miss the kick-off."

Lepiniere was watching Dabber pulling the conductor's box out of the rack and hopping about agitatedly. The only other person in the room was a conductress, and she was gesturing to Dabber behind Lepiniere's back and tapping her head as if to indicate that she thought the driver was a little loopy. Dabber was aware that some of the other busmen said that Lepiniere had been born in France, his mother had weaned him on red wine and left him in the hot sun for long periods and that's why he had gone slightly loopy. However, Dabber guessed that it was probably just anxiety or a mild mental condition, and that Lepiniere needed help and tolerance, rather than mockery.

The rest of the football specials were already long gone, but Special Bus B was still in the depot. Lepiniere snatched the duty card from Dabber and tried to head out of the door, but Dabber protested.

"Hey, give us that back. I can't get the waybill done without that."

At length, after Lepiniere had danced about and rat-a-tatted on the counter with great impatience, constantly urging Dabber on, the pair rushed out into the garage where there was a big board with the duties of all the crews. Beside each duty was chalked the fleet number of the bus which had been allocated to that crew. Driver Lepiniere immediately scanned the board, his head whirling this way and that, his eyes flicking and dashing all over the place. But some funny man had rubbed out three of the chalked digits from their bus number, so instead of a four-digit number there was only an 8 followed by three blanks, and every bus in the whole depot started with 8.

All the jazzers, the rush-hour overtime buses, were back in, fuelled and lined up, plus many other buses as well, so Dabber and Lepiniere didn't know which one they had to take. They couldn't take just any bus. Lepiniere was hopping about because they were already ten minutes late and he didn't want to miss the kick-off.

He started to run about, looking for a maintenance man, and found one at last, not in the garage but in the rest room. The maintenance man had his feet up on a chair taking it easy, having a cigarette and looking at *Peanuts* by Schulz in the *Daily Sketch*. He looked up, startled, with his cigarette paralysed in mid-air, when Lepiniere and Dabber rushed in.

"What's up?" the maintenance man said, and he gradually and with difficulty made out what the gibbering driver was on about.

He came out slowly and sedately with them, because he had been on the job for thirty years and there was no way he was going to hurry for anybody. He slowly looked at the board and stared at it, and mused on the problem. He wiped his chin with the newspaper containing *Peanuts*, scratched himself here and there and thought a bit more.

Eventually he pronounced, "Some bastard's rubbed a bit of the number out."

"I know, I know," screamed Lepiniere, "but which one should we have? Which one we got to take?"

"Now let's see," said the maintenance man, rubbing his chin slowly again. "Football Special B? That's a football bus, ain't it? That ain't a normal service run. That's the one that goes out to Hartcliffe, ain't it? Now, which bastard did I put on there? I don't know what I put on there. Not 8028, because the clutch is knackered, so it definitely ain't that. 8421, the brakes is all shot to hell, so don't take that bastard whatever you do. I don't know. I just don't know. It could be 8132 – I don't even know! Could be that 'un on the end there, 8244, but I just don't know. Tell you what, think I'll go and check. Wait here."

He wandered off. He was on duty all through the night, so he didn't give a monkey's toss about anybody else's problems. He was gone ages and Lepiniere couldn't keep still; he was striding about and looking at his watch as if he was mad. He stared into one of the inspection pits, walked around it and stared hard into it again like he was thinking of jumping in and committing suicide.

At last the maintenance man came back, looking at this and that on the way and still not hurrying.

"8308," he said. "That's the one. I had a feeling it was that bugger all along."

Lepiniere and Dabber were into 8308 very fast, and then just as they were on the forecourt of the depot, Lepiniere slammed the brakes on, beckoned Dabber around to the cab and said, "Don't let the bastards ring the bell too much – I don't like a lot of effing bells."

And then they were off at top speed through the darkened streets with the crowd flocking towards the ground and the kick-off not far away. The bus hammered over the Parson Street Bridge and along Hartcliffe Way with the engine racing and the governors only just reining it in before they slid to a stop in the darkness at Bishport Avenue, where the crowd of football supporters had not a friendly word for Dabber.

All they greeted him with was, "Where the hell you been? We're going to miss the sodding kick-off."

On the way back, on the long downhill stretch of Hartcliffe Way, Lepiniere put the gears into neutral to pick up speed. That bypassed the engine governor and they picked up speed fast, way past the company's limit and very dangerous. The bus raced along in the wet with the cold air sweeping in over the platform and the whole bus lurching from side to side. It must have nearly touched fifty and then, thank God, before they all got killed or seriously maimed, the driver braked, pulled the stick back into gear so the governor took over again and they sped along normally. *That was scary*, thought Dabber, and he hoped Lepiniere wouldn't do that again.

Lepiniere had probably scared the hell out of himself as well, because he drove impeccably the rest of the way to Duckmoor Road, where they parked up the bus and raced to Ashton Gate for the match.

CHAPTER 5

Dabber and Melody wandered all over the bustling central area and the inner suburbs of the city. They explored narrow cobbled lanes and sometimes found a little pub or café that never got much passing trade. If they went in there was usually dead silence immediately, and everyone stared at them because they were strangers.

Whoever was behind the counter would say, "Yeah?" and jerk his head, all grim-faced and unfriendly, as if Dabber and Melody were going to rob the place.

There would be continuing silence while Melody sat down and everyone in the place would listen and watch while Dabber went up to the bar to order. He would take the drinks back to Melody and sit beside her and the whole clientele would gaze at them as if they were freaks as the two young lovers took their first sips and lit cigarettes and stared back.

And then slowly the silence would break and the locals would look away and start to talk to each other again, and Melody and Dabber would sit and whisper together. They saw some amazing quaint characters in some of these rickety, hidden-away places.

Once they found a tiny pub no bigger than a kitchen, with bare stone walls and rough wooden seats. The place was so small that there wasn't even room for a bar; the drinks were served through what looked like a stable door, the kind where the top half swings open so that the horse can look out.

The proprietor, a grey-haired, bent old man, was sitting swapping tales from long ago with two more old men. They looked at Dabber and

Melody when they entered, but not for too long; the oldsters were too engrossed in some long tale that one of them, struggling with a heaving, wheezy chest, was slowly recounting.

Melody sat down at the table with them because there was nowhere else to sit, while Dabber went up to the stable door and leaned on the bottom half.

There was no sign of anyone serving. He hung around and waited, looked here and there with interest, walked a pace or two away and leaned on the door again. He looked around once more. The landlord saw him and gave a cursory nod, but was clearly not going to move until the long tale had finished. He kept glancing at Dabber because Dabber was waiting to be served, yet all the elderly man wanted to do was just keep sitting there nice and comfortable while swapping stories with his two friends.

After a seemingly interminable time the bent old man telling the story stopped and wheezed a couple of times, took a long drink and said, "Yes, it was different in them days." The other two agreed.

The landlord slapped the table in great satisfaction at the tale, went round and emerged behind the stable door, jerked his head at Dabber and said, "Yeah?"

Well, Dabber had a job not to laugh at the absurdity of it all, but he got his drinks and sat down at the old wooden table with Melody and the two men.

After a silence one of the oldsters said, "In them days you could have a good night out for a tanner. Bus fare, a few pints and on to the dance. Many's the night I've been drunk on a tanner. And the girls we 'ad. Couldn't do it now."

"Not now," said the second old man, shaking his head sadly.

"Not on a tanner," Dabber said.

The two old men looked at him in semi-shock because he had spoken in regard to their private conversation, but they immediately saw that Melody and he were only trying to be friendly.

"See this?" said the first one, pulling his sleeve back. He had a metal hand, complete with fingers, which the young couple hadn't noticed. He worked the metal fingers. "Bastard Germans did that. You young 'uns don't know what war is, you don't know what it is."

"That's true," Dabber said.

"Look," the old man said, and with the metal hand he gripped his glass, lifted it up and set it down again. "Technology, that is," he said, "technology. Know where that technology come from? Germany! Bastards shot my hand off and forty years later gave me a metal one. How about that?"

Melody said, "You must be very brave."

The other fellow said, "Brave? You 'ad to be brave in them days. Walking on corpses, we were, a lot of the time. Walking on corpses – blood everywhere."

No one said anything for a time. Dabber looked around. Moisture was oozing from the stonework. Four walls, a stable door, a table and two wooden benches on the bare stone floor – that's all there was in the place. The landlord was pulling more real rough ale with big white frothy heads, straight from wooden casks. He brought the pints over and set them down in front of the old men, and he had one for himself.

He said, "Now then, you young 'uns. What you two young 'uns having? It's on the house."

"If it's on the house, I'll have a pint," Dabber said.

Melody said that she would have half a pint. The landlord went off behind the stable door to pull the beer.

Dabber looked around. "Nice place, this," he said.

"Very nice," said Melody.

The first old man said, "Fifty years. Fifty years I've been coming 'ere."

"Fifty years," repeated the second one.

The landlord brought over the drinks for Melody and Dabber. "That's on the house," he said. "Don't get many decent young 'uns in here these days."

There was another pause then while they all drank. Dabber passed round cigarettes and they all sparked up.

The other old man said, "See this eye?" He gestured at one of his eyes. "See this eye? Artificial. Artificial eye, that!"

"You couldn't tell," Dabber said.

"Know where I got it?"

"National Health?" Dabber guessed.

"National Health, my arse," the oldster said. "There was no National Health in them days. Paid for it myself. Twenty quid. Twenty sodding quid. Private. Paid for it myself. Couldn't get nothing off the bastard government. They gave me a black eyepatch. That's all they give me: a black eyepatch. And it was their sodding war I lost my eye in. Last time I seen that eye it was lying in the mud in France. Jerry bullet ripped it out."

Dabber and Melody sat there in that cold little pub late into the evening, but never noticed the cold, and then said long, sorrowful, inebriated goodbyes to the oldsters and wished them well, and the old men wished the youngsters well also.

Melody and Dabber tottered up the hill under the cold, hanging stars to his room. They snuggled up tight and warm to each other all that glorious night, and Melody ministered in a very tender way to his body.

They slept a deliciously long sleep and lay in until late the following day.

Late one chilly afternoon Dabber stood in Old Market, swirling back his hair and shuffling bored steps this way and that as he waited for Melody.

He had nothing else to do while he waited but shuffle here and there and gaze around the famous old street that he had got to know so well. There in the middle of the junction stood a policeman on point duty, swivelling this way and that, gesturing authoritatively at lorries, cars and big green double-deckers. Dabber gazed at a woman on a motorbike revving like mad, and a tired worker on a bicycle who shouted, "What the eff...?" at the snarled-up traffic.

On the pavements groups of weary workers trudged homeward, merry arm-linked schoolgirls laughed and giggled and schoolboys ran about playfully thumping each other. Plump housewives with long dowdy coats and bare ankles staggered with heavy shopping, and an attractive office worker, swinging her hair, ran for a bus and laughed when she caught it. Girls bouncing along in miniskirts drew lecherous looks from youths and jealous glances from older women. Trendy older teenagers with sharp suits and Elvis hair smoked and lounged about. A toddler, hand in crisp packet, looked around in a panic for his mum.

A down-and-out stumbled up to Dabber and mumbled, "Hey, man, can you spare a tanner?"

Dabber pressed two bob into the man's hand, said, "Best of luck, mate," and then recommenced wandering this way and that, looking in all directions for Melody, but there was no sign of her. Over the road a fruit-shop worker was polishing apples and a young street cleaner, after making bored and desultory movements at fallen leaves with his brush, sat on his barrow, lit a cigarette and contemplated the world. An old lady with a wide-brimmed hat and heavy tattered coat muttered in a world of her own. A little girl with big blue eyes and hair in plaits gazed open-mouthed at her.

Outside the Angel Snack Bar the proprietor, slim and smart with a bow tie, stood looking for customers, but his establishment was too pretentious for Old Market. Along the road at the Spring Chicken a driver and conductor, having left their buses, were dashing in for hot tea and to crack a few jokes with the cheerful proprietors. Dabber knew the crew would have to look sharp before the checker found their unattended bus.

Just around the corner was Hell's Kitchen, a dingy café where tattered men gazed vacantly and clutched mugs of tea with cadaverous hands. It was said that in there, the knives and forks were chained to the tables and a sad old tramp had dropped dead one day.

On the other side of the junction was the magnificent White Hart, where young busmen drank, girls flirted and squealed, the jukebox hammered out joyous tunes and Tubs, the genial host, was forever polishing glasses.

And then across the road Dabber could see the Three Horseshoes: one of his favourite cider spots, where he often went when he wanted to be alone, to dream and to contemplate life.

Dabber wandered up and down the pavement and looked up at the big clock on the corner. He had waited nearly an hour and there was still no sign of Melody. A chill wind was rising and he decided to pop into the nearby Punch Bowl for a drink. The landlord was smiling and his young wife, a fresh, rosy beauty with bulging breasts, was flirting and laughing with the customers. She lit a cigarette, posed daintily, dodged brawny arms and wiggled around the tables. She sat briefly with customers, shared whispered secrets and laughed some more. Suddenly she stubbed out her cigarette, ran to her husband behind the bar, threw her arms around his neck and kissed him. He lifted her, swung her round and kissed her in warm reply. She giggled, grabbed his hand and ran daintily up the stairs with flash of thigh and white suspenders. Her husband followed eagerly, slapping her bum, and they disappeared. A sweating busman, on his break, threw back his head and roared great ho-ho-ho's at the ceiling. A pot-bellied, bulbous-nosed customer sitting by himself slapped the table in private mirth. Two merry, ragged fellows sang lustily. A customer rolling a cigarette joined in with noisy laughter.

Dabber went outside again. It started to rain as he wandered slowly up and down and shuffled about. He contemplated the rest of the majestic old street. Over the road outside the Three Horseshoes some customers were lounging, talking tiredly and gazing at nothing. The proprietor of a newsagent next door could be seen inside, smoking and staring dully out of the window.

Dabber wandered along the pavement. There, tucked away up a dark alley, was the 99 Club, where games of snooker were played for high stakes. It was said that illicit gambling went on and some punters were fleeced. Dabber glanced inside.

The boss was shouting, "Smoke up, smoke up, it ain't smoky enough in here."

Dabber went out into the street again and turned up his collar against the rain. In the middle of the street were the underground toilets: grim and dank, where the cubicles needed a penny and perverts watched through little spyholes.

It grew dark, and a steady rain was falling. Dabber wandered up and down once more with his hands in his pockets, kicking stones, staring in shop windows and looking in every direction, but there was still no sign of Melody. She was over an hour late. Dabber checked his watch and looked this way and that. He looked all around one last time and then turned up his collar against the rain and trudged away.

CHAPTER 6

Every day buses were off the road all over the city because of the shortage of crews.

Winter was slowly tightening its grip and a flu bug hit the city. Because the bus company's staffing situation was so desperate the running schedules were all messed up, and every day buses that should have been out on the road were left in the depots. At shift changes up in the Centre and Old Market, when there were no crews to take over incoming buses, the passengers were turfed off and the empty buses were parked up in side streets.

In the canteens men were saying, "It can't go on like this much longer, all these buses off the road. The company's bound to start taking blacks on."

Poody, a thin driver with long bony fingers and a droopy moustache, was saying, "Plenty of them blacks would be all right if they got a chance. The company won't even interview them. Soon as they see a bloke is black 'e's out the door again before he gets his arse on a seat."

"Yeah, well, it's obvious why they don't want 'em, ain't it?" said Skully. "It's because they ain't up to our level of culture and stuff, are they? I mean, we're better than them in culture, ain't we?"

"How do you mean, 'better in culture'?" Dabber, who had been quietly reading a newspaper, looked up and asked.

"Well, our way of behaving, doing things different. I mean, we're more civilised, ain't we? We conquered the world, we established colonies and that. If it hadn't been for us British, them blacks would still be swinging from the trees."

Dabber said, "Let me tell you something. For hundreds of years white people have terrorised blacks, made slaves of them. Any blacks that rebelled were tortured by burning, whipping, branding and things like that. The ones that ran away were hunted down with dogs. Even as recent as fifty or sixty years ago a thousand blacks a year were being lynched in Mississippi and them places for no reason at all, black women and kids among them. White people used to turn up to watch a lynching as if it was a football match. You call that culture? You call that civilised behaviour?"

There was a sombre silence, and then Poody said, "Well, I ain't got nothing against blacks."

"Yeah," said Ratso, "but if them blacks git in they'll be all over the place, won't they? You'll have black coppers, black councillors – you could even have a black lord mayor. Think of that, mate – a black lord mayor of Bristol!"

"A black lord mayor? That'll never happen in a million years in this city, mate," Skully said.

After a time, as the argument about the colour bar raged, Dabber left the group and went over to another table where Greasy was halfway through a big plate of fry-up. Greasy's mousy, untidy hair was dangling almost over his eyes, which always seemed somehow to be out of alignment with each other. At school his lack of interest in the classroom had meant that he finished low in his class, but he had always had a keen interest in figures, especially the nubile and busty variety. He was almost permanently friendly and cheerful and those qualities were important in a job like 'the buses'.

He was not, perhaps, the ideal person to discuss a difficult emotional subject with; nevertheless Dabber said, "You know that bird of mine?"

"What bird?" Greasy said.

"That Melody."

"Yeah?"

"She's disappeared."

Greasy's face took on a strained expression as he struggled to comprehend the meaning of this strange piece of information.

"How do you mean, 'disappeared'?" he said.

"Gone. Just disappeared off the scene, man. There's no sign of her."

"Probably found another boyfriend, mate," said Greasy after further lengthy contemplation. "Wants to give you the old heave-ho but don't know how to do it."

"I don't think so," said Dabber.

"If she shows up, though, you want to watch her," said Greasy.

"What do you mean?"

"Well, you don't know what she's been doing," said Greasy, chewing away at his sausage and chips. He liked plenty of brown sauce and salt and vinegar on them. There was a silence while Greasy forked more chips into his mouth. After he had finished chewing, he said, "I mean, she could 'ave caught summat."

"Shut up, you idiot," Dabber said.

Greasy sliced through a cloud of flitting black midges with his knife and slopped some more brown sauce and vinegar onto his chips. "No, seriously, mate, if she comes back, watch her. I know a bit about these sorts of things. You don't know what the hell she might 'ave been doing. What you need to do, mate, is forget her and get back into circulation." He paused a moment. "Tag along with me one night and I'll show you how to chat up a bird."

But Dabber did not stop looking eagerly for Melody whenever his bus hammered over the Old Market junction. They had lived the sort of existence where neither knew much about each other's lives or when the other was going to appear or disappear. It was the norm that the drifters, the down-and-outs, the alcoholics and the other denizens who hung around Old Market did not ask questions about individual lives. The transient crews who worked on the buses, as well as the feckless young women who hung about the crews, also did not welcome personal enquiries.

Dabber and Melody had just drifted along from day to day, sometimes meeting, sometimes not. Even if they met they didn't do much, just wandered about the streets and went in and out of the cafés and played the machines. They sat in pubs, smoking and staring around, not saying much to each other. Although disorganised, they had always managed to see each other two or three times each week.

But she had been gone for over two weeks now, and Dabber missed her. He often thought wistfully about the times when they would go up to the Downs and wander about in the sunshine like other young people. They sometimes went into a grassy hollow. But it wasn't the ideal place up there on the Downs, with casual walkers blundering about and uncontrolled dogs running around, so usually they would just lie back and gaze at the sky, dream and talk; but Dabber was never wholly relaxed in his mind at these times, because as he travelled around the city on his late shifts he had a few times seen Melody with the stumbling youth he had seen her with before. It had looked as if she didn't want the drunken lad mauling her, but why was she even with him?

Although Dabber was annoyed, he had decided that he was not going to get overexcited or jump in. He was not going to overreact, but just play it cool and see what happened.

And sometimes he had lain with her up on the Downs in the late autumn sunshine, thinking, and afterwards they would wander down Whiteladies Road with their arms around each other.

After she disappeared, Dabber missed those carefree days. She haunted his dreams. Once, while lying on the bed in his bedsitter, he fell into a doze and in a dream he was wandering along a riverbank. Feeling a little shaky, he entered a small café and sat down. He looked around and noticed that the waitress was Melody. She was leaning against a wall and seemed to be thinking deeply about something. After a time she slowly turned and looked in his direction, but her gaze moved on. She looked absently all around the café. Dabber wondered if she had seen him. She had given no sign or acknowledgement; indeed her gaze had passed slowly over him as if he was not there. He wondered if he really was there, sitting in that café. Perhaps he was no more significant than a puff of cigarette smoke. Perhaps he had no bodily substance.

And then, in his dream, Melody seemed to notice him; she took a quick step sideways and stared at him. She stepped again, here and there quickly, then stood stock-still and fixed her gaze on him. A sound like the faraway bleat of a lamb escaped her. Dabber was looking at her with curiosity. She stared at him again and walked a little to the left.

She said, "Hah, it's you, is it?" in a low voice, and slapped her palm lightly on a table. She approached a little way. "What would you like?" she said.

"A cup of tea, please," Dabber said.

"What?" she said.

"A cup of tea," he repeated.

"Are you sure that's all?" she said.

"Yes. How much is it?"

She shook slightly, like a leaf trembling. "Fourpence," she said.

"All right," he said.

"Actually, for you the tea is free," she said. "You're a special customer."

"All right."

"The tea is free," she said. "Did I mention that?"

"Yes."

"And would you like dessert?" she said.

"How much is it?" Dabber asked.

"It might be free for you. I haven't decided. God, you're so handsome," she breathed. "I've been missing you. God!" she murmured again, and bent over him.

"There's a special offer on for you, Dabber," she whispered. "Everything's free for you. Did I mention that?"

Her arms wrapped around his neck and she drew his head against her breasts. She turned his face up and kissed him for a long time, full on the lips.

"I'm sure you want something else, darling," she whispered.

In Dabber's strange dream, Melody's uniform started to shimmer and become misty. It dropped away and her dress slipped from her, and then her underclothes. Finally she was naked.

"I'm sure you would like something else," she whispered again, cuddling him. "Everything's free for you, Dabber, even my desserts. My desserts are special, aren't they? You know how you love them. You can have one now if you like."

He was panting. "Yes, yes," he said. He reached eagerly for her, but

44

as he tried to grasp her it seemed the drunken, stumbling youth he had seen with Melody flitted between them. Melody faded to nothing and his dream slipped away.

CHAPTER 7

The days crept on into a bitter December. On Dabber's early shifts the frozen night would still be gripping the city when his alarm clock hammered its bitter reveille. Sometimes Dabber had only been in his warm bed for four or five hours when he had to roll out, grab a cup of black coffee, get out of the house and race along the frosty, deserted streets under the staring yellow streetlights to the depot.

One morning the pavement was wet and unfriendly, with a sprinkling of snow, and Dabber's feet slid this way and that as he ran. He heard a cough and a whirr behind him and a policeman on a bicycle drew level and shone his torch on the running bus worker, but Dabber had no time for pleasantries and raced on. The policeman slewed around and skidded, put one foot on the ground and wheeled away into the darkness and his loneliness.

At the depot, Dabber said, "Fourteenth four," to the foreman.

He dragged his conductor's box from its slot, slung it onto the back counter and did the waybill fast, for his driver was waiting and the bus, with its mighty engine firing, was shaking and trembling on the forecourt.

They roared away fast, and in the cold and the darkness at the initial pickup point at Filwood Broadway the first passengers were huddled. It was scarcely 4.45 on that bitter morning. Straight onto the bus they got: women with headscarves, talking and laughing with loud, dirty laughs; and men, reluctant and weary already, and taciturn, for it was too early for them.

The women were cleaners, going up to the city centre to clean offices, and then they'd be rushing back home to kick the squealing

46

kids off out to school and lay into the old man if he was still lying in that warm bed that he was so fond of. They sat downstairs, these women, for such was the custom; and upstairs went the men, often thin and old, worn out from long years of work, shabbily dressed, silent, morose and alone with their thoughts.

The ceiling of the upper saloon was stained brown and yellow with the smoke from a million cigarettes. Many of the men of the upper deck had not much life left in them. They had their old-age pensions ahead of them, and their cigarettes and a few pints when they could afford it. They sat hunched in their seats up there on the top deck, hollow-eyed and probably brooding about work and home and the pub and wondering what the hell it was all for.

Dabber's driver was young – mid-twenties or thereabouts; a silent type with a thoughtful face and a healthy red glow to his cheeks as if he had just been running. He was serious and had spent a lot of time studying the duty card before they left the depot. Dabber knew that there would be no flankers – the little dodges the busmen used to make the job more bearable – with him up in the cab. There would be no running sharp, extra cups of tea or running off service to make up time.

After this early run far out to the eastern edge of the city they turned and came back, and at about 7.30 the office workers started to appear, and then the school kids. After that the housewives were out on the stops again, yanking the arms of reluctant toddlers and struggling to get pushchairs on board.

And throughout this time there were passengers moaning and whining, complaining about fares and missing buses and the weather, and threatening to report the crews for this, that and the other. In the middle of this, Dabber and his driver had to try to stay on schedule in the midst of the traffic jams, and then they finished the first half of their shift and hurried to snatch what was left of their break and a bite of breakfast in the Old Market canteen.

After the break, Dabber and his serious young driver went out again and took on a bus on the number nine route and it all started again, with the wind whipping thin snow onto the open platform as the bus went along.

There were buses off all over the place because the company couldn't get the staff, and the empty buses were parked up in Broad Plain, Anchor Road and other side streets, while the foremen scratched around for crews.

Dabber and his mate ran their bus in to finish the shift in Old Market just before one in the afternoon, and then it was ten minutes waiting to cross the road to get to the paying-in office. There were four lanes of traffic going like the clappers of hell this way and that along Old Market Street, and every time Dabber stepped off the kerb some vehicle came hurtling along close in, and tried to take his toes off. He tried a couple of runs at it, dodging through a couple of lanes, was defeated and had to retreat fast to the bit of kerb where he started.

But, hallelujah, eventually he was across and heading to the paying-in office and the end of his shift.

Days passed. There was still no sign of Melody, and late one Friday night, against his better judgment, Dabber found himself with Greasy staggering through the drizzly, dark streets with two girls who had been looking hopeless and dejected in the Pelican at closing time.

"Where to?" said Dabber, his arm around a girl with peroxide-blonde hair piled high, who in between drags on her cigarette had informed him, in a harsh voice, that her name was Veronica.

"You can come up to the flat if you want," she said, and stopped to drag deeply again on her Craven "A".

The other girl, the one Greasy had an arm around, a thin, sour-faced girl named Bella, added, "But we ain't fussy if you bloody come or not."

Along West Street they wobbled, the four of them, with Dabber and Greasy tilting bottles to their lips every few steps, causing the arm-linked foursome to lurch about this way and that, banging against the wall sometimes and only just managing to stay upright. Once Greasy staggered into the road, pulling the other three with him, and a car came hurtling out of the deep city gloom, just missed them and sped away, horn wailing at this near-elimination of the young drunks.

"Shit," said Bella, disentangling her arm from Greasy's. "Shit, you nearly got us wiped out, you nutcase. Walk properly. What the hell's the matter with you?"

But Greasy started giving great drunken belly laughs, stepping with big, silly steps into the road and jumping back quickly. Cars hooted as they sped along before vanishing into the far distant gloom.

Dabber was mostly just shuffling along with blank eyes and crazy thoughts, still clutching a bottle and with his free arm around Veronica.

Then he decided to copy Greasy, and started shouting, "Whey-hey!" and, "Hey-ho!" and jumping around also, but Veronica yanked savagely at him and said, "Don't you sodding start, for Chrissake."

Dabber turned his collar up high; then against the drifting rain, took a last swig at his bottle, stared morosely for no reason into purple, oily pools in the gutter, and then lapsed into booze-raddled gloominess and contemplation of the probable horrible fornication to come.

As the strange conjoined quartet staggered through the dreary streets their progress was viewed by two ragged down-and-outs who were just settling down for the night on piles of rags in a dirty doorway. The two old men shook their ancient heads sadly and wonderingly as Dabber and Greasy and the two girls lumbered away.

In the bleak and cold foyer of a high-rise block in Barton Hill Veronica shook the rain off herself and said, "It's a wonder we got here instead of the sodding hospital, the way you two loonies carry on," and she started up the bare concrete stairs.

When the four reached the top floor, Greasy, panting and gasping on a cigarette, grumbled, "Ain't there no lift in this place?"

Bella, who was just putting her key in the door, looked hard at him and said, "Shut it, will ya? The lift's noisy. My mother's asleep in here – it's her flat."

Inside the flat it was all darkness. Dabber smelled a strong, stale odour of beer and smoke and guessed they sure as hell were not the first men to be brought back to that dismal den. He struggled to muster some sensual thoughts, but only had more visions of probably disagreeable bodily interactions to come with Veronica.

The four of them blundered around in the darkness and then Greasy staggered to a sofa, fell onto it and lay on his back, panting.

Bella stared at him, muttered, "For God's sake…" but then went over and pushed onto the sofa beside him.

Veronica, down on the floor already, reached up and pulled Dabber down on top of her. There was silence then while they all orientated themselves and gathered drunken thoughts. There was a bout of kissing and groping and things were reaching a climax when Greasy, for no reason at all, suddenly stopped mauling his partner and said, "Ain't there no lights in this place?"

"What the hell you want lights for?" his partner, Bella, said.

"I just wondered why there was no lights," said Greasy.

"There's no lights, so shut the hell up, will ya?" said Bella.

On the floor in the darkness Veronica had her arm around Dabber's neck, pulling him to her while her free hand was exploring his body. Dabber was languidly stroking and squeezing her breasts.

On the sofa there was heavy panting and then a sudden thump as Greasy fell onto the floor.

"For goodness' sake," said Bella. "What the hell's the matter with you?"

Greasy was moaning, "Oooh, I think I broke my sodding backbone."

"This is great," said Bella, "just bloody great." She got up, lit a cigarette and started to walk about furiously.

Greasy was just lying on the floor, silently watching her, and then he said, "You ain't got a spare fag, have you?"

"No," said Bella. She stubbed out her cigarette and got down on the floor beside Greasy again. They kissed and rolled about for several minutes, then Greasy started to laugh, rolling about and chortling for no discernible reason. "What the hell you laughing at?" said Bella.

"Nothing," said Greasy, and then nearly choked himself with laughter once again.

"I'm fed up with this," said Bella. She got up, lit another cigarette and started to stalk about again. "This is bloody great," she muttered, "just bloody great." She stopped walking and stared silently down at Greasy in the semi-darkness.

"I thought you had no more fags," said Greasy.

"I got none for you," she said. After a time she stubbed out her cigarette and got back down on the floor. She started to nuzzle Greasy and run her hand up and down his chest inside his shirt. Greasy tried to stroke her breast and slip his hand under her skirt, but she slapped him off. Then she turned her head towards him and kissed him on the lips. He pulled her to him and they kissed again.

"I'm sorry about the fag," she said, "but I just haven't got a spare one."

"I'll do without," he said.

She kissed him again and rolled onto her back. "We could have some fun tonight," she said.

She tried to pull him on top of her, but all of a sudden he sat up. "Where's the toilet in this place?" he said.

Bella pulled away from him and stared at the ceiling. "For God's sake," she said.

"Where's the toilet?" asked Greasy again, standing up.

"There's no toilet," said Bella.

"What do you mean, no toilet?"

"I mean there's no sodding toilet," said Bella.

"There's bound to be a toilet," said Greasy.

"It's not available."

"What's that supposed to mean, not available?"

"It's through the bedroom and my mother's in there," said Bella.

"What we supposed to do for a piss, then?"

"There are no facilities for that sort of thing," said Bella.

Greasy stood there for a minute and then he got down on the floor again. "No facilities?" he muttered.

"Stop bloody grumbling," said Bella.

"I just want a piss," said Greasy.

"Please don't use language like that in my presence," said Bella.

Greasy didn't answer. He leaned over and put his hand on Bella's breast. She slapped it off.

"Don't sodding try that," she said. She hopped up and sat on the sofa. Greasy got up and sat beside her. He put his arm around her and tried to pull her close. "Bugger off," she said. She moved to the far end of the sofa and sat there grim-faced with her arms crossed. Greasy was gazing at her.

"What the hell you looking at?" she said.

"Nothing," Greasy said. He looked away and then just sat gaping.

Dabber was lying on his back, half-asleep, his mind wandering in a strange fog. Through it he saw dark woods, his head being slapped this way and that, punches in his stomach. He saw grim child institutions, grey figures with gloating faces and a sweaty, fat, naked housemaster bending over him. He felt a smelly bare body pressing up against him and groaned.

"What the hell's up with you?" Veronica exclaimed, pulling away from him. But Dabber was up and scrambling for his clothes.

"Let me out of here," he moaned. "Just let me out of here."

Veronica was on her feet fast and scrabbling for her clothing. "What the hell's the matter with you?" she said. "What the hell's up? You some kind of nutter, or what?"

Dabber just muttered, "Oh, God. I got to get out of here."

As the two young busmen rushed down the smelly, unlit stairs, Greasy said, "What the hell was that all about, mate?"

"I couldn't do it, man," said Dabber. "I just couldn't do it."

Greasy was silent and then he said, "Well, at least I can have a piss now we're away from that barmy pair."

They were silent, then, as they trudged through the wet and dismal streets for the sad walk home.

CHAPTER 8

On late shifts, crews who were based on Old Market took over their buses at about three o'clock in the afternoon and spent the first two hours conveying harassed housewives, whining toddlers and stroppy school kids home. After that the early-finishing workers were coming out onto the streets at the beginning of the evening rush hour. For the crews it meant another two hours of sweating and stress, but as soon as that was all over it would be time for them to have a break.

Down in the dismal underground canteen the crews would line up for their cooked meals, have a bit of repartee with the kitchen staff and then find a seat. Mostly the men ate in silence, glancing at any copies of the *Daily Mirror* or *The Sketch* which had been left lying around, and only occasionally entering into prolonged conversation with their colleagues. Half a shift – which was often more than four hours – with the travelling public was quite enough to knock a man's brain off the rails and it could take food and a bit of silence to get it back on track.

Only after an interval down in the canteen would the real conversation start to flow. On one occasion Dabber was saying, "Yeah, whatever you think, those blacks suffered a lot in the past, whipped and chained up and all that. They were taken away from their homes and families and made into slaves. And in this city here, Bristol, a lot of the slave traders came from here."

"You on with all that namby-pamby stuff again, mate?" said Ratso in an angry tone.

"I'm just telling the facts," said Dabber. "It's true, a lot of slave traders came from here."

"I've heard that said," Ratso replied angrily, "but there's never been no proof. Show me the proof and I'll believe it."

"Go up that museum up near the top of Park Street, mate," Dabber said. "It tells you all about it in there – even the bloke that gave the money to build that museum, and the university building next to it, one of them Wills lot, his ancestors made their original fortune from tobacco plantations."

"Yeah, but they didn't have no slaves," Ratso said.

"I don't know about that," said Dabber, "but did any of their profits come from slave-produced tobacco? Those staff up in that museum will know. I'll ask them next time I'm up there. They're brilliant, them staff – answer any question you got. Tell you all about it, whatever you ask. Tell you about everything. Some of them never stop talking, telling you stuff. Yapping about stuff you never even asked about – an' a bit more besides. In the end, you're just glad to get away."

"Yeah, I suppose you're one of those brainy buggers that's always in museums an' suchlike, but you don't know nothing about life, mate," said Ratso with a sneer.

There was a silence then, before a conductor with yellowing teeth chipped in. "Wherever the money come from, that museum's still a magnificent building. I used to be a builder and I know quality when I see it. That museum is built of Pennant stone, faced with Bath stone ashlar, and when I see the pedimented entrance, them coloured marbles, the intricate door handles, them electroliers..."

"What the hell's electroliers?" said Greasy.

The ex-builder stared at Greasy with the scorn of a man who has a little knowledge. "You don't need to worry about electroliers, mate," he said. "You ain't educated enough to worry about electroliers. What I'm saying is it's classic, that building – classic architecture."

A conductor nicknamed Rulebook put a brown carrier bag on the table. He said, "I concur absolutely with what you say, sir. I have in this bag not only a copy of the full rules and regulations of our job, but also Ministry of Transport material, cuttings, leaflets and other assorted ephemera, and I have lots on slavery and on the buildings of this city. As a matter of fact, I visit the City Museum and Art Gallery regularly in order to ensure that my knowledge is entirely up to date and comprehensive. Always I pause at the entrance to admire the magnificent Middle-Jurassic oolitic limestone of the outer façade. And inside the electroliers our friend was referring to are actually branching frames of ornamental design which support the overhead lights, and the marbles he refers to are simply breathtaking. One has to see to believe the white Sicilian marble used for the steps, the green cipolin of the pillars, and the cream and black pavonazzo of the door surrounds. Also, may I mention the superb terrazzo flooring? Yes, the Wills family were certainly generous with their donations to this city."

"Yeah, but where did the money come from?" Dabber said. "Was it from slavery?"

"The origin of the wealth that enabled such buildings to be built is, I agree, an extremely debatable matter," said Rulebook. "However, I was merely praising the simply marvellous architecture."

"It's a disgrace when you think of where the money came from to build some of the buildings in this city," said Dabber. "That Georgian house off Park Street, for instance – a rich geezer called Pinney had that house built. He had slave plantations over in the Caribbean. A lot of his slaves sweated and died cutting sugar cane just so that Pinney could make a fortune and build his fancy house. He even brought a slave over here to wait on 'im hand and foot. Yeah," Dabber continued, "the amount of buildings in this city built with slave money don't bear thinking about."

Rulebook said, "That is quite correct. I absolutely agree with you. I have researched the subject at some length. For example, Ashton Court – the Smyth family that owned it had shares in slave plantations. Arnos Court is another place that was built by a slave trader. Most of the big houses in Queen Square and King Street, loads of big houses up in the old part of Clifton, Redland Court – that's now the private girls' school, houses on Park Street, the Colston Hall…I mean, one could go on and on, but I do not agree that any of them should be knocked down. You cannot alter history. Perhaps it would be sufficient to place a small plaque on each of them giving some account of the history."

"Yeah, I can go along with that," said the ex-builder. "I mean, if you knocked down all the houses in Bristol that was built with slave money there'd be bugger all left. The least we can do is welcome them blacks coming on the buses if they want to."

"You're all talking a load of bollocks, you lot," said Ratso, and he dug his fork savagely into his meal.

Dabber and his driver had to go out again then and take over a bus for the second half of their late shift. He always looked for Melody as his bus travelled all over the city, but there was just no sign of her. He used to think to himself: *I wonder if she's still knocking about with that rough-looking lad, the one that always looks like he's half-drunk. What does he mean to her? She never seems to tell me the truth. I mean, all this two-timing stuff – what the hell's going on? I'm just going to ask her straight out. Funny thing is, she always acts keen to see me – always loving. I don't get it. Man, it's a mystery.*

But that night as the second half of his late shift started, Dabber did not have time to dwell on the subject. Crowds of early drinkers were out, going up to the city centre for an evening's boozing, and then later the same revellers were heading home, all squinty-eyed, muttering and fumbling drunkenly for their money. When the last passengers were safely deposited at the terminus on the last journey of the night it was a hammering run, then, empty, back to the depot with the great Gardner engine shuddering and wailing, the pistons screaming *whuppeta-whuppeta-whuppeta* and Dabber, the conductor downstairs, struggling to count up his takings, being thrown this way and that as the bus hurtled along through the still, black night.

CHAPTER 9

Unknown to Dabber, Melody had reappeared and was standing on the corner of Old Market, swinging her little handbag and scanning the buses that went past to see if she could see him.

She showed little interest in the busy life of the street, which bustled about her as she waited. She watched the pub doorways to see if Dabber emerged from any of the hostelries, but he didn't. Once she saw a drunk roll out of the Old Market Tavern and pause for several moments holding the door frame. Melody watched languidly as the man staggered first one way, then the other, took a few jerky steps to the right and steadied himself against a wall. He tottered forward a few paces and held the wall again for dear life, all the while staring at the pavement as if in disbelief.

He wobbled forward, did a quick series of jerky sidesteps to the left, balanced precariously on the edge of the pavement, swayed back and forth and then collapsed onto his backside. After he had sat there gazing blankly round, muttering and cursing, he pushed himself up and staggered around again. Melody watched him as he wobbled his way up the pavement and through the door of the Gin Palace.

After wandering up and down some more, listlessly swinging her handbag and looking without much interest at the everyday life of the street, Melody crossed over to the White Hart. She pushed open the door of the back lounge where the young busmen drank, but inside there was only the usual collection of bar-haunters.

But over the road in the Spring Chicken café, Melody had success. Dabber was there, playing the machines with Greasy. He was bending over, engrossed in the game. Five in a line on one of the café's pinball machines paid two hundred cigarettes. No one had ever seen it done. Dabber had his back to her. Melody did not disturb him, but found a seat and sat down. She watched the pair of young busmen shoot a lot of balls, and once they got four in a line. They tilted the machine to try to get five, but it had a built-in alarm and immediately flashed up the words *tilt-tilt-tilt*, and sounded a siren.

The proprietor called out, "Hey, you boys – no tilting my machine."

Dabber laughed and called out, "No one ever wins on this thing, man. You got it fixed, or what?"

Suddenly he noticed Melody. He strode quickly towards her. "Melody!" he exclaimed. "What the hell...? How long you been sitting there?" He grabbed her and hugged and kissed her.

"I didn't know if you wanted to see me again," she said.

"Of course I do," he said.

"I thought you might have found someone else," she said.

"Course not!" he exclaimed. "What would I want with someone else? But where the hell you been? Where'd you get all them nice clothes? Hey, never mind. I've missed you. How long you been sitting there?"

"Not long. I've been looking all over for you. It's taken me ages to find you."

He hugged her again. "We've found each other again. That's all that matters," he said. "Here, have a go at this machine. You might be luckier than me and Greasy."

Melody got up and pulled the lever. The balls whizzed around: *whang-whang-whang*. She remembered how to do it all right.

"I never was lucky," she said as the balls sped everywhere but into the winning slots.

Greasy said, "Give me another go."

He took over the machine and began to wallop the balls around. He got four in a line again and only one ball left. Two hundred cigarettes were almost in his grasp. He left the machine and stalked away, walked back again and stared at the machine.

"Holy shit," he muttered, "two hundred fags. I don't know if I can do this." He took the lever in his hand and eased it back. "I got to do it, I got to do it," he muttered. "This time." He eased the lever some more, hesitated, and then for some unaccountable reason he turned and looked sideways at Melody.

"You disappeared for a bit, didn't ya?" he said.

She didn't reply.

Greasy concentrated on the machine again and then, as if he was too nervous to release the lever, he turned to Melody again.

"Make much money at it?" he said, still holding the lever, preparing to let the ball whizz round.

"Much money at what?" Melody said.

"Whatever you've been doing, walking the streets or summat. I mean, it looks like you made a bit with them clothes you got on," Greasy said.

"Get effing lost," Melody said.

She shoved the machine violently and the alarm went off.

"Hey, I had four in a line there," protested Greasy. "I could have had two hundred fags." But Melody was already stalking out.

"Jeez!" muttered Greasy, staring after her. "What was up with her? Two hundred fags. I could 'ave had them."

"You're an idiot," Dabber said. "Just shut your mouth in future about Melody, will ya?"

He went out and found Melody in a cold, dark doorway in an alley behind the Spring Chicken.

"I should have whacked that stupid bastard for saying what he did," said Dabber.

"Don't worry about him. I can handle creeps like that," she said. She pulled Dabber to her and they kissed. Melody said, "Let's go in the sodding pub."

They went in the Pelican, found a comfortable table in a warm corner and Dabber went up to the counter. While he waited to be served he listened to two drivers swaying about in great conviviality. One of them, waving his cigarette about in one hand, was slurring out one of the bus crews' recurring gripes:

"Some Muller Road driver dogged me for a trip and a half! Out to Hartcliffe, then up to Southmead, back down to Hartcliffe and back in to Old Market. Bugger wouldn't overtake, hardly picked up any passengers, but I was stacked out."

His companion said, "Yeah, that's how arguments start. Just looking for trouble."

The first speaker said, "I tell you what, an hour of that bugger dogging me to stop, leaving me to do all the work, I nearly got out the cab, opened his door and gave him a whack."

"Nah, you don't want to do that," the other said. "Get the push from the job for that. You can talk your way out of a lotta things, but not fighting. Get the bullet definite for fighting."

"Well, if he tries that again, I'll whack him, bullet or no bullet."

Dabber got the drinks in, and when he sat down again he said, "But where the hell you been, Melody? You look real smart. I mean, you just disappeared. What happened? You never said anything to me."

Melody was quiet for some time, and then she said, "It wasn't anything I could tell you about, Dabber. Me and my friend was looking for someone, but we didn't find them, not here in Bristol or up in London or anywhere. I had to look smart for the places we went to. Whatever that bugger Greasy thinks, I saved up a long time for these clothes. We had to go to places and meet important people. We didn't find who I was looking for. Maybe I will find them one day, I don't know. I don't want to say anything else, so don't ask me. Maybe I'll tell you all about it one day, Dabber, but just for now I want to keep it for myself."

She smoked defiantly and didn't say anything more for quite some time while Dabber sat and wondered, and then she said, "My life's been shit so far. I just want to have a bit of happiness and settle down and live a normal life like any other girl."

"I'll help you," Dabber said, "but maybe I could help you more if you told me what's going on with you and that lad, and you disappearing and all that."

"I can't tell you that," Melody said. "Not now, but I will one day."

There was a long silence, and then she said, "You know, when I was just young my father pissed off and my mother turned to drink. She was waving a bottle about all the time, ranting and raving. Living hell, it was. The house was a tip. Drunken blokes turning up all the time. When I got older I used to get out of there as often as I could. My friends from school wouldn't come near the place. My mum would shout at them and swear and stagger about. She turned real crazy in the end. I put up with it for a long time, but then she kicked me out and I haven't been back since."

"The world's a bastard sometimes," said Dabber.

They held each other tightly. Later they walked over the frozen streets to her bus stop, and with a sad heart he watched her bus pull away.

But Melody, for all her mysteriousness, could be playful and a tease when she felt in a mischievous mood. The little auburn-haired vixen must have sensed how overjoyed Dabber was to have her back because she toyed with him like a piece of kids' plasticine for a week or two. At her whim, whenever she felt like it, she played with him and pulled him this way and that, stretched him, squashed him, left him for days on end, then came back and pulled him apart all over again. But Dabber was happy to go along with it and let Melody lead him here and there. He was helpless in the face of her attractiveness. And then Melody stopped her games and became serious and romantic, and clung to him often.

Melody was working in the Corona soft drinks factory in Kingswood on the production line, checking the bottles as they came clinking and clanking and rattling past on the belt. And she said she sometimes wished those sodding stupid bottles had vodka in them, not lemonade, and she sure would have a big swig now and again when the foreman wasn't watching.

She said that sometimes it was so cold in that factory, what with the big doors constantly opening to let the delivery lorries in and out, that the workers sometimes had to wear coats and gloves to keep warm. Dabber thought that the girls in there must have got so cold and fed up watching those bottles that their minds were probably far away most of the time, on dates and dishy lads and dresses and all that kind of thing.

Melody and Dabber knocked about the pubs and the cafés mainly, just as they had done before she disappeared, and he sensed that as the weeks went by a change was coming over her. She didn't mess him about so much, and they got closer to each other. Sometimes when she spotted him in the street or a café, she would call across to him with her sweet little-girl voice: a big "Yow!" or something, or maybe just an excited girlie squeal.

But anyhow, the sound was all round and soft and beckoning, as if she'd hooked her little finger into his shirt and was pulling him. It was so beautiful to hear, that summons. He would rush across and she would nestle up really close to him and cling to him as though she needed support in her life.

Dabber could see that Melody had fallen in love with him. But he also knew that she was still not playing straight with him, because while he was whirling round the city on the back of his bus he kept seeing her on the pavement again with the stumbling, rough-looking youth.

Dabber never mentioned it to her though, but it tore a rip in his heart every time he saw the two of them together.

CHAPTER 10

One bitter night, just before Christmas, Dabber and Melody sat in his room, huddled together listening to the little gas fire moaning its sadness at the end of its thin rubber tube. Melody liked to sit late at night with the light off as they cuddled and listened to the sighing of the fire. The two of them would talk a little bit of nonsense and do a bit of rolling about and messing around with each other.

But mostly they were just silent and happy to sit there, each with their own private thoughts.

Occasionally the voices of revellers down on the pavement floated up to them, and sometimes, as clear as slivers of ice, isolated remarks would reach them:

"Did you hear about Rachel?"

"…carrots are so useful…"

"…just his underpants…"

"I mean, whatever was he thinking?"

"He appeared to have an unbalanced buttock."

Just isolated bits of conversation from the lost and distant souls meandering past outside in the cold and moaning night.

Once Dabber and Melody heard, as clear as anything, the lonely boom of a ship's siren down on the river, and the two young lovers knew it must be high tide to get a big ship up that far, past all the mud banks. And maybe it was coming on foggy as well, and the captain was sending out a warning that he was on his way.

The young pair sat there as content as anything, listening idly to the occasional sounds from outside, the soft sibilance of the gas fire and the little creaks and groans of that big old house.

Then all at once there was the slow, muffled slop of feet on the stairs, a shuffling along the landing and then silence, a long silence, as if the person outside was waiting and listening. Dabber shushed Melody.

He left his chair quietly and crossed the room slowly, and just as he reached out for the door, there came a soft, hesitant tap. He opened the door fast and the landlady was there: Mrs Racks.

She had one hand on the door frame and she slouched a little in her crumpled dress. "I'm alone down there, you know," she said.

Dabber stared at her.

"It's Christmas soon," she said.

"Soon," he agreed.

"I'm just down there in my flat by myself," she went on. "I've got nobody, you know. I used to have lots of friends round here. In every street, I had friends. When I walked down the street everybody I met shouted, 'Hello, Amy.'

"They've all gone now, all moved away. And family, I had lots of family. But they don't last, you know. They move and they don't write anymore. They don't call. Course, I don't blame them. A lot of them are gone, you know, not here anymore. But I get on fine by myself. I don't need anybody, not really. But at Christmas, that's when I feel it sometimes. Christmas is a bad time to be lonely, isn't it?"

Melody had come over and was standing there also. "Look," she said. "Why don't you come in? We're just going to have a drink, actually."

"Oh, I don't like to trouble you," Mrs Racks said, in a nervous rush of words. "I wouldn't have knocked, but I didn't know if you were in. I wouldn't bother you. It's late, you know, nearly midnight. I wouldn't bother anybody at this time of night."

She leaned her head against the door frame and they saw the signs of drinking and misery and loneliness on her face, and felt sorry for her.

Dabber opened the door wide and put on the light.

"Look, why don't you come in?" he said. "We were just going to crack a couple of bottles open. You're very welcome."

Amy straightened up. "Oh, I really don't like to. Oh, my goodness, I'd be intruding."

"Come on in, what the hell?" Dabber said.

Melody said, "Come on in, Mrs Racks."

And Mrs Racks said, "It's Amy. I will come in actually, but only for a minute, now you've asked me, but I won't stay."

Melody took her by the arm to encourage her and made a little face when she smelled the landlady's sherry-tainted breath. They sat Amy down in the rickety armchair, while Melody and Dabber sat together like a pair of lovebirds on the sagging settee. And then they all stared at the tiny gas fire, which by now was spluttering with indignation at this intrusion.

They all looked at each other and then away again. There was an embarrassing silence, and then Amy said, "Well, this is nice. You've got it very nice in here. You're lucky to have each other, you two."

And Dabber, jumping up suddenly, said, "I forgot the beer," and got three bottles out and was going to crack them all open when Amy said, "Actually, I've got some sherry downstairs – I quite like a drop of sherry."

She went down and got it as speedily as her sherry-slowed, stumbling legs would allow. Dabber found a glass for her and she sat swigging the sherry while Melody and Dabber knocked Double Diamonds back straight out of the bottles.

They all sat back then, happy, and looked at each other and started drinking again, and Amy said, "You know, I've got a big flat downstairs, a big empty flat, and I was thinking of having a little party this Christmas. Just for a few people, if you'd like to come? We used to have such good parties in the old days – you wouldn't believe the parties we used to have."

And Melody said quickly, "We'll come, Amy. Of course we'll come."

"We used to walk down the Zigzag and watch the Campbell's steamers and walk about and have a drink in the Bear. Oh, we had some good times in those days."

Dabber got more bottles of Double Diamond out, and Amy gradually became more maudlin. She drank down the bottle of sherry and became hazy and a bit wobbly, and Dabber and Melody were both glad it was an armchair she was in and not a dining chair.

She was late forties or early fifties, Dabber thought, and although she had obviously been hitting the sherry a bit because of the sadness and the loneliness, she was still slim, with a good bust.

Amy said, "I'm glad I knocked. I didn't think you were in or I wouldn't have knocked. One thing I would never do is disturb anyone. No, I would never disturb anyone. I would never intrude."

They sat there until about two in the morning and all was quiet outside. They had no beer left and all the sherry was gone.

They helped Amy down the stairs to her flat and she said, "We used to have picnics in the gardens. Picnics."

Melody said, "Let us know when the party is, Amy, and we'll come. We'll definitely come."

In the Old Market canteen a driver nicknamed Slab was boasting.

"I'm telling you, mates, there ain't nothing easier to get than money. If I ain't got a big, fat pay packet every week I ain't happy." He forked some more greasy food down his throat and went on, "I got to be on the road at five in the morning and still up in that cab last thing at night. Double shifts. Split shifts. Overtime. Rest days. I do the lot. It don't worry me how many hours I do."

"Yeah, we all know that's how you got your big belly – you got it eating too much grub and sitting squeezed behind the wheel, whacking up the hours," a young driver named Cyril said. "But some of us got more pride than that. Some of us got more pride than hanging around the foreman's desk like a dog, ready to grab another bloke's duty."

"If a man's too lazy to get out of bed for his shift, I'm entitled to grab it," said Slab.

Cyril said, "Yeah, you're quick to grab other blokes' overtime, but you're too slow on the road. You got to get on the ball, mate. I just get my toe down and get going. I might be the youngest driver on the Bristol Omnibus, but I reckon I'm one of the best."

Slab said, "Listen, mate, it ain't about getting your toe down and stuff like that, it's about experience. You got people's lives in your hands when you're driving that bus. It ain't about speed, it's safety, mate, safety on the road an' safety of your passengers. You ain't had that red badge five minutes and you think you can drive. Wait until you been on the job twenty years like me and then you might have a bit of common sense."

The young driver replied, quick as a flash, "Yeah, but when you learned to drive, Slab, back in the Dark Ages or whenever it was, there probably wasn't much traffic, just horses and carts and things like that. Things have changed, mate. You've got to be sharp nowadays, sharp and fast."

Slab forked some food into his mouth and chewed slowly, without replying.

Cyril went on: "It's all about speed and reactions now. I've seen you driving, Slab, and it's painful. You got your big belly stuck behind the wheel and it takes you yonks to react to anything."

Slab threw down his knife and fork and looked as if he was going to leap across the table at the young driver. "Listen, mate, I drive with my brains, not with my belly. It's experience and brains you need on the road and you got neither."

"What I lack in experience I make up for with reactions. I reckon I can react faster than any other driver in this company," the young driver said. "I got a fast brain. That's what you need, Slab, not a slow old brain like what you've got. You're like an old carthorse, the way you go around, mate."

Slab was silent for a moment, just staring at the young driver, and then he said, "You got no common sense. One of these days somebody's gonna stick one on you if you keep talking like that. The trouble is, you got a brain but it ain't mature. Your frontal lobes aren't developed enough."

"There's nothing wrong with my frontal lobes," the young driver said.

"Frontal lobes is where all the common sense is. They ain't fully developed till you're twenty-five, and you're a long way off that. That's why you're an idiot, mate," said Slab, and he got up and lumbered out with a slow swagger.

There was silence for a time after he had gone, and then the young driver said, "If they start taking blacks on, that crazy bugger won't be able to grab so much overtime. That'll shut his mouth."

A driver sitting nearby said, "Nothing'll ever shut Slab up. But he's a fair man when you get to know him. Even if blacks come on the job, as long as they don't grab his overtime he'll be all right with them."

There was silence and then Sideburns said, "Them blacks 'ave got a campaign going, marching about and that. And the students are marching about as well, supporting them."

Ratso, who was sitting there with his usual disagreeable expression, said, "Well, they can march about all they want, and them student idiots as well. There won't never be no blacks on this job, mate."

"Yeah, the colour bar is rock solid. Whites only," Skully said.

Ratso added, "That's right. This company ain't going to give way. They've said quite a few times whites only, so whites only it's gonna be."

Dabber said, "We got to look at this sensible, man. Slaves were treated very badly by white people years ago: whipped, chained, raped, killed, all that kind of thing. Loads of Bristol people owned slaves on the plantations. Black people were bought and sold as if they were things, not people. Bristol merchants and slave owners made fortunes through the way black slaves were treated. When the government abolished slavery the slaves got bugger all, not a penny, but the owners got big compensation. The fortunes the owners made have been passed down and some people today are still living easy lives on the back of it. Now, black people can't even get a job on the buses in this city."

"That's got nothing to do with any of us, mate," said Ratso.

"No, not any of us directly, but the wealth of this city came from slavery – the memory of slavery is all over the place," Dabber went on. "Even that depot of ours, Winterstoke – know how it got its name?"

"Ain't got a clue," said Ratso.

"It was named after a geezer called Lord Winterstoke," said Dabber. "He inherited his fortune. But who was he really, this bloke? He was William Henry Wills, one of the Wills family, mate. He was a descendant of the family that made a fortune from tobacco. I don't know if any of their fortune came from tobacco that slaves produced on the plantations, but whether it did or it didn't, this W H Wills, he did a lot of good stuff – he gave a lot of money away. In the end he decided to call himself Lord Winterstoke. There's a portrait of him in that museum up Queen's Road. It's hanging on one of the staircases."

"That's very true about Winterstoke depot," chipped in another conductor. "My depot, Muller Road depot, is named after another bloke that did a lot of good: George Muller. He made his money honestly, not through slavery, and he spent most of his fortune on looking after orphans in the 1800s. You know them big buildings up on the top of Ashley Down? He built them and looked after thousands of orphans in them. So my depot's named after a bloke that did a lot of good with his money as well."

"Who cares about that? That's all in the past, that stuff," blustered Ratso, "and it don't alter the facts. Nobody wants them blacks on the job."

"Who doesn't want them? Have you asked everybody?" said Dabber.

"There ain't no need. Nobody wants 'em. It's obvious, ain't it? If blacks come on the job, the job will go downhill."

Dabber banged his knife and fork down. "It's attitudes like yours that's the cause of all the trouble in the world, mate. People thinking they're better than everybody else – men thinking they're better than women, whites thinking they're better than blacks, rich buggers thinking they're better than the working class – all the discrimination and such-like. I tell you what, mate, there's plenty of black blokes got better brains than you. Plenty of them would be better on the job than you."

When the atmosphere had calmed down a little, Ratso said, "Yeah, well, there'll never be no blacks on this job."

CHAPTER 11

Amaryllis, with Zorbo beside her, was outside the Wills building addressing another gathering of students and curious members of the public.

"Let me remind you," she cried, "that we are here to support the boycott of the buses, which was started by a very admirable young black man, and which is being backed up by many people, both black and white, by famous sportsmen and women, and by politicians, including the prime minister, Harold Wilson.

"And we must not forget that here in Bristol, the very city from which slave ships sailed and merchants became wealthy, black men and women are still being discriminated against in many ways. True, they are not slaves, they are not whipped or chained or shackled, but they are not treated as decent, ordinary human beings. They are refused service in pubs, turned away from bedsitters and flats and refused jobs."

Zorbo came to the front. "This Wills building where some of us have our lectures, yes, it is certainly a magnificent building, but we must remember that it was built with huge profits which the Wills family accrued and which have been passed down through the generations. Did any of that fortune come originally from the ill-treatment of slaves on the tobacco plantations? That I do not know."

Another student had jumped up. "The students of this city certainly do appreciate the magnificent university buildings which the generosity of the Wills family has made possible. We are proud to show our appreciation, not only by study, but by engaging in the fight for social justice and support for those who are not so lucky as we are."

Amaryllis nodded. "Yes, students have always fought intolerance," she shouted. "We must continue to give speeches, we must continue to march. We must make plain our support for black people and work alongside them to persuade the bus company to change its ways."

And then a thin, weedy student in a frayed shirt and shabby jacket jumped to the front. "This is a very worthy protest," he bellowed, "but what does it all mean? Where do we go from here? What are our tactics?"

"Get out of it, you skinny bugger," shouted a heckler. "Come back when you've got a decent meal and a few pints of strong cider down you."

"Strong cider, whoa!" yelled the usual drunk, rolling about and slapping the ground in delight.

And then a white man, about fifty years old, grey-haired, with a neat suit and tie, jumped up onto the steps and straight away started howling and yelling and hopping about. "This is a campaign which should have started years ago," he shouted. "My, this is a great day. Long have I waited to see this day arrive when the citizens of this accursed city would come to their senses and stand up for the poor black men and other immigrants who are treated so shamefully and forced to live such miserable lives in our midst." And then he started stepping about wildly and gesticulating and berating his fellow white citizens before starting off again. "Yes, yes indeed, today is a memorable day in the woeful history of this, our city. Today the eyes of the blinkered have been opened, the darkness of ignorance has been swept aside, the crooked and evil ways of white men have been brought into the light and righteousness has been revealed."

The old gentleman, his head jerking and the veins in his neck bulging, screamed, "This city is awash – awash! – with the foul stench of the slave trade. Corn Street, King Street, Queen Square, Great George Street, the Colston Hall – they taint this great city with the stench of evil." He paused, great breaths of emotion racking his body. "We should all be on our knees praying for forgiveness, yes, on our knees…" The old fellow was waltzing about so much, with his feet dancing here and there, arms gesticulating, spittle flying, that he overbalanced and toppled forward into the crowd. He picked himself up and staggered away holding his back and moaning, "Oh, oh, oh."

He had raised a roar of hilarity from the crowd, and then up onto the steps hopped a slim, bespectacled student in white shirtsleeves and blazing, angry eyes, who immediately started off in a great harangue:

"Brothers, comrades, fellow students and citizens, the only way of avoiding the possibility of the end of civilisation is to rid ourselves of this awful spectacle of inequality and corruption, nepotism and false ideologies." The student's face glistened with sweat and he stamped about, facing this way and that. He stood still suddenly, his angry eyes wide, and then staggered as if from some great emotion, punched the air and shouted, "The pointed swords of justice must be plunged into the hearts of all wrongdoers on this planet of ours, first throughout our whole community here in Bristol, and then throughout this wretched nation of ours, riven as it is with all manner of prejudice and hatred, and then throughout all nations of the world. We must build a great movement encompassing spiritual qualities which banish the deep, clutching shadows of evil. Seducers and fornicators will be banished to pitiless places of torment. Serpents will hang from their necks for all eternity. Diabolical groups and sects must—"

And then, just as the crazy-eyed student was stamping about, gesticulating and yelling, he was brought to a halt by a female student who hopped up onto the step with her bust thrusting and heels click-clacking. She whacked the agitated student in the belly.

"Out of the way, you nincompoop," she commanded. She turned to face the crowd. "Let's have a bit of order here, let's have a bit of common sense," she shouted. "I mean, what the hell are we talking about, here? Racism is what we are talking about. We are not here to listen to bigots or biased individuals or barmy people – we are here to talk about racism, in particular the blatant racism of the company that runs our buses. Only when we have solved that problem will we be some way towards ridding the city of Bristol of this foul curse of racism. We must not desert our black friends. They are fine people."

"Yeah, them blacks is all right. They got good ganja, them blacks. Whey-hey," yelled the drunk, rolling about and slapping the ground in delight.

CHAPTER 12

The night of Amy's party came. Dabber put on a white shirt and swept his hair back with plenty of Brilliantine. Melody dressed in a tight white blouse and a tight short black skirt that showed off her gorgeous thighs, and now and again gave just a flash of the sexy black suspenders holding up her nylons.

She brushed her long auburn hair carefully, and Dabber brushed it for her also, lovingly, until it shone.

They downed some sherry and some beer just before they went out, then laughed and fell onto the bed and rolled around, hot and clinging. When they'd finished they were late and they headed down the stairs in a rush with more bottles in their hands, and only made the party when it was already well underway.

There were long, faded streamers crossing the basement from side to side up near the ceiling, silvery thin strips strewn about, and balloons sticky-taped to the walls with brown bits of parcel tape. Two overweight girls were in the middle of the floor, turning tiredly round and round and gazing sadly at each other. Sitting at the opposite side were Greasy and Rulebook, drinking straight from bottles and gaping vacantly at the scene. There was an old record player blasting out, and beside it a tough-looking character who was in charge of the records and who was singing in a hoarse, cracked voice that seemed to have no relevance to the hit that was being played.

And then in through the door stumbled Old Sam. Old Sam was a heavy, lumbering, good-natured driver who lived comfortably by himself. Dabber was amazed to see him, for he did not seem the party type, and then Dabber blinked and looked again, for following along closely behind and clinging to the elderly driver's arm was Diamond Lil. The pair staggered about here and there, looking for seats, but there were none available, so they made their way to the nearest wall and slid down it drunkenly to the floor.

Immediately Diamond Lil was half-lying on top of Old Sam. She got his face in a strong grip, twisted his mouth towards her and slopped a long, lengthy snog on it, which left poor Sam gasping.

Mrs Racks came over to them with two bottles in her hand and said, "Oh, how nice it is to see two lovers here, how nice. I do like a bit of romance. Have these bottles, there's plenty more on the table. Make sure you both have a good drink."

There was an old piano down the far end, with an unshaven, big-bellied character tinkling away on it at the same time as the record player was blasting out. Also there in the fug of noise and cigarette smoke was Lepiniere. He was on a stool at the far end, and when he caught Dabber looking at him he gave a howl, leaped up and stalked around with strange, jerky steps and wild eyes. Then he poured some beer down his throat, banged back down on his stool again and stared with gaping mouth at the wall.

It would have been a sparse attendance indeed if Dabber had not passed word about the party around the bus crews and the regulars of the White Hart.

And there behind a sideboard, which was loaded with bottles and cans, was the delightful party hostess herself, Mrs Racks, who now wanted Dabber and Melody to call her Amy. She looked sleek and shapely and was immaculately made-up. Her hair was newly cut and permed, and the wrinkled stockings had been replaced by new, sheer nylons. Dabber thought, looking at her, that she had a pair of legs to set any bloke drooling.

She was showing those legs off to the full extent with a smart skirt that ended well above her knee, and the whole lot was set off by an immaculate white blouse, tight-fitting, that showed off her bulging, full – though sagging – middle-aged bust. She was stepping rhythmically and swaying on the spot as she supervised the drinks, gazed around, and every so often took a good gulp of sherry.

She spotted Melody and Dabber and started to come over, and then suddenly went back, poured another wallop of sherry down her throat and came forward again.

"None of my real friends have come yet," she said. Dabber suspected she had no real friends left and that's why she was so lonely.

And then, before Dabber knew it, he and Amy were holding each other tightly and circulating slowly round the room in the middle of the dance area. She felt silky and sweet and he pressed her tightly to himself and buried his face in her soft hair. She turned her face up to him and he kissed her full on the lips. She was rich with perfume, and he would have pleasured an anteater that had that perfume on it.

He was in another world when Melody pushed angrily between them shouting, "Hey, what the hell do you pair think you are doing?"

Amy went back to her drinks sideboard and leaned against it, drinking and looking at Dabber. He looked around for some seats, but there were none left, so he and Melody had to sit on the floor with their legs stretched out and their backs against the wall, which Melody was not too pleased about.

They sat there drinking from bottles. Melody was frosty with him and said, "What you want to go dancing with that old cow for? She could be your grandmother."

"I don't know," he said, "it just happened. She must have grabbed me."

"You weren't making much effort to get away," said Melody sourly.

The two girls of excess poundage were pounding away slowly on the floor and Greasy and Rulebook were still sitting there gaping at the two huge gyrating bottoms in amazement. Rarely could such a mass of moving, wobbling female flesh have been concentrated in such a small area of floor. Dabber was pleased they were in the basement, because he didn't think an upper room would have lasted long under such circumstances.

Then Greasy got up with his bottle in his hand, clutched one of the big-bottomed girls and waltzed slowly round with her, taking a swig from his bottle every now and then.

He was half-cut, Dabber could tell by his expression, but the girl was pleased and made a funny face at her partner, who was now standing at the side and looking most displeased that her friend had got a man and she hadn't. Greasy's head was flopped on his partner's shoulder with his bottle about three inches from his mouth, so that he could suck a drink from it with the minimum of effort when he wanted to.

The other extra-large girl was looking hopefully at Rulebook, but he remained firmly upright on his chair, viewing the whole scene with a stern, disapproving air.

Lepiniere was swaying about on his stool with every muscle of his face twitching and his head bobbing up and down. He mopped his face furiously with a dirty serviette, and then drank a whole bottle of Double Diamond down in one go, got up and walked about sideways for some reason, all jerky and mad. He grabbed another bottle from Amy, who said, "Yes, have a good drink. That's what we're all here for – to have a good time."

Lepiniere, jerking about, said, "Yeah, yeah, good party, missus," and then he sidestepped across to his stool again, just missing Greasy and the fat girl, who were waltzing very slowly, the only ones dancing.

The tough-looking man on the record player was changing the records fast, shouting away to himself, and every so often giving a little jive and a few leg-kicks, and making funny movements with his hands and arms.

Dabber looked at Diamond Lil, who was still snogging Old Sam, and thought that maybe under her hard exterior she was just a lonely woman like so many other lonely people in the world, and that was why she was so pleased to have latched on to bashful Sam.

Amy looked at the couple and seemed pleased that they were being so romantic at her party, even though Old Sam looked a bit groggy as Diamond Lil laid noisy kisses on him.

The piano-tinkler was in a world of his own, pinging away at the keys with wide eyes and an amazed look.

Lepiniere kept getting up and howling, sitting down, crossing and uncrossing his legs, leaning back and leaning forward, scratching his crotch and gazing around with a mad expression.

Amy brought more bottles across for Melody and Dabber and said, "I hope you're having a good time?"

Melody just looked frosty but Dabber said, "Yes, it's absolutely lovely."

Dabber was pleased that Amy brought the bottles across because he was starting to feel a bit unsteady and didn't know if he could have managed to walk across the floor.

He looked across the room and saw that Diamond Lil had her hand across Old Sam's lap and was leaning across, talking very earnestly to him. Sam was listening with an amazed expression. Dabber wondered if it was lovey-dovey stuff she was whispering in his ear, and he chuckled to himself.

But what Lil was whispering about to Sam were her plans for the rest of the night, and Old Sam said, "Oh, I don't know about that – I'm usually in bed by half past ten on my days off."

And Lil said, "Not tonight you ain't, lover boy," and pinned his head back against the wall again with a huge sloppy kiss.

And then while Diamond Lil was up at the drinks table Old Sam lumbered to his feet and went out as sharp as a ferret without saying goodbye to anyone.

Diamond Lil came back with two bottles in her hands, looked round and immediately said, "Where the hell's Sam?"

Someone told her, "He just went out," and she put the beer down fast and legged it out after him.

Dabber pulled Melody to her feet and they danced very slowly, alone, in the middle of the floor.

He rested his face against her hair and breathed her perfume and felt her heart throbbing, and knew absolutely that he loved her.

Amy appeared with two Christmas crackers in her hand.

"These are all I've got," she said.

She gave one to Melody. Melody turned away from Dabber and offered the other end to the man on the record player. They pulled it and both ignored the trinket that fell out of it.

Amy went over to Lepiniere and offered the other one. He grabbed one end drunkenly and pulled. Amy tumbled against him and the cracker dropped to the floor. He put his arms round her and she turned her face up to him and they kissed. He pulled her down with him onto the stool and they kissed some more, then nearly fell off the stool and Lepiniere had to put his hand against the wall to save himself.

Amy freed herself, stood up, smoothed herself down and went back to the drinks sideboard.

Lepiniere sat morosely and then spied the cracker on the floor. He picked it up, gazed at it as if he had never seen a cracker before and then lethargically let it drop.

Greasy and his overweight partner had slumped to the floor at the side of the room and were pawing each other. Rulebook was still sitting upright and observing everything impassively. The other tubby girl had edged closer to him and was looking at him hopefully.

The man on the record player got up, scowled round and began to put his coat on. The record player died to silence. A Christmas streamer drifted slowly down from the ceiling and splayed forsaken on the floor. The unshaven man who had been tinkling on the piano turned round and looked at everyone. After a minute he slid slowly to the floor with his back against the piano and an idiotic grin on his face. Amy's nylons were sagging. She slouched against the sideboard looking at Dabber.

Greasy and his tubby dancing partner were lying on the floor groping at each other's bodies without much enthusiasm. The other overweight girl was leaning tiredly against the wall looking depressed. The cigarette smoke was thick. There now wasn't a sound in that basement flat.

Greasy rolled over onto his back, flung his arm out and started to snore. Everyone gazed at him silently.

The balloons on the wall were wrinkling and starting to drop off. Lepiniere got up with his cigarette still in his mouth and slowly took off his jacket and then his shirt. He sat down again bare-chested and stared gloomily at nothing.

Dabber stared at the fallen streamer. The drinking had stopped.

Melody was looking around. She said, "Let's go. It's a bloody fiasco, this party."

"Yeah," said Dabber.

On their way out, Melody said in a sarcastic tone to Amy, "Thank you for the party."

Dabber said, "Yes, thank you, Amy. It was very nice."

*

Back upstairs, in Dabber's bedsitter, he and Melody sat together quietly in the dark, holding each other tightly.

Neither seemed to want to speak, but then Melody said, "What the hell you want to let that old cow grab you for?"

"I don't know."

"You men spoil everything when you get drunk," she said.

They were both silent again, still holding each other, until Melody said, "You know that person you see me with sometimes?"

"Yeah," he said.

"Well, he kind of used to be my boyfriend."

"Used to be?" Dabber said. "Looks like he still is."

"He's just a friend now. His name's Joe. He used to be a boxer," she went on.

"He doesn't look like a boxer."

"He drinks too much now, like a lot of people. That's his trouble, but he used to be the best in the gym."

"Why do you go around with him?" Dabber said.

"There's nothing between us, nothing romantic. I want you to believe that, Dabber. It's just, there's something important I've been trying to sort out with him, but it's hard when he's always drunk. One day I'll tell you all about it, but I don't want to talk about it just now." She paused and hugged him. "Let's just enjoy what's left of the evening."

CHAPTER 13

However the job went, however conscientiously the drivers and conductors of the Bristol Omnibus Company laboured, however much they tried to avoid problems, stresses occurred and disagreements with passengers happened.

Every day complaints rolled into the company's offices. There was scarcely a thing which some members of the travelling public of Bristol did not complain about: high fares, wrong fares, missing buses, late buses, early buses, dirty buses, fast driving, slow driving, bad driving and rude conductors. The vast majority of passengers on the Bristol buses were fine, honourable, upright and sensible people, but there were also eccentrics, mentally disturbed people, serial complainers and bigoted characters. Always among the latter was a small number who, after a real or imagined slight, took pleasure in writing down drivers' or conductors' badge numbers. Not even the most conscientious worker escaped the 'complaints brigade'.

Each crew carried about a thousand passengers per shift, one shift per day, six days a week, fifty weeks of the year. Then add in overtime, rest-day working, double shifts and all sorts of other stuff and you're up to about 350,000 passengers per crew per year. Well, if there weren't a few upset characters among that lot it would be a miracle.

350,000 passengers per year, all waiting for buses, grumbling, getting on buses, moaning, paying fares, bitching, ringing bells, getting up, falling down, injuring themselves, phoning the company and writing letters with all sorts of cranky complaints about this, that and the other.

And the driver cursing the traffic, struggling to stay on time; the conductor trying to smile through it all, getting the blame for everything because he was the one who was face-to-face with the passengers. Yes, the crews had it all in their ears every shift: missing buses, full buses, dirty buses, cold buses, high fares and overcharging. And the drivers and conductors may have slogged to the depot on foot or on pushbikes in the early hours. No buses for them at four o'clock in the morning in the cold and the sleeting rain.

The complaints that came in from the often bonkers and aggressive passengers who boomeranged about on the buses were typed up by office staff and put into crews' pigeonholes at the depot. The driver or conductor on the receiving end of the complaint would have to go up to the Centre to see the big boss and face a reprimand, a suspension, the sack or any manner of things. Sometimes the crew member, if he had a bit of savvy, would have conjured up some sort of a plausible story, be found innocent and sent back to his duties. Others would leave the office feeling hard done by and disgruntled, cursing passengers, buses, bosses and the whole setup of it all. But to be fair, some of the complaints were justified. Among the men who crewed the Bristol buses in those crazy days of the early sixties was a ragtag, drifting, dysfunctional proportion of strange and irrational characters. Mix them in with the drinkers and the dippers, and the stunts and antics which the travelling public sometimes had to put up with had to be seen to be believed.

One day Dabber found a brown envelope in his pigeonhole and he groaned, thinking it was a complaint against him, but when he opened the envelope, to his surprise, it was not a complaint; it said that now he had reached the age of twenty-one the company would like to train him as a driver. Well, the thought of being up in the cab of one of those powerful, throbbing monsters and driving round that teeming, heaving, vibrant city was something that set his blood racing.

He whacked in his acceptance right away.

Dabber found Melody banging some balls up on the pinball machine in the Spring Chicken.

"I've been looking for you, you bugger," she said.

"I keep seeing you with that drunk lad again," Dabber said. "I mean, what's going on?"

She was silent and looked away, and then she said, "Where did you see us?"

"I've seen you a couple of times – when I'm on late shift."

"It's just someone I used to know. I told you there's nothing between us," she said.

"Yeah, but is it you and me, or you and him?" Dabber demanded.

"He doesn't mean anything to me now."

"You'll have to tell me sometime what it's all about, Melody. Why not now? Why don't you want to tell me?"

"It's something personal I don't want to talk about. We were very close in the past, me and Joe, and we did things together," said Melody. "He's trying to help me with something. I know he still loves me in a way, but I don't feel the same way about him, honestly I don't, Dabber."

"It's just a weird situation. Why is he always drunk?"

"Like I told you before, he didn't always used to be like he is now. He used to be all right, but now he's just gone to pot – I mean, his brain's gone. Too much getting knocked about in the gym, and too much drink. I'm trying to help him straighten out and sometimes he's almost there. I just want you to know there's nothing romantic between us."

They were both silent for a time and then Dabber said, "It's hard for me, you know, Melody, when I don't know what's going on." He turned and looked at her. She looked sad and beautiful. He leaned on the machine without speaking again, and she remained standing silently beside him.

Her auburn hair glinted and shone in a lustrous cascade under the lights of the café, and her moody dark eyes were cast down, not looking at him.

"One day you'll understand, Dabber," she said. She looked away and then looked back at him. "I don't want to talk about it anymore."

They went out into the darkness of the evening with the air hanging still and silent and walked a little way along Old Market until they came to the Pelican. Inside, two or three old men were drinking silently, separately and sadly, and at another table two rough-looking deadbeats were drinking and smoking. A group of bus workers were sitting around another table. The owner was leaning on the bar, smoking and reading a newspaper.

Dabber and Melody sat quietly in that cosy bar. He put his arm around her and she snuggled against him. They whispered a few inconsequential things and occasionally laughed, but Dabber's mind was full of wonderings about Melody and the drunken boxer. They sat for a long time and then went out into the darkness of the lanes behind the Pelican. Melody leaned back against the wall and she and Dabber fondled each other and kissed a lot, then they walked to the bus stop and kissed and cuddled some more until her bus came. He stood and watched the lights of the bus disappearing until he could see them no more.

Dabber stood there for a long time, deep in thought, then he turned, walked back to the Pelican and sat with the group of busmen and women.

Skully was saying, "The thing is, with these blacks, they got different habits and things, haven't they – they live different."

"How do you mean?" said Dabber.

"Somebody said there's, like, ten of 'em in one room."

"Who told you that?" said Dabber.

"It's what I 'eard."

"Well you heard wrong," Dabber said, "They live normal, just like us."

"Yeah, but there's too many of 'em coming in," said Skully.

"Most of the ones who want jobs on the buses are here already, mate," said Dabber. "They're as English as any of us lot, just a different colour, that's all."

Skully said, "Well, I don't fancy working with one of them."

"What?" a conductress immediately replied. "I've worked with black people on other jobs I've had. They're all right: polite and well-behaved, nothing wrong with them."

Diamond Lil, who had a pint of brown ale in front of her and had just sparked up a cigarette, said, "If any of them black 'uns try owt with me…"

"I don't expect any of them's that desperate," Poody said.

She glared at him.

Dabber said, "You don't need to worry about them, if they ever come on the job. They're human beings, same as us. They won't be robbing anybody or mugging anybody."

There was silence for a time and then Skully said, "They'd knacker the job up, though, wouldn't they? They wouldn't do it right."

Dabber said, "What you on about, mate? Some of 'em would probably do the job better than you. They're highly educated, a lot of those black people. Just think of all that talent wasted because they can't get decent jobs. They're forced down to the bottom of the pile, mate. Some of the black people, they got qualifications to be other things – brain surgeons and so on. Instead they can't even get a job on the buses."

"I wouldn't want one of them blacks operating on my brain," said Diamond Lil.

"What brain's that, Diamond?" said Poody.

Diamond Lil was halfway out of her chair, but was restrained by a friendly hand. "You're really asking for a smack round the ear'ole," she said.

After this, most of the busmen and women got up to go, until only Dabber was left. Two young women were sitting at a nearby table.

Dabber was toying with his drink, thinking about the colour bar problem, when all of a sudden he was startled by one of the two young women who had been sitting nearby. She had approached silently and now stood beside his table. He looked at her curiously.

"Excuse me," she said, "I couldn't help overhearing what you were talking about. My name's Amaryllis. I'm a student at the university."

"Yeah?"

"We've got a campaign going."

"What sort of campaign?"

"Supporting the boycott some black people have started against the bus company."

Dabber toyed with his drink without replying.

"All the students are worried about what the bus company is doing," said Amaryllis. "It doesn't seem right. I just wondered what you thought about that."

"Well, I'm against the colour bar, obviously, but why do you want to know what I think?" said Dabber.

"We're anxious to know what the ordinary crews think. If you could give us some information it would really help our campaign," said Amaryllis.

"Well, most of the blokes aren't bothered one way or the other about it. I personally got nothing against black people," said Dabber. "I'd like to see them on the job. It would make it better for everybody: us crews, the passengers and everybody. It's us crews who get all the hassle from the public because buses are off the road."

"That's the sort of information we want," said Amaryllis, "and what would be really useful for us would be to have someone on the inside – just to tell us what the feeling is among the crews."

"Sounds a good idea."

"I heard you talking – you don't seem too keen on what the bus company is doing," Amaryllis said.

"Here, hold on a minute," said Dabber. "I hope you're not thinking about me being your inside man."

"No, not at all. Just give us some information about what the mood is among the ordinary busmen. That's all I'm asking."

Dabber was silent for a time and then he said, "I don't know if I want to be involved. I mean, it's in the regulations – we aren't supposed to criticise the company."

"But you're concerned about this policy," Amaryllis said.

"Of course I am. Everyone should be," Dabber said. "It's wrong that people can be treated like outcasts just because of their colour. Everybody's entitled to earn a living, aren't they?"

"Of course, but nobody need know. If you could just give a little talk, a few words, to some students who are very involved in the campaign…"

"I'd be no good at giving a little talk," said Dabber.

"You've got your heart in the right place. All you'd need to say to the students would be just a few words along the lines of what I've just heard you saying to those bus people."

"I dunno. I don't think I'd be able to tell you very much. I mean, I don't know what the bosses are thinking. I got no idea what the management's plans are."

"Not the management – we know what their attitude is all right.

Just the ordinary crews, what they're thinking. That's what we're interested in," said Amaryllis.

Dabber was silent again.

"Just a few little words in confidence to a few of us students?" coaxed Amaryllis.

CHAPTER 14

Seven in the morning and winter still had the city in an icy grasp. In the bleak darkness of the yard at the Lawrence Hill depot the trainees struggled to get the heavy, cold engines of the ancient training buses to fire. Their frozen fingers were pressed for long spells against icy starter buttons, and the huge engines struggled and groaned and slapped slowly over as if they were in barrels of glue. Sometimes heavy starting handles were brought out and the trainees heaved and panted and sweated with bulging eyes as they struggled to turn the mighty engines.

If all else failed, Scoter, the instructor, standing huddled in his thick company overcoat, cap pulled down low, hands deep in his pockets, would shout, "Get the rag. Get the effing rag." A flaming oily rag tied to the end of a metal rod would be brought and one of the trainees would lie on the frozen ground and thrust it under the engine of the bus to thin the oil. The starter button would hammer again and all of a sudden the surly diesel would burst into life, bellowing throughout the yard and filling the freezing air with thick, pungent fumes.

Scoter's lower jaw had been whacked to the side by about an inch at some time. It was said that he had been kicked by a horse when he was little. He talked out of the side of his mouth and sounded like one of those Martians you see in the movies; all sort of mechanical and toneless.

"Hey, you useless bastards, get those sodding engines started and let's get on the road."

Dabber relished the two-hour sessions on the training buses, even with the hot breath of Scoter on his neck. The partition behind the driving cab of the training buses had been cut away and Scoter was always standing right there behind the learner, growling and grumbling.

"Double de-clutch. Give it a splash of gas. You've stalled the sodding thing. Start it up again, for Chrissake. Don't just sit there, you got to get going again."

Or he would yell in the trainee's ear, "Too much noise coming from that box. You got to take it easy, kid. Make the box your friend. Listen to it. Judge its mood. Treat it like your girlfriend. When the time is right, ease the stick in slow and gentle, *slo-o-ow* and gentle. You've got to listen to the revs and then slip it in *slo-o-ow* and gentle."

It was a nightmare, the training, but through determination Dabber persevered and eventually he was allowed far and wide in the city streets at the wheel of the big training bus. Under Scoter's tutelage he practised on all the routes and a few more places besides, but what Scoter liked best of all were hills of all shapes, sizes and gradients; long hills, short hills, winding hills, narrow hills – and the steeper the better.

There could hardly have been a major hill in Bristol that Scoter didn't order the nervous trainee to take a long run at. And then the skew-jawed instructor would wait, scowling, for the floundering struggle of the learner driver and the scream of the crash gearbox as the bus ground to a halt halfway up. Then Scoter could have a good swear, and that was another thing he liked, a good swear.

But the old bastard pushed Dabber on and eventually the hills seemed to get less steep, the crash gearbox less fearsome, and they reached the summits with ease. And gradually as the weeks went by Scoter stopped scowling and swore less and mostly just sat with his face all twisted and twitching in the front passenger seat, smoking his strong Gold Flake cigarettes and gazing out of the window as the bus trundled along.

But sometimes, unexpectedly, Scoter would leap up from his probably horrible daydreams and imaginings, pull his cigarette from his mouth and yell and curse at the learner. Then he would calm down, resume his seat and his smoking again, with his face now and again giving way to strange contortions. Other times he would suddenly jump up, lean over Dabber's shoulder and impart little aphorisms in a grave monotone, like, "Read the road careful, kid. Always read the road careful. Many's the time a man has come to grief because he didn't read the road careful." Once, while Dabber was driving the training bus down through Bedminster, Scoter had jumped up, leaned over and said, "Always remember, kid, a running passenger is a passenger who is running."

Dabber had thought a long time about the running passenger. He could never quite work out what the significance was, but he supposed it must be something profoundly deep and mysterious, emanating as it did from the depths of Scoter's tormented mind.

Scoter, having delivered one of these solemn little homilies, would sink back contentedly into his seat until inevitably, before long, his face would start jerking and his body would be jolting again as his thoughts returned to who knows where and the demons of his mind recommenced their torments.

Amaryllis had called a meeting of female students in the Students' Union in the Victoria Rooms. There was complete silence for several seconds while she looked them over and then she began.

"I have called you all here because it is women who get things done in this world. While the men blunder about and talk a lot of nonsense, women show common sense – and power. Now here is a chance for us to show our determination once again in this fight for the rights of our friends from the Caribbean, India, Pakistan and other faraway countries. Just imagine if the Bristol Omnibus Company was refusing to employ women. We would fight, wouldn't we – we would fight like tigers for our rights. In fact women will fight wherever there is injustice, and this bus company colour bar is an injustice, make no mistake about it. If anyone doubts our resolve they should remember the great battles which women have fought in the past and in fact are still fighting, especially the battle for equal rights."

And then a thin, bespectacled student spoke. "I absolutely agree. We women were oppressed for centuries, and we still are in many ways. We are slowly moving towards full equality, but it has been a long struggle and we must think not only of ourselves, but of all members of society who are beaten down and suffering."

"That is absolutely correct," said Amaryllis. "Take the suffragettes, for instance – even as recently as sixty or seventy years ago men thought women didn't have the brains to vote. They thought they weren't intelligent enough. They denied women the democratic right to express their opinions through the ballot box, but then the suffragettes came on the scene. They said if women had to abide by laws that men made and pay taxes under laws made by men, then women had the right to vote. There was no messing with the suffragettes, I can tell you."

One of the girls, who had been deep in thought, said, "I know the gist of the story of the suffragettes, but what exactly happened to them in the end?"

"What happened to them? They had to fight, just like the black and Asian people are having to fight now. They could see that the men in Parliament and other people in top positions were not taking them seriously, so they stepped up their protesting – shouting at meetings and that sort of thing. They often ended up battered and bruised and some were even thrown in prison and force-fed, but it just made them determined to fight back even harder. They burned down buildings, chained themselves to railings and disrupted Parliament. Here in Bristol a few suffragettes burned down a new male sports pavilion at Coombe Dingle, which belonged to the university."

"So you think we should try a bit of violence in support of the bus boycott?" said the bespectacled girl.

"Good heavens, no," said Amaryllis. "Our campaign must be non-violent. The dignified campaign of the black people has set the example." She paused, and then went on, "Shall I tell you what happened immediately after the suffragettes burned down the sports pavilion? The male students came along the next day, smashed into the suffragette shop on Park Street, broke the windows, threw all the papers and pamphlets out and had a bonfire in the middle of the street. The police just stood back and did nothing."

The bespectacled student said, "Women students fought another campaign, didn't they, the bluestocking campaign?"

"What on earth was the bluestocking campaign?" asked another of the undergraduates.

"Well," the bespectacled student continued, "it was named after a group of young intellectuals, mostly women, and an occasional man, who met in London about two hundred years ago. One of them wore blue stockings, so the name stuck. When intelligent women got together and started campaigning, naturally enough they called them bluestockings."

"What were they campaigning for?" asked one of the other girls.

"The right to graduate," replied the bespectacled student. "In those days women could not graduate. They could do the courses, but they could not graduate, while male students could. It seems unbelievable now, but in those days people thought that too much education was bad for women. Women were classed as idiots, with no more brains than a lunatic or a baby. The stupid men on the boards of universities said that academic achievement could cause women to lose their femininity. They said it would shrivel their uteruses and cause hysteria."

There was much laughter at this. When they had recovered the bespectacled girl went on, "Yes, those idiots of men said that it would destroy any chance of marriage or a family. Women who had gone through higher education were viewed as shrivelled spinsterish types who everyone should feel sorry for. In 1869, when Girton College was founded, women were classed as not having wills of their own." She paused a moment. "Universities only grudgingly, one by one, gave women permission to wear the cap and gown. Cambridge was the last one to see sense. In fact, it was not until 1948 that Cambridge allowed women to graduate. It was a long battle but I think we have certainly shown the men since then that we have not only willpower, but intelligence. And we are showing it now in our campaign against the bus company colour bar."

"Yes, I'm glad you brought up the bluestocking campaign," said Amaryllis. "It shows that when women start a campaign and are determined enough, they don't give up. There was another Bristol woman who was not only a member of the Blue Stocking Society, but also campaigned very strongly against slavery. Her name was Hannah More. She was a writer and campaigner who gave a lot of support to William Wilberforce, the great anti-slavery campaigner. She also gave financial support to Ann Yearsley, another Bristol woman, who was a campaigner against the slave trade. Hannah More actually lived the last few years of her life here in

Clifton, where we are now, and she lived just long enough to see the act which finally abolished slavery in the 1830s."

"It's amazing what women can accomplish when they put their minds to it," said the bespectacled student.

"Yes," said Amaryllis. "We women know what discrimination is – that is why we are determined to support the black and Asian people in their fight to be treated as ordinary human beings."

Amaryllis was going to continue, but she was interrupted by a creaking, grinding noise and the eyes of all the girls immediately switched to the end of the room where the metal grille of the bar was slowly being raised.

"Thank God for that, I'm dying for a bit of alcohol," exclaimed the slim girl. She led the rush of girls to the bar and there was much pushing and shoving as they all scrambled to be served.

When they had all settled down again, Amaryllis went on. "Talking about buses, I'm sure we all know about Rosa Parks, another woman who made a personal stand for decency and equality. Everybody should know about her. She was a black woman in Alabama who was ordered to give up her seat on a bus to a white passenger. She refused. She just decided she was tired of being ordered around because of her colour, and of being treated like a piece of dirt just because she was black. So she didn't move – she sat tight and the police came and arrested her. They took her photo with her convict number across her front, but what she did sparked a great campaign – a campaign for equal rights for black men and women. That brave person, Rosa Parks, she just decided that she would make a stand for the rights of black people, and that incident on a bus in Alabama started the whole civil rights movement."

Amaryllis paused and then went on, "It's funny, isn't it, that here in Bristol it's the bus industry once again that finds itself treating our black friends as second-class citizens?"

"Yeah," said the slim girl, "what the hell is it with bus companies?"

Amaryllis was just about to reply when the door banged open and a crowd of noisy male students piled in.

"Well," she said, "we might as well finish our discussion about equality now that that collection of tadpole-brains has come in."

CHAPTER 15

Spring crept in slowly in 1963; the days grew warmer and in the underground canteen of the bus company the long-bladed ceiling fans rocked and moaned. Card schools ran non-stop and Slab was often heard spouting on his favourite subject.

"Broke the ton again this week. 105 hours in. Grab the overtime while it's going, that's my policy." He pulled a wad of notes from his pocket. "This is what it's all about: money. Twenty-five quid I've pulled in this week. That's more than any other man on this company."

"But what's it all for, Slab? What's the point of working yourself to death like that?" somebody asked him.

"I ain't working myself to death, mate," Slab said, shoving food into his mouth.

"Yeah, but sometimes you don't look good, Slab," they told him. "You wanna ease up a bit, take it easy."

Slab shoved more food into his mouth, chewed slowly, spread his arms wide and said, "No chance. I'll be off this job an' lying in the sun on some beach over in the South of France or Africa or someplace, while you lot are still slaving away on here."

"You'll soon get fed up lying on a beach," said someone, "an' what are you gonna do when you get skint?"

"What you got to understand," said Slab, "is I'm a man of the world, know what I mean? I'm a hard worker, can turn my hand to anything – I've never been afraid of hard work."

He forked some stew up and slapped it back onto his plate. "I mean, look at this crap they give us to eat in 'ere. It ain't good enough.

I want a bit of high-class grub, a bit of high-class living."

"When you gonna be going, Slab?" asked a conductor.

"Soon as I can, mate, soon as I can," Slab said. "I tell you what, soon as I've got the money, I'll be off over there, *toot sweet*, living like a king."

"You're king of the overtime grabbers," Cyril, the cocky young driver, said. "That's the only sort of king you are."

"Listen, my friend," Slab said, "all the overtime I do I get fair and square. Anybody like me looking for extra work is entitled to grab it. What's wrong with that?"

"You won't be able to grab as much overtime when the blacks come on the job," said Cyril.

"What do you mean, 'when the blacks come on the job'? The colour bar's still on, isn't it?" a conductor from Winterstoke depot exclaimed.

"The colour bar's on its last legs, mate. The company's gonna back down," a driver from Lawrence Hill said.

"Well if that's right, they'll be flocking in, man – from the West Indies, India, Pakistan, all them places, taking white men's jobs," said Ratso.

"The blacks won't be taking no one's job," Dabber said. "There's plenty of jobs around. Look at the buses that's off the road every day because there's no crews, all those buses parked up in the depots and up side streets. There's plenty of jobs for anybody that wants one."

The driver from Lawrence Hill depot said, "I used to be a driver on the buses up in the Smoke. They got black conductors up there. One night all the lights on the bottom deck fused. I looked back into the bottom deck an' all I could see was two white eyes moving about here and there. But I'll tell you what, when you get to know them, them blacks is just the same as white blokes."

Dabber said, "Yeah, they'll be all right. They don't worry me. A man's colour don't make no difference to me."

Rulebook looked up from his meal and said, "That's right. I read all about the slave trade. We sent ships across from here to Africa to load up with slaves and take the poor souls away from their friends and families across to America to sell for big money. Then the ships loaded up with sugar or tobacco, which was brought back to England

and the rich gentlemen sold it for huge profits. There is certainly no doubt that we in this country are in the debt of the black community and we should assist in any way we can."

"Yeah, but it ain't that," Ratso said. "It's their habits and all that stuff, ain't it? They'll be down this canteen, jabbering away with stuff what none of us understands. How will we know what they're up to? And the passengers, they're gonna be scared to death, ain't they, late at night, with a black conductor on the bus prowling about."

"That's a load of crap," the ex-London driver said. "Them blacks is all right. Work sodding harder than a lot of white blokes, I'm telling you."

Rulebook said, "During the course of my research I have made several interesting and unusual discoveries. Do you know, for example, that one common way to test whether a slave who was on sale was healthy was for the potential white buyer to lick the slave's cheek after the slave had completed a hard task of physical labour? If the sweat tasted sweet, then that indicated that the slave was in good health and—"

"Shut up, Rulebook," several people shouted.

There was silence for several minutes and then Slab said to Cyril, the boastful young driver, "Was that you on the telly last night, mate, spouting away a load of rubbish? You want to be careful what you say. You got to realise them reporters is just looking for controversy. They egg you on, man, to say stupid stuff. All that stuff you said about none of us lot wanting blacks on the job wasn't true. I tell you what, mate, I'd rather work with a black bloke than with an idiot like you."

"I never said nothing controversial," said Cyril.

"You got too much mouth, mate," said Slab. "My advice: for your own good, keep your trap shut in future. You ain't supposed to speak to the press anyway. That's in the regulations."

"I never said much," protested Cyril.

"Just as well, mate, because what you did say was a load of bollocks. You just spouted away on the spur of the moment when them reporters shoved a camera in front of you. You fell for it, so you said a lot of stuff that you thought would make you famous, being on the telly and that."

"Oh, shut the eff up, you fat bugger," said the young driver. He grabbed his duty card and rushed out before Slab could respond.

CHAPTER 16

A few days after meeting Amaryllis in the Pelican, Dabber was standing on a stage in the Students' Union building in front of a large number of students. Amaryllis was standing beside him.

"I don't know if I can do this, Amaryllis," Dabber whispered. "Man, I'm nervous. I can't speak to all this lot."

"You'll be all right," she whispered back. "Let me say something first and then I'll introduce you. You'll be all right when you get going."

Amaryllis moved forward. "Thank you all for coming, my fellow and sister students," she began. "We are here tonight to talk about the Bristol Omnibus Company colour bar and the protests which are going on against it. As you know, we are supporting the campaign organised by the black people. Our own campaign is gathering momentum and to give us a little inside information on what the ordinary bus crews are thinking we have Dabber, a conductor from the bus company, here tonight. Before he speaks, though, I'd like to quote to you a little something which reflects the great longing for freedom and equality which I'm sure must be felt by every oppressed and downtrodden person on this planet. What I'm going to read to you is from Article 1 of the Declaration of Human Rights."

She glanced at a piece of paper she held. "The Declaration of Human Rights," she read, "says that 'all human beings are born free and equal in dignity and rights. They are endowed with reason and conscience and should act towards one another in a spirit of brotherhood.'" Amaryllis looked around and then said in a firm voice, "The declaration goes on to say that everyone has the right to work and to free choice of employment." She paused. "I want to emphasise that: *the right to work and to free choice of employment.* Now that's exactly what the black and Asian population of this city of Bristol are fighting for: the right to go about their daily lives without discrimination or harassment, and in particular the right to take jobs on our local bus service."

Amaryllis paused and then went on, "Now, we are lucky to have Dabber here to talk to us. As I mentioned, he is a conductor working for the bus company and he is going to give us a little information about the feelings and the mood among the regular bus crews." She motioned him up.

Dabber rose to his feet and looked around. Hesitatingly, he began. "Yeah, well, as Amaryllis said, I'm a conductor on the buses here. Now I haven't given a speech before and I'm a bit nervous, but what I want to say is when I seen the way black people are treated it was a bit of a shock to me when I first come across it, and I can't see any reason for it. Maybe I haven't had as much education as you students, but I read the papers and plenty of books and stuff and I think I know a bit about the world. I know this racist stuff isn't right and people have got to speak up about it." Dabber paused and looked around the audience, but seeing only interested faces, he went on. "Now Amaryllis just gave us a good introduction about that human rights stuff, but I'd like to say straight off that there's more to human rights than bits of paper. It's translating them rights into action that's the important bit. There's racism all over the place and what the bus company is doing is a classic example. I mean, why are they not hiring black staff when there's buses off all over the place for shortage of crews? What's the mentality of it?"

After pausing, Dabber said, "It's us crews who are on the receiving end. We're the ones who get all the crap from the passengers. It can start even when we're off duty. We might be walking along the street, minding our own business – someone sees our uniform and starts having a go at us about the buses, blaming us for it all.

"Or a driver and conductor might be waiting on the pavement at the takeover place to take over a bus – there might be a big queue of people there and they're all jumping about because there hasn't been a bus for God knows how long. When they see a couple of busmen standing there the abuse starts and the driver and conductor are just standing there, innocent, waiting for their bus to come in. People start having a go at them, real nasty sometimes. But it's the management that's got the colour bar on, not the blokes."

"But is it just the management?" shouted a student with a red face and wild eyes. "What about that vote at Eastville depot, where the bus crews voted against taking on black workers? That wasn't anything to do with the management."

"Yeah, I heard about that vote," said Dabber. "It was wrong for anybody to vote like that. I can't give any excuses for it. Eastville's just a small depot and as far as I know it was just a show of hands, not a secret ballot. It takes a lot for a bloke to vote against something when all his mates can see which way he's voting."

A burly, curly-haired student shouted, "What's your own opinion, Dabber, as to why the management have this colour bar policy?"

Dabber paused for a minute and then said, "I think it's a relic of them slavery days. I been thinking about it a lot and reading about it a lot. This city was big in slave trading in the old days, with loads of money coming in. Bristol got rich on the backs of slaves. The bus company hasn't caught on yet that times have moved on and black people got a right to be treated just like anybody else. I think whoever put this colour bar on must think we're still in the old days, slavery and all that, when black people weren't considered to be real human beings, like they were inferior."

He paused. "I mean, I travel all over the city on the buses and I see all these big old grand houses and you wonder where the money came from. Loads of people were in on it, the slavery business, making money – not only merchants and tradespeople, but ordinary people who'd never seen a slave plantation, never seen a black person. They just bought and sold black people through dealers like they were things.

"People thought you were a pillar of the community, a member of the gentry if you made money like that. And a lot of the wealth has passed down through the generations to people today."

Dabber, getting fully into his stride now, went on. "I work on the country buses as well, sometimes, and it's not only in Bristol where the big houses and estates are, it's out in the countryside as well: Ashton Court, Blaise Castle, Dyrham House, Clevedon Court, Tockington Court – they're all over the place, big houses built with slave money."

"What's the attitude of your colleagues towards this colour bar, then?" called out a student.

"Me and my colleagues? Well to tell the truth, most 'em aren't all that bothered about it. There's just a few that go around shooting their mouths off and they're the ones who get all the publicity in the papers and on the telly and suchlike. They give the rest of us a bad name. I've come across a few aggressive blokes who are against black people, but most of us ain't worried whether new staff are black, white or whatever. Most of the blokes just want to work peaceful without all the nasty stuff."

"Why do you think these few bigoted colleagues of yours have these racist attitudes?" shouted the curly-haired student.

"Well," said Dabber, "probably because they never really got to know any black or Asian people before. I mean, new blokes come on the job, they hear regular staff and the management spouting racist stuff and they pick up the idea that that's the way to go. Who can tell?"

Amaryllis stepped in. "Yes, prejudice can start in very innocent ways. It may be isolated remarks made by parents in the presence of a child which can mean that that child grows up with a wrong view of certain members of society, or in this case of the buses, one or two busmen or women saying the wrong thing can lead gullible members of bus crew to become prejudiced."

"Yeah, but if the blokes could meet some black people, though, and talk to 'em, they'd see they're just ordinary people," said Dabber.

"How many of your colleagues have this racial prejudice, Dabber? A few? A lot? What's the percentage?"

"Well, I don't know exactly," said Dabber. "I've met a few, but the Bristol Omnibus is a big company – it reaches out miles every side of the city. It's got loads of depots and thousands of workers, so I can only tell you what a few of the blokes think, not all of 'em."

"When do you think it will end – this prejudice and discrimination?" called out a student.

"I dunno," said Dabber. "It'll start to end when the company drops its colour bar and begins to take on black and Asian people. It'll never truly end until everybody, including myself, stops talking about 'black' and 'white' or whatever and just starts talking about 'people'. But there ain't a hope of that happening until all the prejudice and discrimination in the world is over, and I can't see that happening for a few hundred years."

And then Amaryllis was on her feet beside Dabber. "That's an excellent note to end on. I would have liked Dabber to go on, but some of you, unfortunately, have lectures to go to. I would like to thank Dabber very much for his talk today. Obviously he doesn't want to stir up a lot of trouble for himself by word getting out among the other busmen that he's been speaking to us, but he's certainly given us a lot to think about. How about a round of applause for him?"

There was a great roar of approval from the audience, and then everyone was heading for the exit.

CHAPTER 17

The air was still and crisp for days at a time. The change seemed to slow everything down. Even the traffic seemed quieter and the passengers were calmer and more contemplative.

Melody was in the Spring Chicken during one of these calm, still days. She was pulling morosely at the handle of the pinball machine, pinging the balls around without much interest. After a time she rested her head on the machine. Dabber entered and stopped when he saw her, then he went up and put his arm around her.

"Where the hell you been these past couple of weeks?" he said.

She looked up at him. "I been thinking about things," she said.

"Thinking? What about? Hell, never mind thinking, let's go over to the Hart."

"Not now," she said. "I don't feel like drinking. Let's just walk somewhere."

"Walk somewhere?" Dabber said. "What do you want to walk somewhere for?"

"Because I'm fed up," she said.

He pulled her to him and they wandered along Old Market. They walked over Lawrence Hill and trudged through the dusty streets towards Redfield. Melody didn't seem to want to talk and they walked in silence.

The number eight and nine services ran on that road, both running on ten-minute frequencies. And as they hammered past, some of their crews recognised Dabber.

The conductors leaned off the backs of their buses and shouted,

"Whey-hey, give 'er it, Dabber, give 'er it, boy!" and the drivers barped merry tunes on their horns.

Melody, though, didn't react to any of it; she just sort of clung to Dabber as they walked and seemed emotionally lifeless. Dabber thought that it was strange, but he didn't say anything to her. He just gazed at the pubs and the drinkers inside who were sinking pints of frothy ale in the late warmth of the afternoon.

Dabber and Melody ambled slowly up the long main street of Redfield. He tried to manoeuvre her into the Fire Engine, a spacious, cool hostelry that had its doors flung open invitingly, but she pulled him over the road into St George Park. They went through the trees and bushes at the entrance and followed the path into the grassy areas. There were swings, a roundabout, a small lake and lots of people taking the chance to enjoy the facilities before the calm days slid away. Melody pulled Dabber away from all that and they found an isolated bench at the side of the park, beneath some trees. He was glad to sit down after the long plod.

He leaned back with his arm round her shoulders and she leaned against him. He stroked her hair and they sat there quietly with the calm of the late afternoon enveloping them.

Eventually he whispered into her ear, "What's up?"

She did not reply. The park was emptying; some children were ignoring their mother's shouts and continuing to run around on the grass.

"What's the matter?" he asked again.

"Nothing," she said, without looking at him.

There was a long silence then. Dabber sat quietly and waited. Eventually Melody said, in a little voice, "Oh God, I got the blues terrible bad, Dabber."

"What you got the blues about?" he said.

There was another silence, while he held her close. Then she said, "There's a lot of things you don't know about me."

"What do you mean? What things?"

She was silent again, and then she said, "I had a baby once, you know."

"A baby?"

"Yes."

"I've never seen you with any baby."

Melody gazed around at the trees and the beds of fading flowers, and the pensioners ambling their slow ways towards the exit. The mother had at last got her urchins under control and was hurrying them off.

"What baby?" Dabber persisted. "Where is it?"

Melody leaned against him in a dejected way and he put an arm around her to pull her closer. She said, in a voice scarcely above a whisper, "I gave him away."

There was a pause, and then Dabber, in shock, said, "Gave him away?"

"It was before I met you," she said slowly. She turned her face up towards him and he saw heartache there. "It was a year ago today." She paused and wiped her eyes. "God, this is a bad day for me. A terrible day," she whispered.

Dabber held her tenderly.

"He was a beautiful little baby. Seven and a half pounds when he was born, with lovely dark hair," she said in a sad voice. "I called him Stephen. And I gave him away. Oh God, I just gave him away. Now I'll never see him again."

He held her tightly. "You never told me about this before." He paused. "What did you give him away for?"

She answered in a slight voice, "Because I wasn't married or anything, they put me in a home just before the baby was due. They treated me horrible in there. All the girls in there were treated horrible."

"What about your mother?" he asked.

"My mother? Her! Oh, she was against me. Called me a slut and never said a kind word to me. There was just me and her at home, you know. I think she thought that when the baby came I would just take the baby and go and live somewhere else, leave her by herself. That's what she didn't want. She was selfish like that. She was no good by herself and she didn't want me to have any sort of life away from her."

Dabber didn't know what to say. Everyone else in the park seemed to be living normal lives and enjoying themselves. It was difficult to imagine any of them having any problems in their lives. They were all leisurely getting ready to go home.

Eventually Dabber said, "Who was the father?"

There was a long silence, broken only by the soft rumble of traffic on the main road beyond the trees. The park was nearly empty now; only a few people who had lingered too long in the cool of the early evening were left. Dabber waited and said nothing. Melody was sitting gazing silently ahead over the grass and the boating lake in the distance.

"You should be able to guess who the father was," she whispered at last. "It's obvious, isn't it? That's why I used to chase around after him."

"The boxer!"

She was silent again, and then she went on, "I wanted some security, somebody solid to lean on. And Joe was all right when I first started to go out with him. He was doing well with the boxing. I thought I had some sort of a future with him, but then he turned to drink. He loved me, but when I got pregnant he didn't seem to understand what it was all about. I tried to talk to him but he was nearly always drunk. I think the other fighters just used him for a punchbag and his brain began to turn funny."

"That's bad," Dabber said. "He should have stood by you. It wasn't right, that, just walking away from you and his little kiddie."

"He didn't exactly walk away. He's still around, as you know. He still wants me," Melody went on, "but he's no good with all the drinking and that. He's a decent bloke when he's sober, I'll say that for him, but when I was pregnant and they took me into that home he just didn't have a clue.

"And my mother, her sitting at home drinking as well, saying that I needn't bother coming back home with a baby. Pressure. Just pressure from everybody. Nobody tried to help. Everybody was just trying to get the baby away from me, saying I wasn't mature enough to look after him."

She paused and wiped her eyes and Dabber pulled her closer and kissed her brow gently.

"I just couldn't stand up to it all," she went on. "I just couldn't work a full-time job and look after the baby and battle against them all the time, it was just too much. You know, sometimes I hate the world." She paused. "Anyway, I went and signed him away. I did it. My lovely little Stephen, and now I'll never see him again."

She wiped her eyes with her sleeve. "Today I put my best clothes on and went and stood outside the place where I signed the papers and they took him away from me. I stood there for over an hour, just thinking about him and wondering where he is and who's got him and if he's being looked after all right."

"Maybe you can still find out, if you make enquiries, I mean," Dabber said.

"What do you think I've been doing? Why do you think I've been going round with Joe all those times? I told you there's nothing between us now, nothing romantic. All he's been doing is trying to help me find out where little Stephen is, to try to get him back. Me and Joe have been all over the place seeing people – welfare people and all that lot. We even went up to London to try to see MPs and people like that, but they just said they couldn't help. Adoption was final, that's what they kept saying." She paused. "So there you are. That's where I've been, the times I disappeared."

Dabber pulled her tightly to him. "I wish I'd been around when it first happened," he said gently. "We could maybe have worked something out together."

She pulled away. "Don't bother with all that 'maybe' stuff. I've had enough maybes to last me the rest of my life. 'Maybe this' and 'maybe that'. Everybody said it. The women in the home kept saying, 'Maybe it would be better if you had the child adopted.' My mum kept saying, 'Maybe it would have been better if you had stayed in at night like any decent girl.' Joe used to say, 'Maybe I'll hit the big time as a boxer.' My God! If I added up all the maybes I've had in the last twelve months..."

They sat in silence then, very close. Dabber said softly, "It doesn't make any difference. I couldn't care less what's happened in the past. It's you and me now, that's all that matters."

He tried to think of something to change the subject. "Are you still up at the lemonade factory?" he asked eventually.

"I packed that in," she replied. "How could I keep that on with all the worries and chasing around trying to find out what happened to my baby? I mean, I used to look around at the other women and blokes in that factory. Some of them have been there since they left school and now they're old. Dead behind the eyeballs, a lot of them: walking zombies. Thirty or forty years watching stupid lemonade bottles go past on a conveyer belt. I couldn't face it. I want a bit more out of life than that. So one day I just packed it in."

"Best thing to do if you don't like a job," Dabber said.

Melody sat up suddenly and he could tell the old fire was back in her. "What did you say that pub over the road was called?"

"The Fire Engine."

"Well, what are we sitting here talking about lemonade for?" she said. "Let's get over there and have a proper drink."

CHAPTER 18

The students were marching again, with banners and much tumult, down Park Street. This time they were chanting, *"Urbi et Orbi...*We back the boycott...*Urbi et Orbi...*We back the boycott."

Passers-by had to move aside for them, and one of them grumbled, "Look at them students, with their stupid chanting."

Someone else remarked, "Useless shower. Waste of taxpayers' money, that lot. Showing off with a bit of foreign mumbo-jumbo."

But other passers-by, when they heard the chants and saw the banners in support of the black boycott, started clapping and shouting encouragement.

At the head of the column, punching the air, was Amaryllis, the very determined third-year student; trailing behind her was Zorbo, blinking and wondering at this young girl who stood for no nonsense.

The procession halted at the Centre for the second time. Amaryllis leaped onto some steps facing the crowd and immediately launched into a speech.

"I don't need to remind you, friends, what black people have suffered at the hands of white people over many centuries," she shouted. "It has been nothing more than one race seeking to maintain ascendancy over another, for white people to make black people their slaves and to treat them with contempt and cruelty. And here in this very city of Bristol, the Bristol Omnibus Company is treating black people with contempt by refusing to employ them as drivers or conductors. They are, however, quite happy to have them doing menial work out of sight in the garages. And they quite happily take the fares of black passengers. They are quite happy to see them then, when they are taking money from them."

An elderly black man who had been part of the crowd came to the front. "May I speak?" he began. "I am not used to speaking, but I would just like to say a few words. We are tolerant, us black people, and most white people tolerant too, but some whites think us blacks can easy be pushed around. Man, I tell you it gives us this feeling of fear. It's not a nice way for an old man to live, all fearful and insecure. Sometimes, I tell you, my soul gets all twisted and despairing and I don't feel like I want to carry on with living."

And then Amaryllis was speaking again. "I have sympathy with you, sir, great sympathy. And it is precisely because of the fear you feel and the discrimination which is shown towards you and all your fellows that we are determined to do what we can to bring about a change in the attitudes of those white people who are hostile towards you. We are starting with this boycott of the buses. The campaign was started by members of the black community. We, the students, have joined that campaign. We also will march, shout and refuse to ride on the buses until the bus company changes its policy."

"They won't let me on them buses because I got no money. That's 'ow I boycott the bastards," chortled the drunk, who seemed to spend all his time staggering around the city centre.

"This mighty city," went on Amaryllis, "this mighty city with all kinds of inhabitants, is shamed around the world because of the actions of one company. Let us not rest until black men and women, if they so wish, and if they are capable, are taken on as drivers or conductors with as little question or comment as are white men and women."

"Yeah, but there ain't no laws against it, is there?" a white heckler shouted.

Amaryllis stepped forward. "No laws against what?" she demanded.

"Being against them spades. An employer can please himself who 'e takes on. I mean, it ain't against the law to refuse to take on a load of spades, is it?" said the heckler.

Amaryllis looked as if she was going to spring forward and give the heckler a smack, but she restrained herself and said, "There may well not be a law against it, my good man, but surely morality is against it, the whole of humanity should be against it and we should be against it."

Some busmen had come out of the bus office to see what was going on. One of them shouted, "The point is, we ain't all against black people, us busmen. It ain't us who decides who gets a job, it's the company what decides who to take on."

A serious-looking undergraduate with long hair jumped up onto the steps. "That is right, my friend. It is not ordinary workers who are responsible for this situation. It is the bus company who is refusing to employ black people. It is the company everyone should be directing their anger towards. Do not blame anyone else."

And then a member of the crowd shouted, "Surely goodwill is needed here, goodwill and tolerance on all sides. We should all be exhibiting warmth and generosity towards our fellow men, whatever their colour."

"That's right," a conductress shouted, jumping up onto the step. "These students here got a point. I'm a woman, and I know what discrimination is. I've worked with black people plenty of times in the factories and places and I'll tell you what, I'd rather work with them than with some of the white staff we got on this job. Every black person I ever come across, they've been honest, hard-working and polite." Her voice rose. "Bring on the blacks, that's what I say."

And then a young earnest-faced student jumped up. "That is most commendable and extremely pertinent. This lady has made very significant and relevant points." He gestured this way and that. "It certainly proves that not all the Bristol bus workers are racists – they are not all against the employment of black drivers and conductors."

But another conductor, just coming to pay in his takings, stopped and shouted, "It's about money, mate. If blacks come on the job they're gonna be grabbing all the overtime. The wages will stay low and we'll never get a decent pay packet."

The conductor was pushed aside by a driver. "The blame for low wages lies with the company," he shouted. "Don't blame black people. There's a lot of bus workers, including myself, who would like to see all this discrimination and blaming other people stop. What I say is, let's have black people on the job as drivers and conductors and people might learn a few things about humanity, mate. I agree with what the lady just said: bring on the blacks and the sooner the better."

Up stepped a young black man. "I thank you for your support, sir. As you can see I am a black man, but I did not think of myself as black before I came here. I only became black when I came here, to Great Britain, to my mother country. But instead of finding a mother's love I have found only rejection and humiliation and loneliness. Let me tell you how it is, for those who have not experienced it. You go for a room and it is taken, you apply for a job and it is filled, you walk into a pub and there is complete silence, you ask a question and no one answers, but everyone is staring at you. You feel full of despair. You wake up in the morning and it seems the sun does not shine. You want your dignity back. Children with their innocent little faces look at you and see how you are treated. They soak it all up and perhaps they learn all the bad things, and so it goes on, generation to generation. That is how it is."

"What do we do, then?" a black onlooker shouted. "What do we do when they treat us like dirt?"

The young black man replied, "What do we do? It is hard to know what to do, but the main thing is not to descend to the level of those who insult us. Do not return insult for insult, or pain for pain. I suggest the answer is not to withdraw, but to politely challenge the other person. Push your position peacefully. Try to persuade the other person to withdraw, but in a way which enables him to maintain his dignity."

"And if that gets us nowhere – what then?" the black onlooker shouted.

"Only the future can answer that question," the young black man replied.

A few nights later when Dabber was stumbling home, half-drunk, along deserted, narrow streets, an empty bottle looped out of the darkness and smashed against his head. This took Dabber by great surprise. He rubbed his head and looked carefully and intensely around the darkness, but could see no one, until all of a sudden, out of the black shadows leaped the drunken pugilist, Joe, Melody's ex-boyfriend.

Joe was screaming, "You been knocking off my tart, busman boy. Nobody knocks off my tart!"

And he whacked another bottle against Dabber's collarbone and blasted a big uppercut into the side of his face. Dabber went down and was nearly out, but as he lay there, all groggy in the great dirty blackness, he opened his eyes into tiny slits and glimpsed, looking down at him, the battle-scarred, snarly face of drunken Joe. Dabber saw that Joe was preparing to boot big, brutish kicks into him.

Dabber's inebriated brain was forced to swing into swift action, and it instantly transmitted to Dabber the reminder that Joe was a trained boxer and so it would be impossible to defeat him in a pugilistic fashion. Dabber's brain therefore swiftly sent him into a variety of unorthodox fighting techniques.

He was up in an instant and bopped Joe on the top of the head with his closed fist. Joe blinked in surprise at this unexpected retaliation.

And while he stood there drunkenly gaping, Dabber started to stagger here and there, sidestepping, staggering forward and stumbling back. Joe gaped at this drunkenness and then came at Dabber with a stumbling rush. Dabber sidestepped unsteadily over the rubble, while Joe, careering headlong after his rush, collided with the mouldering grey brick wall and stared at it unbelievingly for several seconds.

Dabber meanwhile, in the darkness, was still stumbling around, trying to prepare himself for a continuation of the fight. He looked at Joe, and Joe danced here and there at tremendous speed, but this display couldn't last long due to the boxer's recent way of life and drunken condition. He was forced to slow, panting, to a standstill, growling, "Right, you've had it now, busman boy."

He stared around in the darkness, trying to locate Dabber, who was now crouching as low as possible in the black night to make himself blend in and unnoticeable, and also for imagined superior tactical reasons.

Joe growled various uncivil and nasty threats towards where he thought Dabber's hiding place was, but Dabber hopped with great rapidity out of the shadows and tapped Joe, one-two, one-two, lightly on each cheek with his open palm, and then one-two, one-two again, and danced around. But Joe was a boxer and Dabber was startled when a punch hurtled out of Joe's boxing locker and smacked him forcefully on the chin.

As Dabber collapsed, gasping for air, in came Joe's big boot into his belly and Dabber was sprawled on the ground thinking, *Man, I'm done for, I'm finished.* And just as he was thinking this, he saw the big ugly boot coming in again and grabbed it with both hands. Joe was enraged at this and hobbled about over the rubble in the darkness, bellowing and cursing, dragging Dabber here and there. Eventually he wrenched his foot free and in a drunken rage kicked Dabber in the face.

Dabber was stunned, but hopped up all bloodied and cross-eyed and tried to continue. Joe circled his opponent in the darkness, looking for a weakness, while Dabber, still disorientated, was stumbling around.

Dabber saw a double vision of his opponent and charged blindly at one of them, stumbling here and there, but from the other vision an uppercut scythed and Dabber was down and finished.

Weak and exhausted also, Joe went over and stared down drunkenly at his beaten opponent. His befuddled brain surged with joyous victory, but then he remembered something else. He remembered boxing protocol and the code of chivalry towards a defeated opponent. He knelt down beside Dabber and noted that Dabber was breathing heavily, but was conscious. Joe felt his opponent's pulse. It was okay. He straightened Dabber up, arranged him into a more comfortable position down among the rubble, and then he staggered away.

CHAPTER 19

In a multi-storey house in the St Pauls area of Bristol, West Indians have moved in and feel real comfortable, especially today, for calypso music blasting, smells of lovely Jamaican cooking, great excitement, everybody rushing, tumbling downstairs, shoving and pushing in big joyous exit onto street for news just confirmed that bus company is on its back, legs kicking in air like stranded beetle and saying now that black drivers and conductors is welcome like the dear old friends they always been.

Some of the Jamaicy boys got the steel equipment out an' is ripping out red-hot rhythm so loud it doubtless can be heard at far end of the city, for Jamaican fellas got swagger and it seem whoever born under the hot sun of them Antilles got top-speed juice in their veins and spirits kicking so high it a wonder they ever stand still.

Along Grosvenor Road they pour, this noisy, exultant group with the steel blasting, and already gathering more marchers for word spread fast in St Pauls and out onto Stokes Croft, dancing and singing with the procession swelling every minute, and some of the white crowds lining the route are looking at the dancing, jabbering West Indians with squinty eyes, and others is stroking their chins and going, "Hmm…" like they contemplating some deep philosophical problem.

But them whiteys know that things is changing, rushing on so fast hardly anybody got time to put their brains around the new situation. Some of the whiteys are throwing out nauseous banter, others just watching silently, and even those who is outright hostile know they is seeing the thin end of defeat; they say, "Look at them spades," and just sink into silence with gloomy faces.

The black people knew they'd been bowled a googly by the bus company with the colour bar but now they've hit that googly ball right over the fence and out of the ground, and it look like even the Almighty have put seal of approval on the transaction, for the air hanging so warm and sweet and heavy and spirits so high, everyone whirling and dancing and jumping around, all joyful and amazed at how things turned out. There is young West Indian chicks in cotton dresses, bright yellow and green like sun and vegetation of their native lands, eyes gleaming, waltzing around; young black fellas in sharp clothes, shirts and jeans hanging cool and loose, soaring like eagles with vitality, jumping about and yelling and laughing like crazy. There is old Jamaican and Trinidadian hens stepping this way and that, swinging they fat bums side to side in tune with the music, ready to clutch any handsome young male who come within reach.

Some of the black men in the parade, they see whiteys on the side-lines looking hostile. Black men don't want trouble and say to each other, "I tell you, man, if things kick off, I out of here fast."

Others say, "You have nothing to worry about, man. Them whiteys is only puzzled and disgruntled because they know they seeing the future here."

Other young fellas from Jamaica got the eye for white girls lining the route, and they saying to each other, "Go on, man, she giving you the eye back," but young black fellas afraid and fearful, so one white girl suddenly come right over and join in, and she sure know how to dance and keep brushing against young black fella who is overpowered by this and start dancing with her. Well, that is great encouragement and soon four, five, six white girls joining in and dancing as joyful as West Indians with steel band ripping out big euphoric numbers. It so hot that August day that everyone fanning themselves as they march along over the Haymarket, past the Horsefair, everybody jumping about, big sweaty rivulets running down faces, girls' make-up running but who cares, man, this is joyful occasion and we is all here to have a good time.

Some white lads from the crowd is looking with glinty eyes at the young blacks and whispering. Blacks is all on edge and fearful as two or three white youths come bouncing up, high-fiving to the young

Jamaicans, but all white youths want is to say, "Hey, you got any weed, man?" and one of the older black men retorted sharply, "Go away. What you think we is? You think because we is black we go around with pockets full of weed ready to dish out to all comers? Go elsewhere and look for your filthy drugs."

Well, for a minute or two situation teeters in balance and everyone readies for fracas, but white boys not looking for trouble and are genuinely friendly.

"Fair dos, boys," they say, "if you ain't got any, you ain't got any," and they do a bit more high-fiving and smiling and go away peaceful. Jamaicans want no dealings with white youths they don't know, for you never know who is law and who isn't.

However, one or two young West Indians in procession *have* been hitting the weed and are ambling all carefree, with dreamy expressions looking far out into space and thinking world is marvellous place.

White lads see this, come back and say, "Okay, man, if you got none to sell maybe we meet up later and have a puff with you," but nobody in the parade want to take them up on that suggestion.

One of the young West Indians who hardly know what day of the week it is mumbles, "Is it true we can get jobs on the buses now, man?" and old wise black man says, "If you got brains for the job, maybe they take you on, but looking round at some of you dim faces I got my doubts whether you could add 2p ticket and 4p ticket to make 6p. More like you make it 5p or 7p, you is so thick."

All the girls is wearing colourful summer frocks and as they dance breeze wafts through, and occasionally them frocks flicking up and everybody glimpsing thighs and nylons and suspenders, but only for an instant. Girls, as soon as breeze plays its tricks, they quick as a flash put hand down to rectify frock but still secretly pleased that all lads, white and black, got a peek at forbidden areas.

And as the procession reaches the busy shopping areas more and more supporters joining it, white and black, young and old, plus many more just coasting along to see what happen, and when parade reaches the Centre people there is already sitting up and gaping, for they heard the music from a long way off and all at once the atmosphere is heavy and overladen, for when the white people see the blacks parading with music and dancing, whooping and yelling, colourful clothes, white girls dancing calypso with black youths, well, the onlooking whites is all stricken with doubt and puzzlement as they is trying to work it all out.

But quick as a flash to calm their fears, a young, cultured West Indian leaps up onto a bench, holds his hands up, takes his time and when all is quiet, says in loud voice, "Ladies and gentlemen, if you would excuse us, we black men and women is feeling like lords and ladies today with the sun shining hot just like home. We is so happy that we all together in big friendly crowd, West Indians and Bristolians, for today we learn that bus company roll over to give us jobs. Everything going right today, but we is no fools and know that the dice not always going to fall friendly. This just the start and there sure to be foul and difficult times ahead, but for now I propose big party, for we all just citizens together under the big sky that the Almighty created, and the little old world is going to roll on regardless whatever we do so I sure hope we can all get along with each other."

And there, under the big bus company clock, ticking time remorselessly, the party starts: calypso ripping, dancing and singing, the sun shining, the Centre gardens beautiful, the doors of the Horn and Trumpet, the Drawbridge and the Sedan Chair flung wide open and the whole night ahead.

CHAPTER 20

With the warmth of summer came the sadness of the strange, lonely women who haunted and hunted the busmen. They hung around the changeover points, drawn like magnets towards any man with a bus uniform on, especially if that busman was young and handsome.

They rode round on the buses, these women. They possessed an eerie sixth sense as to which buses their favourite crew members were likely to be on. They appeared unexpectedly and frequently, stalking the busmen and desperately seeking attention in their sad and lonely lives.

They craved company and romance and commitment, but their quests were fruitless, because the crews knew who they were and no busman wanted to get in too deep with any of them.

One of the 'bus-birds', as the crews called these lonely women, had been riding round on Dabber's bus on and off for a week or two. She would gaze at him, hang onto his hand when he took her money, and pour out strange, rambling love talk, but Dabber always moved swiftly on up the bus or back to the platform. She wasn't a bad looker, this woman, she had a nice figure, but Dabber did not want to get mixed up with her.

But the warmth of the days spawned a strengthening of the trade in the pubs around Old Market, and an increase in the urges and lusts and lechery of the young men who frequented them.

One afternoon Dabber was in the Hart knocking them back with Greasy and a few more of the lads. It was wild and loud in that back saloon: everyone was shouting and girls were swivelling their hips and swinging their hair, sitting on men's knees and jumping up fast again before the men could get their hands on their breasts or up their dresses. The drink was flowing and the latest hits were howling and hurtling out of the flashing Technicolor jukebox when all of a sudden the door opened and in staggered Old Sam with Diamond Lil, and the pair were cuddling and kissing and stumbling with fuddled expressions. They collapsed onto seats, lips still glued to each other, and fumbled drunkenly with each other's clothing.

Diamond Lil glanced up and saw the whole lounge watching and said, "And what the hell's wrong with you lot? You want your 'eads smacked or what?"

With difficulty everybody shifted their gaze away, not knowing where to look, but soon coins went in the jukebox and songs thundered out again, blokes were laughing like madmen, women were squealing and drinking. The whole riotous scene was crazy.

In the midst of it all Greasy shouted, "Hey, Dabber, that woman over there's giving you the eye."

Dabber looked over and there was the lonely bus-bird, sitting by herself at the far side of the saloon. She was smiling at Dabber with her weird, half-crazy smile. At first Dabber ignored her, but he had drink inside him and the woman was smiling at him with her strange smile. Her nails were badly painted and her full-face make-up all awry, but as he drank more and looked at her more, she looked lovelier all the time. Dabber's mind was confused. He thought of Melody, the girl he loved, and he turned away from the strange woman and started chatting to the barman, but when he turned back the woman was still gazing and smiling at him with her disturbed and longing look.

She had on a low-cut dress that showed plenty of her middle-aged breasts and her hemline was well above her bone-thin knees. She stuck out her nylon-clad legs and crossed them and uncrossed them and smiled at Dabber some more, and pulled her skirt up further.

Some of the blokes were shouting, "Go on, mate, get stuck in."

"Get out of it," Dabber said.

Everybody laughed and banged the tables in delight. Dabber drank more and stared at the woman more, and she kept smiling at him with her imbecilic smile through the cigarette haze.

And then, before he knew it, Dabber was rolling around with her on the grass in the little churchyard of Pip n Jay behind Old Market and she was gasping, "Oh, I love you, I love you."

He rolled over onto his back and stared up at the thin, wispy clouds. Everything seemed sort of still and sacred. The air was warm and soft, with only the faint droning of insects and low rumble of traffic to disturb the peace.

The woman was nuzzling Dabber's neck. He pulled away slightly, but she followed and pushed her mouth into his neck again.

"What's your name?" he said.

"Judy," she said. "Judy... It's a lovely name, isn't it?"

"Beautiful," he said.

She clasped him in a tight hug and glued her lips to his. "Oh, I'm so glad I've found a friend," she gushed. "You've no idea how lonely I was. No idea! I've seen you on the buses so often and I thought you would never speak to me. I couldn't believe it when you noticed me in the pub just now. This must really be my lucky day, I thought to myself. I've found a friend at last."

Dabber closed his eyes against the strange heaving of the sky. "I'm too young for you," he said.

"No, you're not," she responded, kissing him again. "Oh, I love you."

He put his head back and closed his eyes again. "I think I'm going to die," he muttered.

"But my love for you will never die," she breathed. "Never, never, never, never."

She was lying half on top of him, gazing down into his face with soppy eyes and running long, thin fingers through his hair. She forced another long kiss, pinning his head to the ground.

He gasped for air and said, "I've got to go in a minute."

"No, you're not going, you lovely boy, you, you lovely young man. You're staying with me forever."

She planted more kisses on him and tried to undo his shirt with her dirty fingers. "I'm never going to let you go. Never! Oh, how I love you."

The clouds seemed to revolve and the ground felt cold. Dabber raised his hand and fondled her breast over her black dress.

He rolled her over so that she was on her back. He fondled her breasts some more. She moaned and suddenly Dabber thought of Melody and began to find the whole scene he was involved in repulsive.

Chuckles and loud laughter hit them. Busmen were watching them from over the wall at the side of the churchyard. A driver nicknamed Barhanger was there, and Greasy, among others.

"Give 'er it, mate!" Greasy shouted. "Ride 'er, cowboy."

Dabber lurched to his feet and the group of men scarpered with guffaws and shouted crudities.

"What's the matter?" the woman asked, standing up and clutching his hand.

"Those blokes were watching us."

"Take no notice of them," she urged, clutching him more tightly and gazing into his eyes. "It's nothing to do with them what we do. It's us now that's important – you and me. It's our love that's important from now on. That's the only thing that matters, isn't it? Oh, I'm so happy we've found each other. So, so, happy." She started to pull at him. "Where shall we go now?"

"Nowhere," he said, dragging his arm away.

She stood there, forlorn, with bits of grass on her dress, her make-up skewed and her nylons wrinkled and holey.

"Oh, please don't go," she whimpered, clutching him. "Stay with me. We can go somewhere – somewhere nice."

"I don't want to," he said. He pushed her off and began to walk away.

She ran after him and grabbed his arm again. "Please, please, stay. Please. You've no idea how lonely I am."

He pushed her away again. "No. I shouldn't be doing this. I've got a girlfriend."

She trotted alongside, trying to cling to him and sobbing. She stepped back and stared with anguished eyes. "What are you talking about? I thought you loved *me*. When you came over and talked to me in the pub, I thought it meant you liked me. And now you turn like this. I know you don't really mean it. Oh, I do need a friend. If you only knew how lonely I am. I've been getting tablets off the doctor. You don't know how ill I've been. You could make me better. We could be so good for each other and be together forever…" She went on and on.

"I got to go," he repeated. "You're a decent woman, Judy. You deserve someone better than me. I'm no good for you. You deserve someone better than me."

"But you're the one I want. Please stay," she begged.

"I've got a girlfriend already. I got to go," he called back to her, and he walked away fast.

CHAPTER 21

It was 4.30am and the signing-on room was getting busy. The noise and hullabaloo were reaching a crescendo when the door opened and immediately a strange and unnatural silence fell on the room. Everyone stopped moving and stared towards the door.

Dabber, who was just filling in his waybill, looked also and saw with amazement what everyone else there saw: in the doorway was a big, imposing black man, and the new arrival was in full conductor's uniform. His shiny black face and glistening eyes were beaming a great friendly smile as he gazed around, and then a low voice at the back of the room exclaimed, "Blimey, the banana boat's pulled in."

The new arrival heard the remark, but he ignored it. He placed one black hand on the doorjamb, leaned sideways and slowly looked around, calmly observing everything: the big round clock, which was always accurate to the minute, for time was important in a place like this; the layers of racks for the conductors' boxes; the huge, complex duty rotas up on the wall; the long, flat-topped counter with its partitions where the conductors counted their takings; and the notices pinned up all over the place.

Finally the big black man looked at Quade, the foreman, standing red-faced and impatient as always behind his counter. And slowly the black man took his hand off the doorjamb and stood there, relaxed and easy, and then slowly advanced across the room.

The men parted silently to let him through and the black man stood respectfully in front of Quade and said, "Good morning, sir, my name is Amos. I been told I am allocated to the first number nine bus for my first shift here in this depot, so if you would just kindly point me to a conductor box and point me to my driver I sure would like to get started."

Another low voice in the room said, "Boy, I sure would like to see just what's inside one of them black men. I heard that all they got inside 'em is a lot of sawdust and their heads is made of solid wood."

Amos heard this remark also, and he turned and looked directly at the side of the room from where the voice had come and said in a slow, sad voice, "Well, there sure is no need to look inside me, my friend, for I just the same inside as all you white guys. I just ordinary muscles and bones and kidneys an' stuff, and my blood is red blood, jus' exactly the same as every other man on this old rolling world we all got to share."

The foreman was angry now, for all he cared about was that big round clock and the time, and he said, "Right, that's enough of this. We got buses to get out on the road."

And immediately the room was mad again with frantic activity and hullabaloo, and out of the throng Old Sam approached, put his arm around Amos's shoulder and said, "I'm the driver of the first nine, kid. You're on with me. Come over here and I'll show you where to pick up your box and then we gotta get on the road fast because we're down the pan already."

Later that morning the fourteenth four was parked up waiting for its time at the far-flung terminus of Blackhorse. The estate was as quiet as the grave. Dabber, sitting in the downstairs saloon, saw the flicker of a match up in the cab as his driver lit a cigarette, and then the driver hunched up comfortably over the steering wheel for the nine minutes' layover time. An alarm clock went off as clear as anything in a nearby house and then all was silent again. The only other sounds were faint cracks and creaks as the bodywork of the bus settled down after its ten-mile haul from the depot.

Dabber settled back, lit a cigarette and closed his eyes. All was peaceful and quiet and then, in the silence, a faint sound started to flicker and fade and flicker again in the distance, like the faint, faraway buzz of a wasp.

The buzz slowly grew louder and Dabber opened his eyes as the noise of a powerful diesel engine reverberated through the sleeping estate.

He stood on his platform and watched the lights of an oncoming double-decker rapidly approaching through the darkness. Some driver was running at least twenty minutes sharp, Dabber thought. It was well under the arm to run that much sharp so early in the morning. It wasn't acceptable. Running sharp was for times of need: to work a flanker on a crew from another depot, or to grab a cup of tea. Everybody understood that. But at 5.30 in the morning there was no legitimate need for it.

The other bus pulled in behind, its heavy radiator halting inches from the rear of Dabber's bus. Up in the cab of the bus, grinning, was Slab, the overtime king.

Slab pulled open his cab window and started boasting straight away. "Know what happened this morning, mate? Ten minutes late, that's all I was, just ten little minutes late, an' that bastard foreman had given my bus away. Give it to some new twat that only been on the job five minutes.

"Know what 'e said to me, that bastard foreman? He said, 'Well, driver, you should make more effort to get here on time.' Me, a driver that's hardly ever late. I told the bastard straight, I did – that sodding foreman. 'I could walk out of 'ere right now,' I said, 'walk right out an' wrap the job in. You'd like that, wouldn't you? That'd wipe the smile off your face. Me, the best driver in the depot, the most reliable, the one what does the most overtime. You'd be a driver down then all right, wouldn't you? No sodding spare left. What'd you do then, you idiot? Well, you better give me a new shift straight away or I'm out of 'ere.' That's what I said to 'im, the sodding non-entity. He didn't know what to say to that. Just stood there shuffling 'is sodding papers, an' two minutes later he gave me this shift. I tell you what, mate, 'e won't take no shift off me in future, not after what I told 'im."

He looked at his watch. "Well, mate, no time to talk – this is when I get a bit of kip." He slammed his cab window shut, and in the darkness of the cab slumped his heavy body forward over the steering wheel, rested his bald head on his fat arms and his huge shoulders were soon rising and falling like giant pulsating pasties.

Dabber stood and gazed silently at the sleeping overtime king. For all Dabber knew Slab was not dreaming mad dreams of champagne and scantily clad women on the French Riviera, but having nightmares about his wife at home. Perhaps she was a sour-faced woman who bossed him about, demanded a big pay packet every week and slouched around smoking all day. Perhaps Slab's means of escape was in his fantasies of a life elsewhere: in the dream world he called *el mundo*.

Dabber cackled to himself as he readied himself for his return journey.

At another terminus, Old Sam was lowering himself from the cab of the first number nine. He walked round to the back of the bus and onto the platform where his conductor, Amos, was just filling in his waybill with the details of this first journey.

"You're managing okay so far, kid," said Sam. "You having any trouble with that waybill, let me know. I know how to fill them bastards in."

"No trouble at all, sir. They taught us all that up at the training school."

"And less of that 'sir' stuff," said Sam, stuffing tobacco into his pipe. "Sam's the name. And I got to say, them bells you gave me all the way up were real sharp. We kept on time all the way up the road and we got a few minutes now to put our feet up."

"There weren't many passengers, so it was easy," said Amos, "but I 'spect from now it going to be real busy, what with the rush hour just coming up."

"We'll be all right," said Sam, lighting his pipe and giving it some pulls. "Don't you worry about it if we gets a bit late or stuff like that. Every bus does in the rush hour. It ain't nothing to worry about." He settled himself into one of the seats, motioned Amos to sit beside him and gave two or three more deep, thoughtful pulls on his pipe.

"I just want to say, Amos, don't worry about those two idiots at the depot who made them remarks about black people. It ain't what the majority of the men on the job think. Me and a lot of the other crews, we're old enough to have more sense. I was in the Second World War, fighting all over the place, and I fought with men from all sorts of countries, black blokes and white blokes, and I always found everybody's just the same when you get to know 'em."

"That's sure true, what you say," said Amos. "I'm young and I ain't had your experience, but I already found out that there's all different sorts of men on this planet of ours, and some of 'em talk nonsense. I heard all about how some white folks think us black men is going to murder and rob people, and rape all the white women. I read all about what some people in the papers been writing in and saying about black men. It's all nonsense."

"Yeah, there's a few idiots about that don't understand things and think just because you come from a different country and talk different that they got to have a go at you. So keep your wits about you, Amos, and try not to react or you'll bring yourself down to their level."

"Sam, it don't bother me. I been and read all about this colour bar here on the buses and I've sure had a few nasty things said, but for the most part the men and women I already met here in this city of Bristol is just the same and just as decent as everywhere else. I know lots about human nature and I know that there's no sure way to happiness. You just got to go out and find it for yourself."

Old Sam said, "You got it there, Amos. You just got to stand tall on your own two feet. I can see you is a steady and dignified man and you can think things out. You're not the type to react rash if white blokes start to give you hassle."

"Yes, sir," Amos said, "I sure always try to keep calm. The world belongs to us all, white and black. It belongs to all kinds of people wherever they come from. We jus' got to get along together and all be friends like the Lord intended."

"That's the way to look at it, Amos, and there's plenty of people will back you up if trouble comes. Just keep that way of thinking and everything will turn out right."

Old Sam puffed on his pipe again and then looked at his watch. "Blimey, we're late. We got to get going." He knocked his pipe out on the edge of the pavement fast and hurried round to the cab.

CHAPTER 22

Middle of the evening and Dabber was on route four, Filwood Broadway to Station Road, with Driver Lepiniere. Dabber had not worked with Lepiniere since the football special and he was hoping for a quiet shift, but he instantly saw that Lepiniere, up in his cab, was moving with strange, jerky movements. A dirty, greasy woollen hat topped his skeletal face. His long, gnarled fingers gripped the steering wheel like claws. Every so often his body shook with some kind of tremor.

Lepiniere had a very simple philosophy of life: everything and everyone in the world was a bastard and passengers were the biggest bastards of all. If you approached the job with that thought in your mind you would not go far wrong.

Right from the start of the shift the number four was running down the pan because of traffic jams, buses missing and huge crowds on all the stops. During the break the driver and Dabber had a pint together in the Hart, and Dabber hoped that would calm Lepiniere down and ease his jerking.

But in the pub, Lepiniere kept making a moaning sound: "Hor… hor…hor."

"Those bastard passengers, ringing the sodding bell," he moaned, swaying about on his stool. "They're driving me bonkers."

After the break they switched to the 6B route but the passenger load never slackened. As the bus headed up the Gloucester Road the passengers were hitting the bell with all the joy of a Saturday night. They turned for the return trip, and all the way back down to Old Market the bus was packed out again and the bell box up in the driver's cab, a few inches from Lepiniere's left ear, was shrilling its strident tones, bouncing and vibrating as if it was going to come off the wall. But gradually the load lightened and the number 6B ran easily out to Hartcliffe with Lepiniere giving the engine a tanking so that they stole a few extra minutes.

At the terminus Dabber and Lepiniere ran quickly into the Hartcliffe Inn to sink a quick pint. Lepiniere was drinking in short, agitated gulps. In between gulps he would get up, stride a few steps, and then sit down. Abruptly, he would get up and sit down again.

"What's up?" Dabber said.

"Those bastard passengers, ringing the effing bell," Lepiniere said. "Ding, ding, sodding ding. It's driving me crazy." He took a long gulp of his beer, got up, pushed his way through the drinkers to the far wall, came back and started muttering to himself. He was staring with wild eyes round the pub.

They ran with a light passenger load back up the route. Lepiniere was driving normally and Dabber hoped that this meant his driver's crazy spell had passed. As they neared Old Market Lepiniere turned and banged on the glass partition between his cab and the lower deck. He made a drinking motion, and as they swung round the corner Dabber dropped off the platform and ran into the Pelican. He got two pints of English India Pale Ale in. Lepiniere came in fast a minute later as soon as he had left the bus with its load of passengers on the stop outside. The driver grabbed his pint and strode wildly about the pub. Eventually he sat down, staring straight ahead and breathing heavily.

"The bastards," Lepiniere was muttering. "The bell-ringing bastards!"

"They were all right coming up from Hartcliffe, weren't they?" Dabber said.

The driver's face was frozen. "If they start again…if they start…"

His hands were trembling and he could hardly raise his pint to his lips. He took a gulp, then jumped up and sat down again, all rigid and upright. Abruptly he got up and pushed through to the far wall, where he stopped, motionless, facing it. He turned and began slowly pacing back. He was sticking one arm out in front of him and one arm back, half-crouching and moving in jerks. He was going, "Hooh, aah," and, "Neeaah yaaherr," in a tortured voice.

He jerked around fast, his face all twisted and distorted, bent low and advanced stealthily across the bar again with his right hand twisted outwards and his left arm pushed far back again.

He stalked slowly up to an elderly customer, straightened up, glared into his face and went, "Huhaarh...huuaaah." Then he stumbled back and sat down.

The landlord came over and jerked a thumb at the driver. "What's up with him?"

"Nothing," Dabber said.

"You'd better get him out," the landlord said.

Dabber and Lepiniere's bus hit Stokes Croft ten minutes late, just as crowds of revellers were staggering out of the pubs, and soon the bus was packed out, with passengers singing, swaying about and ringing the bell merrily.

Dabber struggled round, trying to collect fares. Most of the passengers were slightly if not well inebriated and fumbled endlessly in pockets and bags trying to find their money.

A funfair was in full swing at one place, and another crowd of revellers piled on. A little boy who had won a goldfish in a plastic bag held it up proudly for everyone to see, and the next thing the bag was on the floor, the goldfish wriggled out and the child was crying and squealing.

As it gasped its last, Dabber pointed authoritatively at it and pronounced, "What that fish needs is a pint of beer."

Well, the kid's father thought that was funny, but the mother, all stony-faced and angry, just glared at Dabber and at her husband and said, "Can't you see the little boy's upset?"

The bus was rocking and swerving, and the little child was howling and trying to scoop up the dying goldfish. Passengers were ringing the bells but the driver deliberately drove without stopping past the next stop.

"What's up with the driver?" people were shouting.

"He doesn't like people ringing the bell," said Dabber.

"Doesn't like people ringing the bell?" exclaimed a passenger. "What the hell's he doing driving a bus then?"

An elderly passenger with a bald pate and bountiful, grimy side whiskers came up to Dabber on the platform, pushed his face close with a confidential look and whispered, "Have you ever wondered if it's all real, conductor?"

"All what?" said Dabber.

"The whole thing, the whole caboodle. Everything. I mean, are we really here?"

"I'm here," said Dabber.

The man put a hand sympathetically on his shoulder. "Ah, but are you really, young man? Are any of us? I mean, there aren't many sardines in a tin, now, are there? Not as many as there used to be. I mean, where have they all gone? Who's taking them?"

"It ain't me, mate," Dabber said. "I ain't taken no sardines."

The man put his face close to Dabber. "We don't know about anything really, do we? We sent strong radio signals out into space, you know – that's the cause of it all. That's how it all started. We're impinging on someone else's territory. That's what I think. That's why they're taking the sardines. We should never have sent the signals. They don't like it, those people out there. And now we're in a dummy universe. That's what they've done: put us in a dummy universe."

He looked around suspiciously and slowly and nudged Dabber again. "What do you think?"

"I don't know nothing about any dummy universes or sardines," said Dabber.

He tried to get away to collect some fares but the man clutched his arm urgently.

"I mean, I never thought I'd see the Queen on this bus. She's upstairs you know, in the back seat."

"I better make sure I get her fare then, before she gets off the bus," said Dabber, but the old man tightened his grip on his arm.

"Oh, no, you mustn't. She travels free, you know, everywhere free. She carries no money. You mustn't approach her."

Dabber loped up the stairs anyway, but there were only drunken passengers up there, and no one who looked like the Queen. The passengers were singing, "Bugger off, conductor. We ain't paying no fares," and slapping each other, all lusty and swaying, with bellies full of drink. Dabber went downstairs again and just stood on the platform. He could hear Lepiniere howling up in the cab.

The engine was on full revs and they hammered past stops, not allowing anyone to get off, before rocking to a stop at the terminus. Immediately furious passengers who had missed their stops jumped off and started running towards the front of the bus, yelling threats towards the driver.

Lepiniere had the side window of the cab open and was leaning out, howling in delight and banging the engine cover. And just as the mob reached the front of the bus he put his foot down and roared off, leaving the passengers gesturing and cursing.

Out of the bleak, late-night estate the bus hammered, up to and across the Downs, way off the official route, and descended at full speed the twisting Bridge Valley Road to the Portway, where they slid to a halt. Lepiniere jumped from the cab and ran round to the back of the bus. There was a crazed but jubilant expression on his face.

"I got them," he exulted. "In the end I got the bastards, didn't I?"

CHAPTER 23

The Old Market canteen was noisy, but when a black conductor entered everyone fell silent. The black conductor looked slowly around. Nearly all the seats were filled by white crews, but there were one or two spaces. The black conductor approached a table where three white drivers were sitting.

He put down his cash bag, spread his arms and with a big beaming smile said, "Here I is, new on the job, but sure glad to be here and to meet you gentlemen. May I sit with you at your table, please?"

There was silence from the white men.

"I hope nobody ain't ashamed to sit with me or to work with me, 'cause I sure am happy to sit with you gentlemen and to work on the Bristol buses," said the black conductor.

The white staff regarded the black conductor silently; then one of the drivers gestured towards an empty seat. He said, "The thing is, mate, we never had no blacks on this job before."

"De colour of my skin is jus' the colour I was born in, like you gentlemen was born white," said the black conductor.

"Siddown, then," said one of the white drivers.

The conductor sat down and beamed around.

"We ain't got nothing against you personally, mate," said one of the drivers.

There was silence for a time, then Ratso said, "They don't serve foreign crap in here, mind."

The black conductor said, "I am happy to eat whatever food is here. I was born in this fine country and have eaten many delicious English meals all my life."

"You won't find no delicious meals down 'ere, mate," said one of the other white drivers with a chuckle.

"It's just we don't want any smelly habits stinking the place up, know what I mean?" said Ratso.

"I will try not to have any smelly habits or stink the place up," said the conductor with a chuckle.

Another driver added, "No offence meant, mate. It's just we ain't used to black people, know what I mean?"

Ratso got up, glared at the black conductor and went over to join several other busmen and women who were sitting around a table in the corner of the canteen.

"I tell you what, them blacks'll take over," he said to his new table companions.

"The union should do something about it," said a conductor.

"The union's in with the management, mate. You'll get nowhere with the union," Ratso said. "Bloody turncoats, the lot of 'em."

"Well, somebody should stop any more coming in," said Skully.

"It's too late to stop any more of them coming in. They're here already. Nothing's gonna change now," a conductor said.

"Well, all I can say is the bloody job will go downhill now."

"They only come to get on the National Health and the dole and that, don't they?" said Skully, his shiny bald head seeming to glint with the fury of his emotions.

"We oughta get up a petition, get everybody to sign it," said Skully.

"What bloody good would a petition do?" said Ratso.

"Would you want your sister carrying on with a black bloke?"

"If I see any of them blacks talking to white women…" said Ratso.

And then from an adjoining table Dabber leaned across and said, "Hey, hey, hey, what's all this you lot are on about? Calm down. Us British went to their countries and took over, didn't we? The wheel's turning full circle, ain't it?"

The morning Dabber took his driving test, they gave him old W101, the oldest of the bangers in the training school and the one with the ropiest gearbox.

The examiner sat behind him with his big pad on his knee and his pen in his hand. Scoter was behind Dabber as well, but the instructor obviously could not give the young trainee any help during his drive through the chaos and hurly-burly of the morning rush hour.

The traffic was all clogged up and in a rage, with drivers hooting and snarling, but the old W101 moved smoothly through the chaos, behaving herself for the first time ever. It was as if the old bus was thinking, *So this is Dabber's test, is it? I've messed the kid around plenty over the last few months. I've had a bit of fun with him, but fair's fair, he's still here. He ain't packed it in. He ain't given up. I'll give him an easy ride today, let him get his red badge and then I can start having a bit of fun with the next poor sod.*

It took two hours, that test: out to Hartcliffe, back through the city centre and up Park Street to Clifton and Cotham, along the Downs into Westbury, back to the Centre again and all over the city. The gears slotted in better than Dabber had ever known. Old W101 rolled smoothly and the hills seemed to flatten out under her.

Back at the depot the examiner spent a long time studying his notes and turning the sheets over and back again, making little marks with his pen and looking again at all kinds of things in his documents.

Then he got up and sighed the deepest sigh that ever was, looked as sad as anything, gave Dabber a slip of paper and said, "I've given you a pass, but you've still got a lot to learn, kid." And he shook his head mournfully.

As soon as the examiner had gone, Scoter stepped forward right away and shook Dabber's hand, up and down and up and down, as if he was going to go on shaking it forever. Scoter's face had a feverish expression, the like of which Dabber had never seen before. His features twisted into a strange shape whereby his displaced jawbone skewed upwards and his mouth warped, and Dabber realised with a shock that the contortions meant the old bugger was smiling – an actual smile!

"Well done, kid," Scoter enthused. "Well sodding done!"

Dabber still had a week to go as a conductor before the paperwork and his red driver's badge came through; and what a week that was, with everyone in a drunken, carefree mood. The cigarette girls, the young sexpots from the Wills factories in Bedminster and Ashton, they knew what Saturday nights were for. What a time they had.

In the evenings they flocked onto the buses from Hartcliffe and Withywood, Ashton and Bedminster, some with boyfriends, others in noisy, boisterous groups, to go on wild nights out up in the town. They thronged the streets in excited, raucous gangs, smoking and shouting. The girls with boyfriends would head for the pubs or cinemas, and the single girls and lads would prowl the pubs of the Centre, Broadmead and Old Market. The girls hunted in packs, hitching up their skirts and staring openly and challengingly at the hordes of dishy young men who were out on the town.

And the young men, downing their drinks, ogled with calculating, lecherous eyes the bare, seductive female flesh. If individual girls and lads clicked, new duos formed. Groups grew, diminished, changed, squabbled, made up, but were rarely stable or in one place for long. Then at 10.30 when the pubs shut and the cinemas closed, the young revellers tumbled onto the dark, frozen streets in restless, rowdy gangs, taking over pavements, blocking traffic, running, shouting and startling with their antics any old codgers they came across.

The half-drunk ones stumbled about the streets, with courting couples seeking doorways and other isolated places where gentle kissing and tender fondling could begin.

But sometimes passions got too high, the young people could not contain themselves and there was a rush to the parks or dark back alleys. After an interval the boy and girl would emerge from the alley, arms round each other, and then, squealing and shouting to each other, they would tumble onto the last buses, their hairstyles frequently messed up and their clothing in disarray.

The courting couples would occupy the back seats, for such was the custom, while the single lads and girls would sprawl lazily and noisily over seats towards the front.

The excited chatter would rise to full pitch and Dabber, the conductor, going around the bus taking fares, heard it all. Amid the hubbub and cigarette smoke on the top deck of those late-night buses, the inebriated talk and tales, always at a higher volume than normal, could be an education:

"...crazy bugger tried to..."

"...that tart in the Pelican..."

"...you wouldn't believe..."

"...just couldn't help myself."

Downstairs, a shy-looking young girl was sitting on the long seat just inside the entrance. She was too quiet to want to mix with the boisterous, drunken lot upstairs. A fat old pervert, swaying all over the place, put his hand on her knee and said, "Thinking of that thrill you 'ad tonight, are you, my little chicken?"

"Get lost, you old perv," the shy little thing replied as fast as anything.

The pervert shook his head wildly for a moment and then slowly toppled sideways and began to snore in a beery stupor.

Dabber went back upstairs and the single girls and lads had grown wild. They rolled about and threw themselves backwards on the seats. Some of them changed seats and started messing about and chatting up others. Legs were stuck out into the aisle to try to impede Dabber's progress. Some of the girls grabbed his hand and tried to pull him on top of them as he went past, but he was too busy getting the fares in.

Going down through Bedminster there was a pub every hundred yards, and on each bus stop was a seething, tumultuous mob of drinkers. As soon as the bus stopped – even before it came to a halt – there was a forward rush, and a shouting, chaotic scrum as those pushing to get on battled drunkenly with those getting off. The bus was packed, with about twenty standing and even a few groggy specimens hanging onto the platform.

Dabber really couldn't leave anyone behind with the night cold enough to freeze the soul, but on the bus the heat from packed bodies was tremendous and the noise deafening – singing, shouting, curses and above it all, the revving of the engine.

After every stop Dabber would push and shove through the standing passengers to try to get a few fares in, but within a minute, *wham*, another bus stop and another chaotic pushing match. Another hundred yards down the street and *wham*, another stop, another melee. Off again and *wham*, rocking to a halt and another half-crazed drunken mob battling to get on and tangling angrily with the boisterous lot trying to get off. Round the corner to the London Inn: same again. On a bit further, past the Black Cat and the Red Cow and *wham*, they stopped again and took on another load, struggling and pushing each other in their attempts to board.

Two fast bells and off again. The passengers were rolling about and shouting, some of them too inebriated to find the money for the fare. One old maid was nipping Dabber's backside every time he pushed past, and the wrinkled biddy she was with was encouraging her with sly nudges. Every time Dabber turned round to look at them, the two faces, worn and lined by the years, creased into mischievous innocence.

Pushing through the standing passengers to collect fares on the bottom deck was a battle against the buttocks – some of them huge, others young and shapely.

Sometimes, stuck fast in a sea of buttocks and breasts and bending down to collect a fare, Dabber would find his head nestling against some softly swelling bosom. Usually the owner of the delight would not, or could not move away, but occasionally the lady, to annoy the man she was with, would squeal and her partner would glare at the conductor and sometimes make nasty threats. The woman would be pleased at the jealousy in her man, and would press romantically against him and turn her face to him for a kiss.

There was a punch-up at the Cross Hands stop. A blonde woman getting on recognised a brunette piece getting off. They went for it like a pair of spitting cats – what for, nobody knew, but the next thing the two women were screaming and pulling each other's hair and punching and kicking. Then they were down in the filthy slush in the gutter, rolling around in their good coats and fighting like it was a war.

The men with them, two burly, coarse characters with aggressive, raucous voices, tried to pull them apart, but the men were inebriated also and wobbled about all over the place. One of the men whacked the other in the mouth and the pair of them went down, grunting and wrestling in the dirt.

Dabber could happily have watched the scene a little longer, but the driver was revving the engine and they were off again, racing up over Bishopsworth and down into Headley Park with inebriated people stumbling off in little groups at all the stops.

Upstairs, the girls had quietened down. They were finishing their cigarettes, brushing each other's hair and tidying their clothing. Their talk was more subdued. Blouses were securely buttoned up and coats fastened. Sometimes little mirrors came out of handbags and lips and faces were made respectable. It was time to go back into the family homes, where suspicious mothers would be sitting up with their tight lips and their narrowed eyes ready to scrutinise every inch and every movement of their daughters and to deduce in an instant what the little minxes had been up to.

Running into the Hartcliffe estate, the girls and lads came downstairs singly or in boozy couples and groups. The wild, wanton behaviour was put aside until the next big night out, the next exciting romance-seeking adventure, the next excursion into the big, alluring, crazy world of the city centre.

But not all the restless, tipsy passion had left some of them.

"See you again, lover boy," one girl said, ruffling Dabber's carefully combed and greased black hair as she came down the stairs.

"Night, handsome," another added, staring meaningfully at him with her big, innocent eyes.

A busty girl with copper-coloured hair who came down the stairs stood innocently on the platform and then, as the bus stopped, whispered, "Wish you was coming home with me," before giving Dabber a little kiss and slipping quickly away into the darkness.

At the terminus, the old perv was still snoring away on the long seat. Dabber and the driver lifted him carefully off the bus, took him into the public toilet and gently sat him back against a wall in the corner so that he would be reasonably warm and safe.

Then it was engine at full blast for the depot.

CHAPTER 24

In the Old Market canteen two black conductors, Dion and Jermaine, were sitting at a table.

"You is looking all unhappy and fearful, man," Jermaine said to his companion. "Don't be afraid of these whiteys, they jus' unsure of you 'cause you is strange. Some of them, they never been in proximity with black men before."

"They sure keep their proximity big an' wide," replied Dion, a slim, fit-looking young West Indian. "I had pride in this uniform when I first put it on, but I have not pride now, the way I have been treated. I just don't feel comfortable here. I don't feel like I belong."

"What the hell the matter with you, boy?" said Jermaine. "When you wear that uniform you is part of an organisation. You got to walk like you is proud, like you belong. You ain't walking alone. What the hell you not feel comfortable about?"

"I jus' don' like it here, man. I thinking of going back home to the sunshine."

"What you talking about, man? Things still bad in Jamaica. You is walking round like you is defeated, man. You ain't defeated. You only defeated if you let that feeling grab you inside. You as good as any white man."

"I know what you is saying, brother," said Dion, "but I don't feel easy, man."

"Listen to me, man, I been in Bristol a long time. I was one of the first spades to come here. You just got to walk tall an' keep your head up an' you will find most whiteys is friendly. You ain't got nothing to be ashamed of," Jermaine said.

"I ain't ashamed, but why my driver ignore me? He treat me like I don't exist. He stay up in the cab, never speak to me." Dion gestured with his knife. "I tell you, man, I feel like stick 'im, stick 'im."

Jermaine said, "Take it easy. Put that knife down, boy. It no good waving a knife around. Next week you might have real friendly driver who chat to you, sit down here with you, take you to the café, to the pub. That put a big smile on your face, I bet."

"Well, I will see."

Jermaine leaned forward. "You know, Dion, my friend, let me tell you something. There be plenty friendly people here, but a few who are not friendly. You see, Bristol is an old town with some tired old attitudes and values. When you arrive you see the streets clean, the flower beds all full of colour, the big an' tall buildings and the citizens, most of 'em working hard at all kind of things. The whole city seem so nice, standing proud with green hills and countryside round about. Only thing that strikes you is big, dirty river flowing through, but that neither here nor there. On the whole you think this is a nice place and the people nice, but it is a city of two faces, my friend. On the surface, everything nice and pleasant and the people beaming and friendly to each other, but knock the top off this city, boy, and you see something different, you see a side that ain't so nice. You see what black men see every day, and I ain't gonna weary you with the details of what we see because there ain't no need to repeat what we all so familiar with."

Jermaine took another drink of his tea and pulled on his cigarette before he spoke again. "Now I want to talk to you about another town with two faces, a little town in Alabama in the deep south of the USA. In the 1930s this little town, Scottsboro, had maybe a couple of thousand souls, mostly white. Jus' like Bristol it was a clean and well-tended town. The people, on the surface, easy-going folk with warm, cheery faces greeting each other friendly, like, and most everyone knew everyone else's business. The place lay amid green and fertile hills, just like Bristol, and it might be thought that in such a place where the citizens seemed so kind, mild and God-fearing that nothing could bring hate and ugliness to those same souls. But Scottsboro was in territory where friendly-faced white folk felt it in their marrowbones that black citizens must be subjugated – they must be kept down by any means.

"Now it so happens in 1931 in Alabama two white girls were hoboing on a freight train – riding on top the open freight cars for a free ride, like it was the custom and a normal thing to do in them times. Now onto the train hops a group of nine coloured boys and what goes on between them and the white girls is anybody's guess, but top and bottom of the story, someone notified the law that there was coloured kids on that train and they was hauled off by a posse of the sheriff's men an' slung into jail. The two girls was questioned as to what they was up to on that train. They seemed happy at first and didn't make no complaint, but under a bit of questioning as to exactly how friendly they been with them coloured boys, the two girls was under a bit of pressure. They cottoned on real quick as to what them white law officers wanted them to say, so they says they sure as hell never said a friendly word to them coloured boys, in fact them coloured boys had just grabbed the two of them and raped them there on the flat car, all nine of them boys.

"Now there wasn't a mark on either of them two girls when they was examined, but that didn't make no difference. The nice white people of that pleasant little town was just hassling and thirsting to hang them black boys right there and then. Kindly faced old ladies was saying, 'We oughta string them black fiends right up,' and others were full of nasty made-up stories about what 'them awful black brutes' had done to the two girls.

"Well, you can imagine, them nine black kids was all fearful because in the deep south of the USA, any black man accused of raping a white woman – it was death by the electric chair, or strung up from a tree if the local people got hold of them first."

"But if them black kids had done nothing to the white girls…" said Dion.

"Didn't matter if they did or they didn't. Once they had been accused that was it."

"What do you mean, 'that was it'?"

"What do I mean? Guilty, my friend – sentenced to death. All nine of 'em."

"Did they really execute them?" said Dion.

"No, but them black kids was behind bars and had it hanging over them for years: convicted, appealed, convicted again, on and off. Some sentenced to up to a hundred years in jail. It destroyed the lives of every one of them black lads. Later one of the girls said she wasn't raped at all, though the other girl just went about cracking jokes about the whole thing. Course that didn't make no difference to the way them coloured boys was treated."

"But it's not like that in Bristol, is it?"

"No, it sure ain't that bad. In Scottsboro, in that little community, black children played with white children jus' like they do here in Bristol. But sometimes the hating disease of a few grown-ups infects little children's minds and something happens that no intelligence that I know can explain. Maybe a psychologist feller could tell the reason, and I guess plenty tried in the past to do so. It just seems that somehow hate is passed down from generation to generation and it needs something or someone to come up with an idea to break what is happening. It needs education – education for the young children."

The pair were silent then as they saw Ratso coming towards them from the other side of the canteen. Ratso banged the table.

"What the hell you two jabbering about? You in our country now. If you comes over 'ere and works on the buses you got to speak English what normal people can understand, not all that monkey-talk stuff."

Dion immediately picked up his cash bag. "I going now," he said to Jermaine.

Jermaine also got up. "I also must go. I am due back on the road."

The West Indian conductors got up and walked out together.

As Ratso headed back to his table, Dabber, who had witnessed the whole incident, got up and waylaid him.

"You could have been a little more polite, mate," said Dabber. "There was no need to talk to them like that."

"What you on about?" said Ratso. "You're an idiot. You ain't been on the job five minutes. You don't know nothing about the situation. I was just telling them blacks to speak English. We're entitled to know what they're on about, ain't we?"

Dabber said, "Far as I could tell they were speaking English. And there's polite ways of talking to people. Those blacks is on the job now, they're bus crew just like us. You don't insult your mates."

Ratso said, "I was just telling 'em to speak bloody English. What's wrong with that?"

"It wasn't polite, the way you did it," said Dabber.

Sometimes the busmen had to work split shifts – an early half-shift and a late half-shift, with a few hours off during the afternoon. During that terrible off-duty time, when it wasn't worthwhile to go home, the locked doors of the pubs would stare mockingly. During these legally enforced hours of closure the cruel wind would often whip flakes of snow along the unfriendly streets and desperate men would huddle in their coats against the penetrating cold while wandering the streets craving alcohol.

They crouched, silent and staring with misery as long as they could over cups of stewed tea in the cheap cafés. They suffered and they waited, that legion of haunted men. They watched the clocks, and each minute seemed an eternity.

With a quarter of an hour to go to the marvellous time for which their hearts craved, they left the cafés and the cold doorways and the hostile park benches and started to plod, heads down, to their pubs. Outside each set of closed doors they stood, silent and miserable, the fever for drink raging inside them. They stood there helplessly as they listened for the sound they craved: the bolts being drawn back, the key turning in the lock, and the hellish final seconds until the doors opened.

And as the sounds commenced and the seconds passed, each man would gradually edge a few steps at a time towards the door, each wanting to be first in, first to be served, first to raise that first marvellous pint to his mouth. But none could seem, even to his fellows, to be anxious, to be desperate; the pretence must be kept up until each had his glass and each had had that first long, long swallow. And then, oh God! Everything was marvellous again; the talk could begin, the jollity could break out and the jokes could be cracked. Another hellish afternoon's closed period had passed and another fantastic drunken evening had begun.

During these terrible afternoon closed periods Dabber often spent time in the Bristol Omnibus social club at Lawrence Hill. The club was an upstairs room, large and bleak, but its austere appearance masked a warm and welcoming place. There were benches with the covering ripped and the stuffing poking out, wooden upright chairs and a machine dispensing tea in cardboard cups. At night, the bar would be open and busmen could relax with pints of Toby bitter.

In this sparsely furnished hidey-hole for bus crews, this refuge from the taxing masses of the travelling public, Dabber lazed about on many afternoons watching the snooker, having the occasional game and observing the characters.

Once he saw a conductor pull something wrapped in dirty newspaper from his pocket and lay it reverentially on the bench beside him. After a lengthy interval of regarding it with an air of anticipation of some great pleasure to come, the conductor unfolded it carefully as if it were treasure, and all it contained were slices of scrawny, uncooked bacon.

The man looked at the bacon and gazed at it, and then suddenly, he grabbed a slice and rammed it into his mouth. His face contorted and strange tremors ran through his body. After every swallow there was a great smacking of his lips and wiping of his mouth, and then he would bend with great eagerness and pull out another piece of bacon from the filthy newspaper.

Another busman was using a magnifying glass to read his newspaper. He had a green conductor's badge in his lapel. Just as well he wasn't a driver when he needed a magnifying glass to read a newspaper, Dabber thought.

A small, sad-looking conductor with a hunched back was spending his time rolling and smoking matchstick-thin cigarettes. He was completely silent and immersed in his task, save that every few minutes he looked up and yelled, "Yo-de-lay-ee, yo-de-lay-ee-o," for no particular reason.

Only a few among many interesting characters in that busmen's club.

CHAPTER 25

In the canteen Jermaine and Dion, his fellow West Indian conductor, were talking again.

Dion was saying, "When they get some sun in this country, man? It rain all the time. It dark till nine o'clock in the morning. And it cold as hell."

Jermaine chuckled, "It winter here, you fool. That why it cold. What the hell you expect in British Isles? You not in sunny Jamaica now, man."

"I been here four months and no ackee and saltfish in this canteen – not one day ackee and saltfish."

"Don't worry, man, you soon get to like shepherd's pie and spotted dick and then you be like real Englishman." Jermaine roared with laughter.

His companion said sourly, "I don't want to be like damn Englishman."

There was a pause and then Jermaine said, "What route you on?"

"Sixes."

"What your driver like?"

"He a bastard. That him over there – fat man."

"What wrong with him?"

"What wrong with him?" exclaimed Dion. "He never speak to me, man. Two days now and he never speak. At end of journey he just sit in cab smoking. Never come round to back of bus to say hello."

"My driver real friendly," said Jermaine. "He chat to me at end of journey. Buy me tea in café."

"Why he not sit with you down here in canteen, then?" said Dion.

"That's jes' the way they are, the whiteys," said Jermaine. "It take time to be *intee-gra-ted*. It hard for them and it hard for us. We jes' got to be patient and keep going and I tell you everything come out right in the end."

"I tell you, man, I is on verge of going back to Jamaica," Dion said. "This country not like they tell us. It not friendly. Britain, our mother country? Hah. British do not even know where Jamaica is. And weather here lousy. When we going to get some sun?"

"You cannot alter the sun, my friend," said Jermaine. "It pop in and it pop out and you never can tell what going to come next out of this British sky."

"And some people is just seeking all the time to humiliate us and to show they is superior," said Dion. "Why they do that?"

"Ah, it just a few, very few," replied Jermaine. "Most of the citizens of this city, they is very civil and polite to all comers. You have just to be polite to them and they be polite back, apart from a few who don't even be polite to them fellow whiteys."

"Well, I got news for them few who thinking all the time to humiliate us," said Dion. "They is failing. They just showing they not worthy of respect as decent human beings. What so bad about the colour black that it make whiteys behave so hostile?"

Jermaine put his hand on Dion's. "Let us leave the subject now," he said. "It is not good to talk too much about what happen in this city which has welcomed us."

The Jamaicans were not the only ones who were grumbling. For months complaints had been flying around about all manner of things, especially shift work, pay and the food in the company's canteens.

"That Old Market hellhole of a canteen…it's a wonder we ain't all down with stomach bugs," Slab shouted over a pint in the White Hart one night.

Greasy chipped in that he'd found a dead cockroach in his chips in the underground canteen. "Man, it was nasty," he said.

"Dead cockroach, mate? That's nothing. I saw mice running about in the bogs down there."

"I 'ad a bit of stew once…" said a conductress, but the recollection seemed to overcome her and she fell silent.

"And all them little black midges that flit about when you're eating…" said Greasy.

"I just want to get over to them sunny beaches where all them French birds are, an' the high living," Slab shouted.

"What do we get when we complain? Nothing, zero, zilch," complained an overweight driver, hopping about and rubbing his belly as if he could already feel a bit of food poisoning coming on.

"The sodding company don't care," shouted somebody else.

"How come we never see none of the bosses? How come none of the bastards ever come and talk to us?" said Ratso.

"Because they're too busy sitting on their fat backsides up in the offices. They ain't going to take any chances of coming out and meeting us face-to-face, are they?" shouted Skully.

Amid this barrage of complaints and crew shortages, the bus services somehow managed to stagger on.

Friday! Throughout the company, at all the depots and at the central points, the pay packets were dished out. The crews who worked the Old Market routes collected their packets from a room above the canteen in Carey's Lane. The room was bleak and the staff who guarded the packets lounged on chairs, smoked and cracked jokes. It took up most of the day, this dishing out of the money, because individual workers did not pick up their wages until they came in for their shifts.

One Friday Dabber picked up his wages and then went down into the canteen to pass the time. There were a lot of blokes down there and the atmosphere was crazy, what with blokes just picking up their packets. But at the centre of it all, and already boasting and waving his pay packet in the air, was Slab.

He was talking and bragging as he stuffed himself with food. He had put his wage packet on the table beside his big plate of fry-up. He wanted everyone to see how thick his packet was.

"A hundred hours," he was boasting. "A hundred hours last week. There ain't no man beat that. No man here beat that."

He was talking and eating at the same time, forking the food into his mouth and swallowing it down into his belly as fast as he could. You could tell he was just interested in shoving it down as fast as possible so that he could get out on the road again and earn more money.

He stopped eating and waved his fat packet in the air once more. "There ain't no man in the company picked up more than me today. Into my pocket this goes, mates – into my pocket towards my life of leisure. I'll be eating like a king soon, lapping up the sun far away from this place."

Some of the blokes started sniggering.

Slab glared. "You won't be laughing when I've got my big stash. You won't be laughing when I come back all suntanned an' relaxed and you lot are still slaving away on this job."

The card schools were in full session, the players' arms going in and out and cigarettes being smoked, taken up and put down like clock-work.

Slab looked furious at being ignored. He prodded his fork savagely into a pile of black pudding and bacon and shoved it into his mouth.

All at once he looked strange. He was still chewing away, but saliva and bits of food kept spewing out. His face twisted and Dabber, who was looking at him, thought, *Slab's not well – he's eating too fast.*

"Yeah, them hot, sunny beaches..." Slab started again. "When I get over there..." Then he sat immobile and stared forward. He sat like that, like a statue, with a fat, expressionless face for about ten seconds. Then he took off with his boasting again. Once more he stopped, gave a moan, looked down and made an attempt to spear a bit of sausage with his fork, but he never made it. Another groan came from him and his bald head wobbled about.

Then a sound, "Uhgheaarraagh," came out of him and Slab just flopped slowly forward, face first, into his fry-up, with a bit of bacon hanging out of his mouth.

His knife and fork clattered to the floor as one hand reached out towards the fat pay packet lying beside him on the table, but he never reached it.

And then Slab was still.

Busmen and women stopped eating and looked across curiously. The card school was paralysed in the middle of a hand. Some of the canteen staff came out and stood silently.

Then one of the men near Slab prised his eyelid up and after a moment said quietly, "I think he's a goner."

Nobody moved or spoke for about half a minute, then the cook came over, gently eased the bacon from the overtime king's mouth and solemnly draped a tea towel over his head. Somebody else tucked the fat pay packet away into the dead man's inside pocket.

The card school was still stopped and the players were looking across. Everyone just stayed silent and shocked. When the men arrived to get 'the king' out of there, he looked bigger in death than he had ever done in life. He lay flat on his back on the stretcher, his fat belly pushing the blanket up and his feet sticking out. The two men struggled and panted as they manoeuvred him out of the dining room, past the smelly toilets and round the corner.

Some of the older busmen followed the stretcher reverently, as if they were in a cortège. That was nice to see. And the two men panted and sweated as they heaved Slab's body from the warmth of that stuffy canteen up the bleak stone stairs and into the grey, sepulchral gloom of Carey's Lane.

CHAPTER 26

Dabber had been driving for almost a week after swapping his green conductor's badge for a red driver's badge. He felt somehow superior up there in the cab instead of having to sway about on the open, windswept rear platform. A lot of Scoter's sensible advice had been forgotten.

Dabber was impatient on the stops: always desperate for starting bells from his conductor, always eager to get going, knowing that strung out along the length of the route behind him were other buses driven by more experienced drivers who knew how to pull all the flankers and stunts of the job. Dabber frequently imagined that these buses were gaining ground on him, closing fast. Immediately when he got a starting bell he would punch the accelerator to the floor, whack the lever into second, up to third, pull it back into top and hurtle along, engine thumping, and then it was ease off, foot on the brake and pull into the next stop – and the next, and the next, dozens of stops, hundreds of them, never ending. And all around, the mighty roar of Bristol's traffic: cars hooting, vans and trucks revving, horns blasting, drivers cursing, motorcyclists weaving, cyclists shouting and wobbling about.

And in the midst of all the chaos, Dabber driving, trying to blot out the roar of the traffic and thinking about the last few peaceful days with Melody in the bedsitter. They had got in a few bottles, cuddled and kissed, had a good drink and rolled about on the floor or the bed with the gas fire popping and zizzing at the excitement of it all.

And then at night, when Dabber was not on late shift, they had gone out and laughed in the snow and joined in the drinking in the Quadrant and the Portcullis and the Greyhound.

Afterwards, with the streetlights coruscating on the fallen snow, they strolled back to his room with their arms around each other. When they got in, they left the light out and sat in the dark over the little gas fire until it had infused some warmth into them. They sat back on the ancient settee, held each other and listened to the sighing of the gas. There wasn't a sound in the house or outside.

"I like it in the dark when we're here just by ourselves, just you and me," Melody whispered. "Darkness is nice when you're inside, somewhere safe. I always feel safe in here when night comes. It's so quiet and peaceful. You just feel as if there's no shit going on anywhere anymore."

Dabber put out the light and pulled out two bottles of George's Pale Ale. The young lovers sat there in the gloom, drinking straight from the bottles.

"I always dreamed that one day I'd have evenings like this," said Melody. "Just me and someone that cares for me, sitting together in the dark and being happy."

They sat for almost two hours and then they crept into bed and pulled the bed sheets and blankets up tightly around them.

Fragments of talk were floating lazily in through the shutters from the passers-by wandering home outside:

"…but what about…the connections?"

"…beef dripping…"

"It resembled a gherkin…"

The two young lovers lay in their warm bed quietly listening to the late-night wanderers meandering past outside. And then just before they fell asleep, Melody pulled him close and whispered in his ear that she was pregnant.

In the Old Market canteen a group of West Indian conductors were sitting round a table.

Jermaine said, "You had an insult. Big deal, man. What they call you? Monkey man? I had insults before. Insults is nothing, my friend."

"I don't like it," said Dion. "Why people think they can insult me?"

"You is taking it all serious, you fool," chuckled Jermaine. "I told you before, you got to hang loose, boy, take it easy. White men get insults, women get insults, everyone get insult sometime. That jes' the way it is in this ol' world."

"They ain't got the right to call me 'monkey man'. Who they think they are? They think they still rule us? I tell you, man, I had enough."

"Cool down, man. Take it easy," said Jermaine. "You is all full of fury. It no good going through life full of fury."

"Woman on bus, she put gloves on before she take ticket from me. Why she do that for?"

"Maybe she thinks she get black colour from you, man," said Jermaine with a chortle.

At a nearby table, white crews were talking. "Listen to them black 'uns over there laughing," said Skully. "I bet they's talking about us. All that pidgin stuff. They could be planning to slit our throats, man."

Dabber said, "Don't be stupid, man. They're not planning to slit anyone's throat. They're just talking. They got a right to talk, haven't they?"

"Yeah, but you don't know what the bastards are saying. Why can't they speak proper English like us?" said Skully.

"They were speaking English, mate," said Dabber.

"Not proper English like what we speak, though," scoffed Skully.

"There's plenty different ways of speaking English," said Dabber.

Across the canteen the two West Indians, Jermaine and Dion, became aware that the white staff were talking.

"Look at them whiteys, man," Dion said. "They is talking about us."

"Let them talk, they ain't harming us. They entitled to talk. There ain't no law against talking," said Jermaine.

"I don't like it, man," Dion said. "Why no one sit with me? Every time I come down here no one sit with me."

"Give it time, my friend," Jermaine said. "Everything smooth out. We is just getting used to each other. How long you been here, man?"

"Three months. Three months and only few white men speak to me. How long it take for them to get used to me?"

"Don't worry. They all be friendly soon. We just do our job and keep going and soon we all be big happy family," said Jermaine with a chuckle.

"Big happy family? You is dreaming, man," Dion said.

CHAPTER 27

Melody was now as close as anything with Amy, the landlady. The little bit of irritation Melody had felt about Amy cuddling and kissing Dabber at the party was forgotten, and one evening when Melody and Dabber were sitting as cosy as could be in the little bedsitter Amy knocked on the door and came in with a bottle of Bristol Cream sherry and some little crystal glasses.

She sat down in the old armchair and made herself as comfortable as anything. She had obviously carefully combed and brushed her hair, which was now showing tinges of grey. The sleeves of her cardigan reached down almost to her fingertips, but her middle-aged bust, although sagging slightly, was still full and stood out proudly. Her mid-thigh-length skirt revealed most of her smooth and well-formed legs.

Dabber gazed at her and thought, *She's good-looking for her age. She's a bit of all right. Yeah, I could go for her all right.* And then he thought, *Hell, what a bastard I am, thinking like that when Melody's pregnant.*

Dabber and Melody could see that Amy was lonely. She drank and talked and shared out the sherry with quick little movements, and she gradually came alive with the drink.

She said, "The trouble with tenants is, you got to watch 'em. If you don't watch 'em, they whip everything. I caught a couple once just going out the door with a sodding armchair. Just caught 'em, I did, in the nick o' time. For the love of God, they'll whip anything, tenants will, if you don't watch 'em."

She was knocking back the sherry as she continued, "I 'ad a bloke in once, in the top flat, 'e couldn't go out the door until 'e'd checked every sodding thing twenty times. He'd come down the stairs and then back up again to check he'd locked 'is door, then back up again to check he'd turned 'is tap off, then back up again to check 'is gas was off all right. That man, it took 'im twenty minutes easy to get out the front door. He was up and down them stairs so much I thought 'e was going to wear the buggers out."

In between talking, she glanced around the room once or twice, taking everything in, and then she said, "My goodness, how nice you've got this place."

Well, that was all down to Melody, who looked after the place a lot better than Dabber. It was cosy sitting there talking, the three of them, hunching forward and trying to get some heat out of the gas fire and drinking the sherry. When the bottle was finished, Amy went down-stairs and came back with another bottle and shared that out among the three of them and told a few more yarns about tenants.

When they were well down the second bottle of Bristol Cream, Amy wobbled to her feet and swayed about like she had half a pound of rubbery spaghetti in each slipper and said she'd better go and leave the two young lovers to themselves.

She'd gone a bit down the stairs when she suddenly panicked about something and pulled herself back up, very tottery on her legs. She grabbed the sherry bottle, which she'd forgotten, and took another big swig. Well, Melody and Dabber had to help her down the stairs after that and put the bottle inside her flat where she could get at it easily.

Dabber and Melody went out then, and walked through the frozen streets with the sky as clear as a pane of glass and the yellow stars so far away in the great vastness of the night sky. They went to the bridge and stood looking out over the gorge, hugging each other, with the air so cold and bright it took their breath away. They stayed so long that the bridge keeper must have thought that they were contemplating suicide and came to look at them.

Then it was back to Dabber's room, where they cuddled up together in the cosy bed under some new, fragrantly scented pink sheets that Melody had chosen. The sheets must have turned her on, for she was as gentle and loving as anything before she dropped off to sleep.

Dabber lay awake for some time in the darkness, thinking about everything: Melody and the baby and what the future would be like. And then he thought of Joe, out there somewhere in the city, rolling around the pubs every day, or perhaps in the boxing ring if he was in a fit state. Dabber wondered what would happen if he and Joe came face-to-face again. As he was lying there thinking, Melody muttered something softly and snuggled up to him. He held her tightly.

One evening, they were all in the Hart: Dabber, Rulebook, Poody, and on his usual stool up at the counter, Barhanger. There were loads of other busmen and women in as well, plus several West Indian and Asian conductors who were sitting and drinking quietly. The jukebox was howling and the smoke was as thick as mist.

Everyone was well lubricated. Barhanger kept shouting drunken, nonsensical phrases: "What's the score? Who's next? What the hell gives? I dunno. Don't effing worry."

Dabber queued and pushed and shoved to get served. The barman pushed him a pint of EI over and Dabber fought back through the swaying, noisy mob and stumbled onto a stool beside Rulebook and Barhanger.

"Aaah," sighed Rulebook, as smart as ever in his company cap and immaculate uniform. "All this rash drinking we do, I'm not sure it's good for us. Perhaps it's because we are all despondent at what life has to offer."

"Yeah, we're all hanging on the side of this crazy planet hurtling through space at about a million miles an hour and nobody has a sodding clue where we're heading," said Snakeface, a skeletal conductor with a viperish face.

"And if you looked down on the human race from the window of a spaceship," Dabber said, "you'd realise one thing straight away: most of the people down on this planet are bonkers."

"The common man is ground down by work and strife, his life becomes useless and futile. Nevertheless, I say *bibamus*. Let us drink," called Rulebook, thrusting his glass high.

"Yes, *bibamus*, whatever that means," someone else shouted. "Let us drink now and keep drinking, and have a drunken old age. Let us shout from our deathbeds, 'Jeez, that was one hell of a ride, that life was.'"

"Yeah, we live our lives, work hard, pay taxes, put up with halfwits and awkward buggers on our buses..."

"We mess around, we fornicate..."

"We stagger around bewildered, baffled, picking up gut rot, foot rot..."

"Bellyache, backache..."

"Athlete's foot."

"You'll never get athlete's foot, mate – you're not an athlete."

"I'm fitter than you, mate."

"Prove it. Do a headstand."

"What the hell I want to do a headstand for?"

"Give us another pint, barman. I ain't living my life to arrive at the grave with a body bulging with muscles."

"Or chubby red cheeks like a newborn babby."

"All our days of bitter travail sweep silently into a black eternity," shouted Rulebook.

The busmen and women paused whatever they were doing and sat in quiet awe for a few moments, pondering the profound meaning and truth of this observation.

And then someone shouted, "Let's 'ave a bit of fun while we're alive. Eff worrying about heart disease."

"Or liver failure."

"Let's keep fornicating."

"To hell with all the scientists."

"Psychologists, psychiatrists..."

"Quacks, doctors, pill-peddlers..."

"Bugger them all."

There followed a long silence while all the busmen and women took a drink and drew on cigarettes contemplatively.

"It's never been proved, you know – none of it."

"What's never been proved?"

"That cancer stuff – smoking and cancer. Never proved."

"There's always some meddler wants to stop people doing things."

"Yes indeed, *les petites misères de la vie*," intoned Rulebook. "There is always someone who wishes to control what other people do. Nevertheless, various scientific studies have shown that smoking is indeed deleterious to human health, and there is evidence that cancer can be a result. However, smoking aside, may I also say that other studies have revealed that it can be beneficial to health to indulge in a modicum of pleasure, including the partaking of moderate amounts of alcoholic liquor? We should undoubtedly respect our bodies and cherish every moment that we are alive. However..." he leaped to his feet and thrust his glass high into the air, "to Bacchus, Bacchus, I say."

"Who the hell's Bacchus?" somebody exclaimed.

"The god of wine, my friend," declared Rulebook, thrusting his glass high once more.

"Yeah, to Bacchus. We only live once, so we might as well live it up," a half-cut drinker shouted.

"*Aux bons vivants*, to those who live it up," cried Rulebook, his glass high once again, and everyone started shouting and clinking their glasses against other glasses in great drunken merriment.

"Yes, yes, we must keep working flankers, drinking and fornicating until the final shift and the last ring of that sodding passenger bell," a man yelled.

"We must hammer down the route, ignoring all the bells and all the checkers with their little notebooks and skid the sodding bus sideways into the terminus for the final time."

"A few weeks on the old-age pension and then we drop dead, most likely."

"I tell you what, if I meet up with God, I'm gonna tell 'im it hasn't been up to much, this life."

"Yeah, but who says God exists? Has anyone ever seen 'im?"

"Why don't he ever show 'isself?"

"Yeah, why don't he never come down an' shake our hands?"

Everyone was shouting and laughing and swaying with the madness of it all, but Old Sam was sitting lonely and silent by himself and looked as if he scarcely had the enthusiasm to puff his pipe.

Dabber said, "What's up, Old Sam?" and Old Sam, in miserable tones, said, "It's Diamond. She's too much for me."

And scarcely had he said it, than the door of the pub banged open and Diamond Lil herself entered, furious-faced. She spotted Old Sam, marched over and gave him a smack round the head.

"That'll teach you to play around with my emotions," she said.

"I ain't played around with your emotions, Diamond," said Old Sam, all downhearted, rubbing his ear.

"And my body, playing around with my body," said Lil.

"But I ain't played around with your body," protested Sam.

"No, but you been thinking about it, 'aven't you? I know what you been thinking – you been thinking dirty thoughts about me, 'aven't you?" said Diamond Lil.

"I have not," said Sam.

"Yes you sodding well 'ave," she said, and she gave Old Sam another slap around the ear before marching out.

Some of the blokes were rolling around laughing, but others were saying, "What the hell? You should have smacked her right back, Sam."

But Old Sam said, "No, no, I could never hit a lady. I could never hit anyone."

Someone said quietly to the others at his table, "You know, I feel sorry for Old Sam. He got married when he was young – set up house and everything. Then the war came and he was sent overseas. Two or three years he was away. When he came back it 'ad all gone to pot: wife drinking and smoking, messing around with other blokes. Sam couldn't take it – stood it as long as he could and then got a divorce."

The men were all quiet and contemplative at this, and then, just as the sympathising with Old Sam was at its height, the door banged open and Greasy came in, all beaming and seeming in the highest of spirits. He was followed closely by a blonde young woman about five feet ten inches tall, with a very short skirt, a tight sweater and a rather large pair of breasts. The eyes of every bloke in the lounge were immediately swivelling about and going round and round at the magnitude of her chest, and all the women in the place were squinting and glaring at her in fury.

Even Rulebook was heard to mutter, *"Mon Dieu, quelle poitrine."*

Greasy and his new girlfriend pushed in beside the busmen and Greasy immediately started talking with great excitement.

"We got a council flat now, man, brand new. When we knew the sanitary bloke was coming round to inspect our old place I got a plan worked out. I threw dirty water and crap all over the walls. I scraped some fungus up from outside and stuck it up in the bathroom. Then I got a dead rat off a tip and chucked it down in the bedroom. When the geezer sees the place, he goes, 'Oh dear, dear. Oh, my goodness, this habitation is shocking. You can't go on living 'ere, I'll 'ave to get you a new place immediately.'"

The blonde girl with the big breasts whacked her elbow into Greasy's ribs. "There's no need to tell them all that," she said. "Give us a fag, will ya? What the hell's the matter with you?" Greasy took his packet out, lit a cigarette in his own mouth and handed it to her. She snatched it without any thanks and sat staring straight ahead, twiddling a beer mat with her free hand, smoking and looking as bored as hell. All the busmen were sneaking glances at her and marvelling at how such a beauty could look so sour and morose.

Everyone else was drinking and laughing and falling about while the blonde sat there with her twisted and disapproving expression, and then she got up to go to the toilet.

After she had pushed her way, with her supercilious nose stuck in the air, through the crowd of ogling blokes and women giving her the evil eye, one of the busmen said to Greasy, "Blimey, what a pair of mammary glands your girlfriend's got."

Greasy's mouth opened and his beer glass froze in mid-air. He said, "What's a mammary gland?"

Rulebook, who had been leaning back against the wall looking half-asleep, instantly came awake. "Our friend is referring to the magnificence of your girlfriend's bosom."

"Yeah, she 'as got a decent pair of knockers, 'asn't she?" said Greasy.

The blonde came back and downed the rest of her drink in one go. She held the empty glass in front of her and turned it this way and that as if she had never seen an empty glass before.

Greasy said, "Would you like another drink, Luella?"

Luella said, "Well, I ain't going to sit here all day with bugger all."

While Greasy was up at the bar, she twiddled with the beer mat again and looked as mad as hell. Nobody dared speak to her. She just stared straight ahead and smoked her cigarette with big, furious gestures.

The jukebox was hammering at the air and beating at the walls, the smoke was swirling and hanging and everybody's senses were twisted and captured by the madness of it all.

One or two blokes were laughing at some private joke. The laughter was infectious and spread, and soon all the blokes in the place were convulsing with merriment and slapping each other on the back.

Greasy was whey-heying and yelling and enjoying it most of all, but the blonde gave him a mighty whack in the belly with her elbow and said, "Shut the hell up, will ya?"

At that, the hilarity of the men increased and blokes were banging the wall and spluttering beer all over the place and slapping each other to near exhaustion. One or two staggered out into the lane, weak with laughter, and slid slowly down the wall at the hilarity of it all.

CHAPTER 28

The man was sitting with his feet resting on a pile of oily engine parts as he sat as immobile as a waiting vulture. He looked calm, but his body at that moment was tense. His body craved strong drink, but his fingers gripped only a mug of cheap coffee. On the floor next to him was an upended wooden crate on which stood a half bottle of milk and a dirty bottle of Camp Coffee and Chicory Essence. He had a stump of unlit cigar in his mouth. The man's pocket was empty.

Although he sat without moving, his senses were alert. Suddenly he sniffed the air. Money had come onto the site. Without looking, the man was aware of Dabber. Dabber was looking at the second-hand cars which were for sale. The man's fingers tightened for an instant and then relaxed. The prey was within reach, but had not been given enough time. The man's addled but long-seasoned brain knew that a customer must be given time, just as a punter viewing the whores in a dingy street on a dark night must be given time.

The imagination of the prey must build, the brain must simmer, the senses must boil over until the merchandise looks like paradise, and it is at that moment that the wallet opens.

The man knew all this, but he did not get up. He waited as a pimp waits, secretly watching through his half-open door as a pimp squints through a crack to ensure the suckers do not get away. As he waited the man tried to stop the trembling of his body as it craved drink and sensed that there was money within reach.

As Dabber looked around the stock of old bangers he drew closer to the office, and the dealer panted as Dabber and his money drew closer. And then Dabber was in the office, his euphoria at the thought of owning his very own car sky-high and his thoughts a little silly.

"I want a good quality car, one that attracts attention, especially with the girls," said Dabber.

The dealer took a slow drink out of his coffee mug. He examined Dabber silently and then he said, "If it's a quality car you want, sir, you've come to the right place. This is a high-class establishment."

"Show me," said Dabber.

The dealer was studying his potential buyer again. After lengthy scrutiny, he said, "'Ow much money you got?"

"About fifty quid," Dabber said.

The dealer put down his coffee cup and stared hard at Dabber. He got up slowly.

"Follow me," he said.

The two went out and stopped beside a big black four-door car. The man launched into some well-rehearsed patter. "First-class condition, first-class condition, this motor. Austin 16. One of the best cars they ever built. Previous owner, a very successful businessman. Kept 'is financial situation under wraps, just like you, sir."

The dealer patted the long black bonnet and put his dirty shoe on the running board. "This beauty'll give you no trouble," he said, and he stroked the car affectionately. "This car was designed for successful men like yourself, sir. They built 'em right when they built this model. For a ride in this conveyance, sir, the birds will promise you anything, anything."

Dabber looked at the car and strolled around it. He looked inside and then he stood and looked at it again. The dealer was silent. He opened the bonnet and Dabber looked at the engine. The dealer opened the boot. He wound the sunroof back a bit and closed it again. He did all this without speaking.

Dabber looked hard at the car. He imagined the pleasure of urging it into full speed, the throbbing of the gear lever and the roaring of the engine.

The dealer saw all this in Dabber's face and burst into professional eloquence. He spoke of the car as if it were an object of rarity and beauty; he said it was a treasure, a classic; one that all Dabber's friends would envy. The dealer caressed the car, he breathed on it, he almost kissed it, and he polished a bit of the bonnet with his sleeve. He talked enthusiastically and mentioned the car as a prize, a rare specimen, and an absolute bargain. The dealer looked like he wanted to cuddle the car, take it to bed and give it a good doing up the exhaust pipe.

"You'll be the envy of all your friends with this one, sir," the dealer said again. "None of 'em will have anything to touch this beauty."

"How much is it?" Dabber said.

"Seventy quid," the man said. He rolled his cigar around and bared his nicotine-stained teeth in a horrible smile. He had on a worn jacket and dirty trousers, cheap, bulky rings and a metal trinket on a chain round his neck. His face was wrinkled and yellowy and cunning. "For a customer like you, sir, I'll knock a fiver off," he said. "Sixty-five quid and it's a deal."

Dabber was silent.

"I mean, think of the birds…" the dealer said.

"Is it guaranteed?" Dabber said.

"Guaranteed? Everything I sell is guaranteed, son."

"Is your business reputable? I mean, can I trust that you won't fiddle me?"

The salesman gaped. "Fiddle you? Never," the salesman said. "I mean, my name's your guarantee. I see executives and suchlike driving round every day in cars I sold 'em. Never had a complaint yet." The dealer paused, rubbed his nose and then opened the door of the black car. "Hop in, son – I'll give you a run," he said.

The man got a starting handle out of the boot and gave the engine a turn. He swung the handle again and it kicked back and rapped his knuckles. "Damn," he said, and clutched his hand. He swung the handle again. He heaved and struggled with the starting handle, so keen was he to feel the customer's money. The engine fired; it fired and raced and it sounded fine. The dealer got into the driving seat with Dabber in the passenger seat. They drove around the block and came back. There was a lot of smoke from the exhaust.

"Cold engine," said the dealer. "Be all right in a minute, sir."

They stood and looked while the big engine ticked over and the car vibrated. The smoke died away and the exhaust was all right.

"Sixty-five pounds is too much," Dabber said.

The salesman took the unlit stump of cigar from his mouth and thought for a moment. "I can knock another two quid off," he said. "Sixty-three quid."

Dabber was silent.

A twitch had set in on the dealer's neck. "Give me sixty, fifty-five," he said.

"Fifty-two is my limit," said Dabber, and he turned away with an unconcerned air.

The dealer's fingers were twitching now; they moved towards Dabber's neck and then they drew back. The dealer didn't want to go back to his office with its dirty mug and its Camp Coffee and Chicory Essence. He wanted strong drink. He held his trembling hand out for the money.

A few minutes later Dabber roared off and away down the road.

The dealer watched him open-mouthed. His fist opened and closed in frustration and then he hurried fast towards the pub.

The strike came fast. Complaints about hygiene in the canteen, pay and shifts had been building up and then, as if on a signal, buses were leaving their routes and running into the depots.

Outside Winterstoke depot men were gathered on the verges throwing their arms about and yelling, "Better pay, better grub. Better pay, better grub."

Ratso was striding about shouting, "If them bastard bosses don't change their minds and give us what we want, we'll stop the wheels, we'll stop the sodding wheels for good."

"What use would that be?" someone else demanded.

"It would show those bastards we ain't putting up with their crap anymore. They think work's all we're good for – working till we drop," Ratso shouted.

"We slave away all the effing time: early shifts, late shifts, split shifts, weekend work, overtime. We never get a decent rest, do we?" another driver shouted.

"We just plod away like a lot of sodding donkeys."

"Suffering all the time."

"And we go down the pub whenever we can," shouted a conductor, with a big belly laugh that had all the sad humour of a long-suffering busman's life about it.

"Them bosses, though, they don't suffer. There ain't no slaving away for them. They got it easy, sitting there in their posh offices, doing bugger all," shouted Ratso.

"How come we never see them, the bosses?" came a shout.

"Because we would suss them out. We'd see what useless bastards they are."

"Yeah, that's right, they got to keep hidden away so we don't see what useless buggers they are."

"They piss all over us, man. We've had enough," shouted Skully.

By half past eleven, all over the city, on dozens of routes and hundreds of stops, long, hopeless queues of would-be passengers formed. When the realisation dawned that there were no buses, all across the city angry people started walking, their feet beating out a refrain of contempt at buses, crews, fares, managers, timetables and all the rest of the shambolic city transport setup.

The crews who gathered on the grass verge outside Winterstoke depot were now highly excitable; some balanced on the wall and others pushed them off for a bit of fun.

An angry voice shouted, "No messing around. This is serious. We stick together. No blacklegs, no scabs, right?"

"What'll we do now?" somebody else shouted. "I ain't standing here much longer."

A cry went up: "There's gonna be a strike meeting up in Queen Square."

"Let's get up there," someone else shouted.

They set off in a long, straggly column, whooping and yelling, punching the air and chanting, "One out, all out. One out, all out."

It was taken up by the rest: "One out, all out. One out, all out."

Up Ashton Road and North Street they marched, the cry changing to "Better pay, better grub. Better pay, better grub," and then, "No blacklegs, no scabs. No blacklegs, no scabs."

Past the Star and the London Inn and into the main street of Bedminster they marched. Each pub they passed seemed to see a slight diminution of the number of marchers, but always striding proudly along with the white busmen were several new coloured staff, including the first Asian conductor to come to Winterstoke depot, a brown, wiry Pakistani. On account of his cheery countenance under all circumstances, the men called him Smiler. He did not say much, but Dabber had taken him in the Hart a few times and he was good company. He was probably the first coloured bloke ever in that back lounge where the busmen drank. He would not touch alcohol and stuck with soft drinks, but he was easy to be with. The blokes took to him quickly. They said, "Hey, that little brown conductor, that Pakistani, he's all right, man. He slots in. You can have a laugh with him."

And there Smiler was, walking erect and proud along the Bedminster streets, supporting the strike.

"It's a sodding long walk, this," somebody grumbled.

"I wish there was some buses running we could 'ave hopped on," Greasy said with a moan.

Shoppers were gaping at the marchers. People came out of houses and business premises just to have a laugh at the busmen.

"Now you know what it's like for us when the buses don't turn up," a bystander called.

A nattily dressed young man on the pavement shouted, "I got a date with a bird up Filton tonight. How am I going to get there with no buses? I was looking forward to a bit of rumpty-tumpty."

"I've never walked so far in my effing life," Greasy grumbled.

Some of the blokes were nipping into shops for cigarettes and bars of chocolate. A few dived into pubs and did not reappear.

The marchers reached Queen Square and excitement rose as they saw the crowd of busmen and women from other depots who were already there.

Clerks in collars and ties were leaning out of office windows around the square shouting witty remarks. Passers-by were gaping.

Suddenly Ratso emerged from the crowd and leaped up onto the base of a statue of King William III on horseback. He held his arms up, and when he had got the mad scene quietened, he started straight in.

"Comrades," he shouted. "We've been sold down the river before and now we've been sold down again." He was gesticulating and jumping about from side to side on the narrow platform. "It's all these blacks what have come on the job that's the cause of it all. It's them what's keeping our wages down an' stinking us out with their smelly food." Ratso had got himself so worked up and was flapping about so wildly he nearly fell off the plinth. "The question is, comrades," he shouted, recovering his balance, "the question is, what the hell are we going to do about it?"

There was a tumult of cheers and jeers and suggestions as to what he could do.

Suddenly he was pushed aside and he stumbled headlong off the platform as someone else jumped up to harangue the crowd. To everyone's astonishment it was Lepiniere. Dabber was amazed to see that Lepiniere seemed quite rational and in control when he began to speak. He must have had a bit of therapy or something, Dabber thought.

"The point is, comrades," Lepiniere shouted authoritatively when the crowd had stilled, "what are we working for? We're working for a pittance, that's what. How many hours do we work? Every hour God sends. Who cares about us? Nobody. The management don't care. The public don't care. They don't give a toss so long as we're there morning, noon and night to keep the buses running for 'em. We're like slaves, mates, slaves of the modern world. Ten quid a week basic – it don't bear looking at."

The crowd was quiet all of a sudden.

"An' another thing," Lepiniere yelled, "the canteen we got to eat in is unhygienic and the food they give us is crap. Look at the responsibilities we got, mates: thousands of passengers we carry every week, hundreds of thousands every year. The most precious commodity there is, comrades, in our hands: human lives. And what do we get? What reward do we get? What recognition? We get a kick up the arse, that's what we get. We need a decent wage, we need a top-class canteen and we need decent grub."

This was more like it, the men thought. Those who didn't know Lepiniere well thought he was excellent, a born leader. Even passers-by were listening attentively.

Rulebook was standing by himself to the side, a serious look on his face. He muttered to himself, "Dear me, this should not be happening. It is irregular. Withdrawal of labour like this is quite unacceptable. It is against the regulations."

Lepiniere's voice had suddenly changed. Up on his plinth, he had been asking the crowd how much money any of them had left at the end of the week.

"Nothing, I bet," he shouted, answering his own question. "Same as me, nothing." And he pulled his pockets out to demonstrate.

A good point, Dabber thought, a very good point. The bloke could make a public speaker. Who would have guessed it?

"An' then," shouted Lepiniere, "there's all the ideology, comrades, all the authoritarianism, and the martyrs and suchlike. We got to engage with our fellow workers in our struggles. It's a critical time, my friends. We got to take back what the rich bastards 'ave taken from us."

Lepiniere had the crowd in his hands. In the distance the bells of the famous church of St Mary Redcliffe started to ring. Lepiniere paused and seemed to be listening, and then he screamed, "Bells, effing bells. Everywhere I go there's effing bells."

The bells of the famous old church continued their sombre chimes. Lepiniere had his hands over his ears and was moaning and rocking about.

People were staring. "What's up with him?" they were saying. "Why doesn't he keep going?"

Lepiniere shouted, "The hunchback, the hunchback..." and then he stopped.

"What's he on about? What hunchback?" the crowd was muttering.

Lepiniere stood there, up on the plinth beneath the statue. He seemed to be transfixed, one hand held out as though he was just going to illustrate a point. The bells of St Mary Redcliffe quickened their chimes.

"Listen to them!" Lepiniere screamed. "They're everywhere. Those bastard bells, they've followed me 'ere. They drove the hunchback crazy and now they're driving me crazy."

And then the bells of the cathedral joined in, ringing merrily and loudly over the square, enlivening and heightening the joyous peals of St Mary Redcliffe.

Lepiniere screamed. He sank to his knees and began pounding the statue, the majestic statue of King William III, with his fists.

There was muttering in the crowd. "What the hell's up with him?" people were saying. "He must be a nutter."

Dabber muttered to himself, "Something must have clicked over in poor Leppy's brain again – a wire's got crossed. He looks like he needs more therapy."

Lepiniere was sobbing and laying his head against the statue. "I can't take no more of those bells," he cried. "They've done for me." And he began to slide down the statue. When he was on his knees at the base, he clutched the statue desperately and raised his tortured face upwards as if praying. "Save me," he sobbed. "Save me from those effing bells."

Rulebook had a very concerned look on his face. "Dear me," he muttered to himself, "the poor man is demeaning that magnificent Rysbrack statue. It is surely the most magnificent equestrian monument in the country. Someone must step forward and help the poor man, otherwise the statue may be irreparably despoiled."

And then, as if he had heard the words, Amos stepped majestically forward. Amos, the West Indian, with his huge bulk and his grave manner, gently helped the sobbing Lepiniere down and a couple of blokes grabbed him and helped him away. Amos held his hands up and the crowd gradually fell silent.

"My friends," shouted Amos gravely. "My friends, this is no good. This is very bad. I am new to this job, as you know, and I do not know fully all your customs, but I do know that today we have a just cause." He paused; everyone had fallen silent. And then Amos went on in his dignified manner, "But we are not creating a good impression here. If we want to win this dispute and obtain our just demands, we must be sensible, we must be civilised, otherwise we shall not be taken seriously and we shall fail."

There was silence in the crowd. Even the office workers hanging out of their windows were listening.

"We must surely understand one thing," Amos went on in his dignified, deep tones, "while we are on strike we will get no pay. While we do not work, we will get no reward. Let us leave it to our union leaders to negotiate for us or those of us who are out will forfeit all sympathy."

Ratso, furious and hopping about, shouted, "What the hell do you mean, 'those of us who are out'? We're all out, ain't we?"

Amos shook his head sadly. "I am afraid not, my friend. Some of us have already seen a number nine on the road. It was driven by, what do you call it, a blackleg? If you will look over there towards the Centre you will see more buses going along."

The crowd turned in the direction his finger was pointing and angry shouts went up as buses running on service were spotted in the distance.

Amos held his hands up again for silence. "So you see, not all are on strike. A few continue to work. While they work, we have no strength. While they work they get paid, and we get nothing."

The assembled bus workers were listening intently now. "What I suggest," he went on in his sonorous West Indian accent, "is that we all go back to work. There is nothing to be gained now by staying out. We have succeeded in making a powerful point. Let us leave it now to our union leaders to sort out."

Amos got a lot of applause at the end of his speech, although one or two bellicose cries could still be heard.

The rain was slashing down again. Men and women started to drift from the square. Members of the public who had been standing around enjoying the proceedings were putting up umbrellas and hurrying away.

The windows of the surrounding offices were now shut against the downpour, the clerks no doubt back to pushing their pens this way and that.

Greasy's uniform was clinging to him as the rain poured down. His mousy hair, usually a tangled mess, was plastered flat and fervour was racing through him.

"Whey-hey!" he cried, slapping a wall in excitement. "What a great day, no more work." He punched his fist into the air and stomped along exultantly as he joined a group of busmen who were heading for the pubs.

CHAPTER 29

A new notice went up in the depot. Busmen and women crowded round to look, for it was not the usual company notice about changes to routes, rotas or about complaints from passengers. This was a far more interesting notice:

ONE NIGHT ONLY

PEACE AND TOGETHERNESS PARTY

For all bus crews, to mark the ending of the iniquitous colour bar of the Bristol Omnibus Company and to celebrate the amicable working together of all crews: white or black, British or from lands across the seas.

Free Drinks – Music – Jollity
Date and Venue to be announced

"What's this all about?" Barhanger shouted.

"Free booze. If there's gonna be free booze I'll be there," shouted a conductor.

"An' me too," cried someone else.

"Who's organising it?"

"Dabber's organising it."

"Yes, I'm organising it," said a voice behind the men, and turning around, they saw Dabber.

"What's it all about, though, Dabber?" Barhanger asked.

"Well, the situation is," said Dabber, "a few of us white crews have combined with some of the new black and Asian bus blokes and have chipped in from our own wages for this party. It's for the true spirit and friendship of all the bus crews in Bristol, white or black. I've appointed Rulebook as Master of Ceremonies on the night. He'll be making sure it runs smooth and keeping everybody in order."

"Rulebook in charge?" somebody exclaimed with a groan. "That's bad news. Give us some good news, Dabber. Is it really gonna be free, all the booze an' suchlike?"

"Why, certainly it will be free," Dabber responded, and then he was overwhelmed as a great cheer went up and blokes were slapping him on the back.

Jermaine was one of the first West Indian drivers to pass the public service vehicle driver's test. He was all misty-eyed when the examiner at the driving school handed him his pass certificate and old Scoter, with his twisted smile, shook his hand up and down, up and down and said, "Well done, kid, well bloody done."

Jermaine was immediately seized with a powerful *joie de vivre*, the sort only those who have the blood of hot Caribbean islands in their veins know about. And when he received his red driver's badge a fortnight later, he knew that that was the final tick he needed to drive a bus with fare-paying passengers and he danced around like it was carnival time.

The day of his first shift as a driver, he bounced into the signing-on room with his red badge gleaming in his lapel and it seemed as though he was twice the size, he was so proud and high in spirits.

He strode up to his conductor, his young West Indian compatriot, Dion, who busy preparing his waybill, slapped him on the back and said, "Aright, my *yute*?"

Dion scarcely glanced at him.

"I am your driver today, boy," said Jermaine.

There was still no response from the conductor.

"I pass my test easy, man. I got the red badge now," said Jermaine. "No more of that stupid conductor's stuff for me." And he made a big, contemptuous gesture at the conductor's box. Dion, who was now engrossed in lighting a cigarette, gazed silently at him.

Jermaine marched out of the signing-on room like a general leading an army, while Dion ambled behind with the cigarette hanging out of his mouth. As they waited for their bus at the changeover point, Jermaine started to walk backwards and forwards, gazing this way and that.

"What the arse wrong with you, man?" said Dion.

For a moment it looked as if Jermaine, in his new status, was not going to lower himself to have a conversation with a mere conductor, but at length he said, "I am looking for our bus. I am the driver. We must not make any mistakes today, my friend. I do not wish to lose my new red badge."

His conductor once more gazed at him, threw his cigarette end in the gutter, and said, "Ease you'self up, you fool. You is all tense."

"I ain't tense. I is relaxed," said Jermaine.

"When you is up in that cab, you make any mistakes today, man, they will have that new red badge off you faster than a dog have a rat," said Dion, and he chortled.

Those words made Jermaine very nervous and he started to think about all manner of things, but as the bus which they were to take over approached, he strode to the head of the queue, drew himself up and announced, "I am the driver who is taking over this bus now," and he pushed his lapel with its gleaming red badge forward so that all the queue could see it. "Look," he said. "Driver's badge. I will be your driver now. You will all be safe with me." And he beamed a big West Indian smile.

As soon as the incoming driver lowered himself from the cab, Jermaine leaped up into it. He spent time adjusting the seat and then slowly caressed the steering wheel, running his hands lovingly over it as if he was stroking a kitten. He fondled and patted each control in turn, checked the angle of the mirror and craned his head this way and that. He slowly tensed each arm so that his biceps swelled, flexed his fingers and beamed happily around his little cab. He sighed a deep sigh of contentment.

In this state of euphoria he was startled by two sharp dings – the starting signal – from his conductor. Jermaine sat stock-still. Seconds passed. He remained frozen. Two more dings rattled the bell box inches from his ear. Jermaine immediately started to flounder, reaching for this and that, pulling and pushing the gear lever, depressing the clutch and flooring the gas pedal. And then he sat immobile again and grew pale. The words of his conductor, Dion, flashed into his mind: *You make any mistakes today, they will have that red badge off you faster than a dog have a rat.*

Once more the bell shrilled its harsh metallic urgency into his ear. He looked back through the window behind him. All the passengers on the bottom deck seemed to be looking at him. The conductor on his platform was staring in his direction and then the conductor was walking along the lower deck towards the cab. The small communication hatch between the lower deck and the driving cab slammed open and Dion yelled through, "Shake you backside, man. What the hell wrong with you? We gonna be late."

Jermaine pressed the starter button. The engine roared. The bus shook. He grasped the steering wheel as though it was going to save his life and he gazed fixedly ahead. Cautiously he pressed the clutch pedal, slowly he pulled the gear lever and nervously he put his foot on the gas. The bus took off in almighty jumps and jolts and then moved smoothly ahead.

For the rest of that first week, Jermaine drove slowly and very carefully. He stopped gently at all the stops, obeyed every bell from his conductor, beamed at passengers, and always the words of his conductor were in his mind: *You make any mistakes they'll have that red badge off you faster than a dog have a rat.*

But the frozen, panicky looks which had previously flickered on Jermaine's face were gradually replaced by pleasant, tranquil expressions as he mastered fully the intricacies of the crash gearbox and learned to pull smoothly into and out of bus stops. But as time passed he started to copy some of the little tricks and stunts employed by his fellow drivers. He increased in confidence, and sometimes when there were no passengers on board he tried little swerves and other playful things.

As more time passed Jermaine grew to love the big green buses which he drove, and he gradually developed his own philosophy:

if people were waiting on a stop, he would happily pull in and let them board. If someone was near a stop, just a few yards away, but trotting towards it with hand outstretched, Jermaine would also stop, but he grudged it big time because the person was not actually on the stop. However, the big happy deal for Jermaine was when a potential passenger was some way from the stop, running hell for leather towards it and signalling frantically. In this case Jermaine would sail on by. That kind of thing always made his day and he wore a big beaming smile for a long time afterwards.

So Jermaine gradually became used to all the ins and outs of driving the buses of the Bristol Omnibus Company on the routes to which he was allocated: the fours, the sixes and the nines. He really came to love each individual bus and he quickly learned little flankers with timekeeping so that he and his conductor could grab illicit cups of tea here and there. He became very popular with all the conductors he worked with.

But one thing Jermaine's heart desired, one thing his high-speed West Indian blood craved, one thing he yearned for with all his heart, was to take a bus up through the St Pauls area of Bristol, where all his friends hung out.

Unfortunately none of the routes of his regular driving duties ran through St Pauls, and the longer he ploughed monotonously up and down his usual routes, the stronger grew his desire to flaunt himself up in the cab of a service bus in front of his West Indian friends in St Pauls.

A big dog fox padded silently under a heavy sky as it scoured the undergrowth beside the narrow road which ran through Clifton Down.

The dog fox was hungry and hoping for a plump young rabbit, but he paused in his hunt as he spotted a car parked in the darkness. The fox crouched as silently as a moonbeam in the undergrowth, his eyes fixed on the car. The fox knew that there would be humans inside the car, and he had learned that sometimes a window opened and a few delicious titbits from the humans' meal were thrown out.

The fox saw that the side window of the car was already open. He was content to wait there in the darkness, his nose quivering and his ears alert as he constantly monitored for danger the many sounds and scents which reached him from the darkness.

The evening breeze was cool; the air sweet and pure and expectant.

The big dog fox heard low whispering coming from inside the big black car parked there in the darkness under the trees. Dabber was pulling Melody to him.

"I love you, Melody," he murmured.

"Get lost, you silly bugger," she said. She turned her face up and they kissed. She leaned her head against his shoulder and shivered. Leaves were brushing against the window. "It's creepy up here," she said.

"It's okay," Dabber said. "Nobody ever comes up here."

Melody pushed closer to Dabber and he held her as she turned her face up and they kissed again.

The fox waited, crouching and alert, in the darkness. He despised these intruders who came up late at night, invading his territory, disturbing his hunting, but he knew that the food which the humans often discarded was good and made the wait and the disturbance worthwhile. He was used to long vigils, for the humans who parked in that lonely spot at night often seemed to spend a long time whispering to each other and making strange sounds.

Inside the car, Dabber was saying, "It's all right, Melody. It's safe up here. It's quiet. There's nobody about but you and me." He began to caress her gently over her dress where the soft mounds of her breasts were.

She looked up at his face in the hint of moonlight which was finding its way into the car. "Are we going to be together for a long time?"

"Definitely," he said. "You're expecting our baby – we'll get married and all that."

In the darkness of the car, Melody smiled.

The fox, squeezing himself close to the ground, heard the low voices and then silence. The whisperings ceased and the only sounds were little creaks and cracks as the occupants continued their strange activities.

Dabber was fumbling about in the darkness trying to unbutton Melody's blouse. She leaned forward to make it easier for him. A trembling eagerness pulsated through Dabber as he fumbled with her bra straps.

The fox, crouching low in the darkness, whined with hunger as he waited.

Inside the car Melody, impatient with Dabber's fumbling, reached behind herself, unclipped her bra and let her lover ease it from her. It was so quiet up there in the darkness of the Downs that Dabber could hear the little whispers of Melody's breath and the sound of his own hoarse panting.

The fox knew that soon the car would be creaking and rocking up there in the darkness as the humans continued their strange activities. He waited patiently for them to throw out some titbit for his supper. The animal's sensitive nose twitched at the smell of the humans and he whined in his sudden desire for a young vixen.

Melody leaned back and closed her eyes. In the darkness she sighed and half-opened her eyes as Dabber fumbled about in the confined space of the front of the car.

Outside, the ears of the fox pricked as the familiar sound of strange moans came to him through the open side window. He wrinkled his nose again at the pungent smell he had come to know well when the humans in their cars came up to this lonely spot. The big dog fox felt his blood quicken as a strange dizziness crept into his senses.

Inside the car, Melody sighed to herself in exasperation as Dabber lurched about in the darkness. She closed her eyes and winced as he landed clumsily on top of her and his beer-raddled breath hit her face.

The fox suffered in his hunger and desire as he crouched motionless in the darkness. It was hours since he had eaten and days since he had been with a young vixen. It was curious how the urge for a vixen came to him as the scent of humans from these late-night cars became stronger in his nostrils.

Inside the car, Melody was staring blankly at the roof of the car while Dabber muttered and swore as he tried to manoeuvre himself about in the confined space.

Outside, the fox all at once rose, his fur bristling. He remained stock-still in the darkness, all his senses alert. His ears had caught the sound of stealthy movement in the undergrowth and his sensitive nose detected the powerful scent of a human creeping quietly through the darkness towards the car.

Inside the car, the two lovers were writhing about in the narrow space of the front seat. So engrossed were they in their frantic activities that they did not at first notice the beam of light shining in on them. The beam, bright and strong, swivelled around the interior of the car; it illuminated the young pair, played up and down and up and down. Dabber, in shock, rolled sideways onto the driver's seat and then a hand came through the open nearside window and started caressing Melody's near-naked body, seeking her intimate areas. She screamed.

A coarse, dirty laugh came from outside. The torch played on the young lovers once more and then the intruder was off into the darkness, cackling as he fled.

Melody was scrabbling for her clothes. "The dirty pervert," she shouted.

Dabber shoved the car door open and half fell out, but the voyeur was gone, laughing and shining the torch back at them once more before he disappeared. Then there was only silence. The hearts of the two young lovers were hammering. Dabber stood there half-dressed and frustrated.

The big dog fox, his frustrations and hunger unsatisfied, was racing as fast as he could away from the crazy world of the humans.

"If I could have got my hands on that bastard..." Dabber yelled, struggling to right his clothing.

There were no stars, no moon, no light now, just a great black threatening stillness, and out there in the bushes, possibly still only a few yards away, the pervert.

Back in the car Melody was crying and pulling her clothing straight. "Get me out of here," she screamed.

Dabber pulled his trousers up, jumped back into the car and drove fast across the Downs. "If I could have got my hands on the bastard..." he repeated.

"Just get me away from here," Melody cried.

CHAPTER 30

The sharp double ping of the bell, muffled by the empty cigarette packet jammed between the clapper and the dome in the driving cab of his number four bus, programmed Dabber into action. He shoved the clutch pedal down and pulled back the gear lever, simultaneously setting the offside indicator going, checking the mirror and giving the engine some gas.

He checked the offside mirror again, starting to let the clutch up as he did so. The rushing stream of early morning traffic never faltered at sight of his indicators. He started to ease the big squat front of the bus out as he let the clutch up further. The bus shuddered and poked a little way out into the overtaking stream. Clutch pedal up further, more gas; the stream of traffic bent, then faltered. A small gap opened and immediately Dabber's foot was hard down, the huge engine bellowing, and they were out and racing for the next stop.

In the long months since getting his driving badge the bells from his conductor or the passengers had become his signals to act in a programmed way, like one of Pavlov's dogs. One bell – stop; two bells – start; three bells – full up. A Neanderthal could have been trained to do as well. Some of the blokes even started to look like cavemen after years on the job, he often thought, as he viewed old busmen chewing away in the canteen.

After many hours up in the cab on a long shift, it became boring. A driver started to think funny thoughts and to try to work everything out. A driver for the Bristol Omnibus Company serviced near on two hundred bus stops in a normal shift and at the end of a day's work there was nothing tangible to show for it: no shiny new tins, no door locks or cigarettes, no loaves of bread. There was nothing but an aching left leg and high blood pressure, the moans of passengers ringing in the ears and the stink of hot engine oil in the nostrils.

They reached the terminus at Inns Court Avenue and swung around for the return journey with Dabber's brain in a frenzy with crazy thoughts and mad, useless figures. Two hundred bus stops per day multiplied by the normal six working days equalled 1,200 bus stops serviced per week – or sixty thousand a year. If a driver stuck the job for forty years, as many did, he would pull in to two and a half million bus stops and make ten million gear changes.

Weigh that up. Work that out. Not forgetting that a crash box needs two ups and downs of the clutch pedal for each gear change, unlike a synchromesh box, which needs only one.

Yes, twenty million ups and downs of the left leg if a bloke stuck the job for a lifetime.

Or consider the eardrums and the whacking they took. On top of the roar of the engine, there were on average two bells for each stop. Two and a half million stops in forty years added up to about five million or more pings, dings or buzzes to torment the nerves. Dabber could see now why blokes like Lepiniere went crazy.

And at the end of it all, at the end of the road, what then? Out of the door with a pot belly, backache, shaky legs, shot nerves, no pension and a kick up the arse.

But into the whole churning, boiling, insane mass of the buses were thrown quiet periods and intense comradeship. There was no closer body of men and women than the bus crews. Once you were in the bus world the circle was tight and defensive. Nothing could disturb the fierce loyalty the crews felt towards each other. It did not matter what you had been in the past: a down-and-out, a banker, a builder, a secretary, unemployed or whatever. You could tell any story you liked and no one would question you, because as far as the crews were concerned a man's past was his own business. Once you were in the tight circle of 'the buses' your comrades would protect you against threats and violence from other road users, from aggressive passengers or from any menace whatsoever. And on top of that fierce loyalty were thrown the delights. Ah, the delights – the tea stalls and cafés, the pubs, the freedom and the fresh air, but above all the girls. *Mon Dieu*, the girls.

The time Jermaine craved arrived one evening when he was on spare duty and sitting playing Myth with white busmen in the Centre canteen. The tannoy blared his name.

"Blud-fiah an' bodderation," he cried and slammed down his cards. "Just when I is winning off you whiteys, they call me out."

He went up the stairs with steps slow and heavy, but when the inspector handed him the slip of paper with his bus and route number Jermaine's eyes nearly popped out and he danced around like he had won the football pools, for it was route number eleven, and route eleven ran up through St Pauls where his cronies were sure to be hanging around.

He bounced over the road to where his bus was waiting. The double-decker, all lit up like a huge illuminated goldfish bowl, was full of sour-faced passengers and Dion, the impatient conductor, was hanging off the platform.

"Hey, my man," Jermaine shouted to his young West Indian compatriot, "we got a St Pauls route here." And he waved the slip of paper.

"Yeah, yeah, yeah, what so great about St Pauls, man?" responded Dion. "Just make haste, my friend. We is ten minutes down the pan already." But Jermaine was already leaping into the cab.

He drove fast out to the southern edge of the city and then turned at Hengrove and trundled back for the return journey, with route *11 Oldbury Court* showing on the destination panel. They picked up passengers and were back on schedule with everything running smoothly. Jermaine hummed to himself – he was so happy, and his West Indian blood raced with joy. They picked up passengers at the Centre and continued on over the Horsefair and the Haymarket. As they turned into City Road Jermaine's elation nearly reached heaven as he spotted some of his friends outside a café. They were just lounging around smoking, swapping ballads and looking this way and that to see who or what might come along. Jermaine barped a big raucous tune on the horn, slowed down and put on the cab light so that his face was all illuminated. His friends looked, and then took a second look.

"Hey, look, there's Jermaine," they yelled. "What the hell he doing driving a bus? That fool not safe with a baby's pram."

Jermaine took his hands off the wheel and steered with his knees. He held his hands in the air and yelled out of the cab window, "Whey-hey, yo-ho-diggety-doh." He swerved around the road and put his left foot up on the dashboard.

He looked across the road again at his friends. More of them were now running out of the café to view this spectacle of a double-decker bus with Jermaine at the wheel. The bell dinged loudly in Jermaine's ear. Passengers alighted and more boarded. Jermaine was seized with a sudden impulse. He swung into a side street with the intention to go around the block to drive past his cronies again. In his excitement he forgot that he was not familiar with those back streets, and soon he started to feel panicked. His conductor glanced out of the window and then looked towards the driving cab in puzzlement.

A fat lady in furs turned around and demanded in a loud voice, "Where the devil are we going?"

A well-dressed gentleman wearing a silk cravat and a trilby hat turned around and enquired, "I say, conductor, I think I may be on the wrong bus. Is this a number eleven?"

Up in the cab, Jermaine looked about here, there and everywhere trying to ascertain his whereabouts. The streets were getting narrower and narrower. His mind seemed to be closing in on him. He floundered across the forecourt of a filling station where the startled attendant, busy filling a car, gaped, and petrol gushed over his foot.

In the lower deck, the stout woman turned around again and brayed, "I demand to know where the devil you are taking us, conductor."

"I will ask the driver," replied Dion.

Behind Jermaine the communication hatch crashed open and the voice of his conductor came through. "The lady ask where are we going, my friend? You is way off the route."

"You telling me what I know, boy," said Jermaine.

"Get back on City Road," shouted the conductor.

"That is what I am trying to do," replied Jermaine. "I is panicking now. How I get out of these precincts?"

"Will you tell me what is going on, conductor?" bellowed the big woman in furs.

"My driver – he want to know how to get out of these precincts," replied the conductor.

"These precincts? Tell the nincompoop to go to the end of the street and turn right, for heaven's sake," roared the woman.

"Go to the end of this street and turn right, for heaven's sake," yelled the conductor through the hatch.

Jermaine turned the double-decker, with all its lights blazing and full of astonished passengers, into the next turning on the right, and then he felt so happy, for there in front of him was City Road once more and his cronies were still mooching around outside the café. Jermaine's elation was sky-high again. He blasted the horn big time: *barp, barp, beep-beep*, swung the bus from side to side and yelled again, "Yo-ho-diggety-doh."

His cronies gaped. "Hey, here come that fool Jermaine again," they shouted. "He is crazy, man. He will get the sack from that job, I swear."

Jermaine coasted the bus along. He opened the side window of the cab and tried to stick a foot out; it nearly got stuck and he pulled it back in again quick. He took both hands off the wheel and gave his friends a big stupid grin as he drove away.

His acquaintances outside the café gazed after him. One said, "Man, that Jermaine, he act like he well cooked."

"I think you is correct," said another. "These streets, they is all right for a smoke and a drink and hanging around with friends, but not for play the fool with double-decker bus."

Now that Jermaine was back on the route he calmed down and soon began to feel like a million dollars again. He crooned to himself and gently swung the bus from side to side. It started to rain and he looked for the wiper switch. As he scrabbled about, peering here and there in the darkness of the cab, the windscreen became a sea of water. Jermaine chugged along, still looking for the wiper switch. At last he found it and the windscreen was soon nice and clear, with the wipers swishing back and forth real nice, everything going along real smooth, and Jermaine up in the cab, so happy. He started to sing loudly, looking about him here and there for he had never driven this number eleven route before, and then all of a sudden, *bam, bam, bam*, the conductor was banging on the glass partition and yelling through the hatch.

"Hey, man, ease up. You have missed the turning."

Jermaine hit the brake pedal. "*Cha*," he muttered.

"You must back up, my friend, back up," shouted Dion.

"I'm backing up, I'm backing up. Ease yourself up, man. What you worrying about?" responded Jermaine as he frantically manipulated the gear lever.

In his panic, he began to reverse at high speed. There was a big crunch. The bus shuddered and stalled. Passengers swung forwards and backwards and Dion landed on the floor. Jermaine sat frozen in the cab.

And then the conductor's voice came through the hatch: "Too fast. You were going too fast, my friend."

Jermaine's brain was now in big confusion. Slowly he got down from his cab and surveyed the situation. A lamp post was leaning over. There was a big dent in the back of the bus. Passengers were looking around with bewildered faces.

"What happen?" Jermaine said.

"You fool, you have hit the lamp post," Dion replied.

"*Cha*, why lamp post in stupid place?" Jermaine said.

"There will be trouble over the lamp post," said his conductor.

"Why trouble? It is still working," said Jermaine.

"And the bus is damaged, my friend. Look, it has big dent," said Dion.

"Ease up. It is a little scratch only," said Jermaine, but he trembled with fright inside when he thought of his red badge.

A portly passenger came down the stairs beaming and waving a bottle of stout. "I say, chaps, this bus is jolly fun. Does it run every night?" he enquired.

"No, it does not," said the conductor, and then he whispered to

Jermaine, "I think we must get out of here."

"Yes, let us get the hell out fast," said Jermaine. He dived into the cab and started the engine.

At the terminus his heart was thumping like a wild thing as the passengers alighted. They were all looking up at Jermaine and some were shaking their heads. One stout gentleman with an angry red face threw him a real sharp look.

Two elderly ladies, arm in arm, looked up at him and one said to the other, "They're really not so good as our own people, are they?"

Dion came round to the front of the bus, shaking his head. "Man," he said, "they is going to have that red badge off you so easy."

"Why you worry, my friend?" said Jermaine. "It has been uneventful journey. All de fruit on de tree is hanging good." But his heart was pounding as if it wanted to break out of his body.

At the depot, Jermaine reversed the bus real crafty into a far corner of the garage so that the dent in the rear was hidden. Next day the bus went out onto the road again and was driven by many drivers before the dent in the rear was noticed. The Bristol Omnibus Company was never able to pin the blame for the damage onto anyone.

But the events of that night shook Jermaine up real bad. He started to drive so slowly and carefully that everyone was looking at him and wondering what happened.

Jermaine hung onto that red badge like a dog hanging onto a big juicy bone.

CHAPTER 31

One night at the end of a long, hard late shift, Dabber had his foot down hard on the gas as he barrelled at high speed all the way back down through that wild, crazy, sex-mad city of Bristol. They dropped the last two or three passengers off at the Knowle West terminus and then it was interior lights off and the mighty diesel engine hammering furiously, *whuppeta-whuppeta-whuppeta*, as they raced through the darkened streets to the depot.

The haste was because Greasy, who was the conductor on the bus, had invited Dabber up to his new flat for a few drinks when the shift finished.

At the depot Dabber pulled his bus forward under the bus-washing machine. The big metal frame inched slowly down over the bus and torrents of water hammered and beat at the front, back and sides of the vehicle. Then the ugly contraption heaved thunderously back up again. When it was clear and the light turned to green, Dabber pulled forward onto the pumps and the old bent-over pump man started to pump in the diesel fuel ready for the next day's work. As he stood holding the nozzle in the tank, the refueller glanced at the upper deck and then looked at Dabber up there in the driving cab.

"There's a girl on the top deck," the pump man said.

"A girl?" Dabber exclaimed.

"You ain't supposed to bring passengers back to the depot," said the old man.

"I don't know anything about any girl," Dabber said.

"It don't end in nothing good when girls come back," said the old man.

"If there's a girl up there she's nothing to do with me," said Dabber.

The old man finished filling the tank. "Put it on eight," he said.

Dabber pulled the bus forward onto row eight and switched off. The girl came down the stairs immediately. She looked around with interest at the immensity of the garage and the ranks of buses parked there. She flicked her long hair back and gazed around slowly like a visitor at a beauty spot.

"Who the hell are you?" said Dabber.

She glanced at him. "I'm with Greasy," she said, and turned away to resume her survey of the garage.

Greasy bounced out of the paying-in room, rushed over and took the girl's hand.

Dabber pulled Greasy aside. "What you playing at? I thought we were going to see your flat."

"We are, mate," said Greasy.

"What about the bird?" said Dabber, indicating the girl, who was still looking around the garage.

"No problem, mate. She can come as well," said Greasy.

Dabber was silent.

The three of them caught one of the night's last number nines up North Street, had a drink in the Hen and Chicken, and then drank some more in the Barley Mow.

By the time they came out of the pub at closing time the buses had stopped running and they had to walk to Old Market. Greasy was well tanked, shouting, "Whey-hey!" and jumping around beside the girl.

As they walked over Redcliffe Hill, Dabber had a sudden inclination to show off with a bit of knowledge. He stopped and slapped the wall of a tall, narrow building.

"See this building?" he exclaimed. "This is the famous Shot Tower, where the world's first perfect shot was produced. Two hundred years ago a geezer called William Watts dropped some red-hot lead into water from the top of this tower and it formed perfect little balls."

"Who the hell's interested in that?" shouted Greasy into the wide, still night.

"Little balls, little balls," sang the girl into the empty echoing streets.

The night was soft, the moon so low and friendly and the air so still that it seemed as though reality had ceased to exist. Even Greasy seemed to be affected. He stopped his jumping around, and just in front of the magnificent church of St Mary Redcliffe, he stood gazing silently upwards.

"Look at them stars," he said. "Them stars is effing wondrous." The three revellers stood quietly, looking up into the clear, cold sky at the sparkling stars so far away.

And then Dabber yelled, "Come on, never mind the stars – we got to get the car."

They piled into Dabber's Austin 16. The girl and Greasy sat in the back and started kissing and nuzzling each other straight away as they bombed through the empty, lonely streets. When the girl wasn't groping about with various parts of Greasy's body she was leaning forward, flicking Dabber's hair and tickling the back of his neck.

"Hey, don't you ever sit still?" he said. "I'm driving here. I got to keep my attention on the road."

"Little me wants a bit of attention," she giggled.

They pulled up outside a council high-rise block in Hartcliffe. Dabber pulled Greasy aside again. He whispered, "Greasy, mate, listen to me: it ain't wise to take that girl back to your flat. Luella will play hell with you."

"She won't say nothing. She knows who's boss in there, mate," Greasy said.

They staggered up the stairs to Greasy's place. There was just the room they were sitting in, a kitchen, and another room with a closed door. There was music blasting up from somewhere downstairs, and overhead it sounded as if someone was heaving heavy weights around: *thump, thump, thump.*

Straight away Greasy started to pull bottles of beer out of the kitchen and the three of them sat there drinking: Dabber in an armchair and the girl pushed up against Greasy on the settee.

Dabber was watching the girl pawing Greasy and trying to slide her hand down his trousers. Greasy had his usual semi-dopey look on his face and it was hard to know what he was thinking.

Dabber said, "What's that noise upstairs?" and jerked his thumb at the ceiling.

"Weightlifter, mate," said Greasy. "Practises all hours. Here, get some more beer outta the kitchen, will ya?"

Dabber went to the kitchen for more bottles. When he came back Greasy was half-lying on top of the girl, panting hoarsely. She was feverishly pulling at his belt, trying to unbuckle it. Dabber was trying not to look at them, but just sat, lethargic and drunkenly content. He took a long swig of beer and all of a sudden a thought came to him.

"Where's the piece with the big Bristol Cities?" he said.

He had hardly said that when a furious female voice screamed, "Don't talk about me like that! Don't talk about me like that!" and in the same instant the door crashed open and Luella flew out. She stopped dead, seemed to paw the carpet with her bare feet like a mad bull for several seconds while she glared round, and then with two bounds she was across to the settee and delivering a mighty whack across Greasy's ear.

"Jeezus," said Greasy, rubbing his ear. "*Jeeezus*. What was that for?"

Well, for an answer Luella whacked him again, across the same ear. As she did so the girl was scrambling off Greasy's knee so fast she stumbled onto the carpet, got up and dived onto a chair at the far side of the room.

Luella stood in the middle of the room, glaring round, panting heavily and with a wild look on her face. She had on next to nothing, and every bit of her flimsy clothing was scarlet: a lacy see-through embroidered bra, a satin wrap which was hanging wide open, and very brief embroidered panties. Her golden-blonde hair was falling down untidily over her shoulders. Her huge breasts were heaving. Dabber was trying not to look at her, but he couldn't help it. She took a step towards him.

"What the hell you looking at?" she said.

"Nothing," said Dabber, and he pretended to have developed a sudden interest in the label of his beer bottle.

Luella's furious look was then directed at the girl. "And who the hell's that?" she said.

"She's called Yolly," said Greasy in a little voice.

"Don't bring no effing Yollies, or any more effing slags back here.

I've told you," shouted the blonde, and she gave Greasy another smack around the ear. She put her hands on her hips and glared at Yolly. "Yolly? Yolly?" she said. "What kind of a namby-pamby name is that?"

"It's short for Yolanda," said Yolly in a little voice.

"And what the hell are you doing here?" said Luella.

"Greasy asked me," said Yolly.

"Greasy asked you?!" Luella screamed. "Well, Greasy better not ask you again," and she gave Greasy another smack round the head.

She stared around, furious-faced, sat down fast in an armchair and scrabbled around lighting a cigarette. She sat back, sat forward and sat back again, as agitated as anything. She smoked furiously and glared at the other three. She crossed and uncrossed her legs and her wrap fell open, displaying her thighs and her flimsy briefs.

Goodness, what a pair of legs she had, thought Dabber, and her breasts were swollen and pushing through her flimsy bra. Dabber couldn't take his eyes off her. Then the blonde bounced up, flung open a cupboard, pulled out a bottle of sherry, banged herself back down and began swigging straight out of the bottle. That seemed to calm her down a bit. Dabber was still staring at her.

"Watch your eyeballs don't pop out," she said, but at the same time she seemed to give him a little smile.

Dabber said nothing and looked away quickly. When he looked back Luella had the sherry bottle between her bare thighs and was gazing at him. She threw her head back, put both hands behind her neck and flung her long blonde hair out backwards. Her breasts were like melons on sale in some exotic marketplace. She pulled the sherry bottle further up her thighs, almost to her groin. She sat there with one hand around the bottle's neck while staring at Dabber.

She gripped the bottle tightly between her legs while still gazing at Dabber. He glanced away and then looked back again. She was still watching him. She squeezed the bottle tightly and sensually between her thighs. Her mouth was slightly open. Dabber glanced away and then looked back. She was still watching him. She took a long, slow drag of her cigarette.

"What you waiting for?" she said.

Dabber gasped. He looked at Greasy.

"Go ahead, mate," said Greasy, "if you fancy it."

Dabber was frozen.

"I think she wants a bit," said Greasy. "I couldn't give a monkey's."

A long minute passed. Everyone was gazing silently at Dabber. He slowly got up, pushed into the armchair beside Luella and put his arm around her. She slowly put the bottle to his lips and tilted it so that sherry ran into his mouth. And then they were kissing and fondling each other. Dabber was panting like an animal.

Greasy was watching them with the look of a man who has only recently realised the contemptuous sexual perfidy of his partner. "Take her in the bedroom and give her a bit, if you want, mate," he said.

Dabber hesitated.

"What the hell you waiting for?" Luella said.

She stood up slowly, sauntered across to the open bedroom door and gazed back at him. There was the faintest beckoning gesture of her head.

Dabber looked at Greasy. He was gazing at the scene with something approaching a sneer. Yolly was leaning forward with an amazed expression.

Dabber took a step or two towards Luella. Her scarlet wrap was fully open and she stared at him. He hesitated and looked all around. There was silence in the room. He looked at the door out of the flat and then looked back at Luella. She had a thin smile on her face and her head beckoned him again.

And then Dabber was stumbling towards the door. "No, man, it ain't no good. This sorta thing ain't no good," he shouted. "I'm outta here, man."

As he blundered down the stairs, he heard Greasy's voice calling, "What's up, Dab? What the hell's up?"

Hours later, back in his room, Dabber jerked awake, trembling and staring fearfully into the darkness. For some reason he was shaking with irrational fear; the sort of fear that preys on disturbed minds and is worse when a person is alone and can't reach out and touch someone and receive human warmth. He sat half-dressed and shivering in the chair, smoking continuously and thinking about Greasy, Yolly, Luella and the unsavoury events of the previous evening. Dabber sat alone without any human friendliness or emotion to comfort him. He felt an urgent desire to see Melody, and as soon as the first light of morning came he dressed fast and rushed out with the wind whipping in on him.

He drove fast up to the steep streets of Totterdown where Melody still had a room that she used whenever Dabber was working long late shifts. The house was large and semi-derelict; the kind which housed many dismal bedsitters and deadbeat tenants. The front door was hanging open and Dabber raced up the dirty, uncarpeted stairs to Melody's room. Almost before he knocked, Melody opened the door.

"Oh, I thought you'd never come," she said straight away, clutching him. "Let's get out of here. I'm fed up of being stuck in this hellhole."

They rushed out along the street to the car and hugged each other tightly in the front seat.

"I thought you'd never come," Melody repeated. "Where the hell you been? I've been waiting two whole days."

"I been working," he said.

"Yeah, and what else?" she said.

They sat for a long time, not saying much, just holding each other. When the pubs were open they drove to Bedminster, went in the Star and sat silently, just happy to be with each other.

After a time Melody said, "I think the baby's coming along all right."

"I'm looking forward to it," said Dabber.

She looked at him. "It's our baby, yours and mine, Dabber, don't forget that."

"Of course I won't," he said. "You just take care of yourself, that's all I'm worried about."

"I will," she said. She was silent, and her thoughts were obviously far away. Then she said, "I won't make any mistakes this time. You know, with my first baby, my little Stephen, I didn't know what I was doing when I handed him over. It was like I was doing it all in my sleep. It just didn't seem to dawn on me what I was doing."

She paused, lit a cigarette and was silent for a long time. "I had no job, no money and even my own mother had turned against me," she went on eventually. "Everybody made me feel that it was all my fault, the mess I was in, and they just seemed to be criticising me the whole time."

"They must have been real bastards," Dabber said.

"They were," she said. "I was just all by myself, you know. From the moment I walked into that home I was treated like so much dirt. The women in there knew I had nobody to turn to and some of them made horrible remarks – they were bitches, making out that I was filth just because I had been with a boy and now I was having my punishment.

"One of the women said I would yell my head off with pain when I had the baby, and she gloated over it. Well, when little Stephen was born, it was bad, I must admit, but nothing like that cow had said. And I thought my baby was the loveliest baby that had ever been born, and I just worshipped him and hugged him every mwinute I got."

"Why did you let them take him away, then?"

"They didn't take him away by force – I gave him away. That's the terrible thing. I gave him away, my beautiful baby!"

Melody looked close to tears. Dabber put his arm around her and held her tightly. It was as if everything else in the place – the bar, the bartender, the customers and even the world outside – had ceased to exist. It was just him and Melody, her memories and her sorrow. She recovered a little, took a drink and drew on her cigarette.

"It's very difficult to explain," she went on, the desolation of the memory evident on her face, "but when a girl goes into one of those homes, she's completely alone usually. There's nobody she can turn to. The women in charge just treated me like a schoolkid that had done something wrong. Well, I suppose they were right in a way. I was just young, young as anything. I didn't know what I was doing." She paused and Dabber bent and kissed her forehead.

After a time she went on. "I kept going over and over in my mind whether to keep little Stephen or to have him adopted. The idea of adoption had never entered my mind, not until those bitches in there started to put pressure on me. It's psychological, all of it. And they keep it up all the time. They kept saying over and over again that it wasn't fair on the baby, me wanting to keep him. They made out I had nothing to offer him."

She drew on her cigarette. "Me, the mother! I would have nothing to offer my little baby. They kept saying what a better life he could have if I let him go to a well-off couple with plenty of money and love." Melody was silent then, as if her mind was far away, and then, "Love," she repeated, the word falling bitterly from her lips. "As if somebody else could give little Stephen more love than me."

Her voice had trailed away and her eyes were fixed as if she could see nothing but that dreadful time. She was crying openly.

She leaned her face against Dabber's shoulder, then sat up straight again and took another long drink. He pulled her close and they sat in silence for a time. He didn't know what to say. There were only two or three other customers in the pub, sitting up at the bar, smoking and chatting among themselves. Occasionally someone at the far side of the pub put a record on the jukebox.

Then Melody said again, "As if anyone else could give my little Stephen more love than me."

"Nobody could have," Dabber said.

"That's the pressure they put on me," she went on. "My mind was all mixed up. I was going mad. I just couldn't think what to do for the best."

"What about Joe? He was the dad," Dabber said.

"That useless bugger? Most of the time he didn't know what day of the week it was."

She reached for her glass again. Dabber lit a cigarette and passed it to her. She smoked silently for a time.

"They kept saying that the sooner I did it and the younger the baby was, the easier he would settle with his new parents." She paused. "New parents," she spat. "I was his mother, for heaven's sake – he was my baby, I was the parent. Me! Not some sodding rich couple.

"Anyway, I did it, I signed," she whispered. "I still don't know why I did it. I wish to God I hadn't. I wish every day of my life I hadn't. And now it's too late.

"After I'd done it and little Stephen was gone," she continued, "I was in what seemed like a trance for days. I couldn't take it in. Then it struck me. I realised what I'd done. I just cried and cried. It seemed like a terrible dream, but it was real. All the pressure they had put on had worked. I didn't realise at the time, but I wasn't thinking straight when I did it. I had gone over and over it in my mind and it just seemed like the best thing to do – to give little Stephen all the things in life that the women in the home said I couldn't give him. And he was gone. He wasn't with me anymore."

Dabber sat silently with his arm round her. There seemed to be nothing else he could do.

She went on. "When I realised what I'd done – what those bitches had persuaded me to do – I went to see the adoption people to see if there was any chance of getting it reversed, of getting little Stephen back. But they just laughed, more or less. They said it was impossible and I had no rights over him anymore. More than that, the bastards started piling all the blame on me again. Making out I'd done a bad thing in the first place by being with a boy and it was only right that I should suffer. And then they said that it must have been my decision to give him away and I couldn't have thought much of him."

After a pause she continued, talking furiously, "That's what they said to me, the bitches. They'd taken my baby and that's what they said to me. That it was my fault. They wouldn't even tell me where he'd gone. Even now, after all the searching me and Joe have done, going up to London and all that, looking for him, I haven't got a clue where little Stephen is."

She wiped her eyes again. "So that's it. I'd been all twisted up and manipulated to give my baby away for a so-called better life, and it was all thrown back at me by those people."

The pub was busier now. The jukebox was blaring and the cigarette smoke was thickening. Dabber went up to the bar and got another pint of EI for himself and a half for Melody. They sat together quietly for a long time then, just smoking and drinking and each thinking their own thoughts.

Eventually Melody said, "But I'm having your baby now, Dabber, and I'm not going to make any mistakes with this one. No one is going to take this baby away."

"We'll look after it together," said Dabber. "No one is going to lay a finger on our baby."

They sat some more and Melody became more cheerful.

Dabber said, "How about coming up the Glen one night? You can still dance, can't you? Dancing won't hurt the chicko, will it?"

"Name the night," she said. "I haven't given up living yet."

CHAPTER 32

It was the last run of the morning for the number four bus manned by Dabber and Rulebook. Dabber's problem now was that the bus was behind schedule. It was stationary at the terminus at Knowle West and could not get going because Rulebook, the conductor, was arguing with a passenger. Dabber, up in the cab, was revving the engine with impatience.

The passenger, a tough-looking workman, was half-on and half-off the bus, and was arguing with Rulebook. The bus couldn't move with this argument going on, and all at once the passenger punched the conductor on the nose and ran off.

Rulebook's cap was pushed back and his coolness and command of a situation had completely deserted him. He ran after the passenger, clutching his nose and shouting, "*Excusez-moi, mon ami, vous n'avez paid the correct fare,*" but the man turned and whacked Rulebook on the nose again.

Dabber pulled open the cab window and yelled at him, "Get back on the bus, you silly bugger."

Rulebook rushed towards the cab, clutching his nose with one hand and the fare book with the other.

"He won't pay the correct fare," he screeched. "That passenger won't pay the correct fare."

"Let's get going," Dabber shouted. "We're late."

"He must pay the correct fare. All passengers must pay the correct fare."

"Don't bother about it, let's get going," Dabber said.

"But he struck my nose and refuses to pay the correct fare."

"View it philosophically," Dabber shouted. "You're the one that's always talking about philosophy."

"But it is not a philosophical question," Rulebook protested. "It is a profound matter. It is a question of ethics and social responsibilities. The situation is not *comme il faut.*"

"What the hell are you on about?" shouted Dabber. "Let's get going."

And then at last Conductor Rulebook was back on the bus. Twelve minutes late, with the bus running in to finish in Old Market where the doors of the pubs would already be open and the fresh ale frothing.

Dabber put his foot down and they tanked at high speed back through the Knowle West estate, around the roundabout and along Broad Walk; then left onto the Wells Road, and a fast run past the George; down the hill, past the Bush, over the Three Lamps junction on green and over the Cut with a rush and the bus running as sweet as anything. They were back on track and on time. Dabber raced from the bridge towards the station, scarcely slackening speed, and that's when he saw a sight which had his foot off the gas and onto the brake pedal fast.

A number five bus was stationary. People were standing on the pavement gazing at something in the road which was half-hidden. Some of the people had hands over their mouths; others were turning away. On his knees on the pavement, weeping and beating the ground with his fists, was Cyril, the boastful young driver. Dabber switched off the engine of his bus, slowly got down from the cab and went towards the crowd. A little girl of no more than four years was in the road, her body a mass of blood and broken limbs. Crouching over her and clutching the tiny body was the girl's mother, her face on the little girl's bloodied chest. The mother was wailing, just wailing, and Dabber did not know that such terrible sounds could come from a human throat.

Someone said that the police and an ambulance had been called. Someone else went into the adjacent business premises and called the bus company. The little girl's mother was now screaming, just terrible screams, and then she fell on the child and hugged her and kissed her and told her that she would be all right. But everyone could see that the little girl would never be all right again. People just stood, silent and shocked. Others, unable to look any more, turned and hurried away.

Dabber stood there looking and Rulebook came and stood beside him, shocked and silent. With a wail of sirens an ambulance and a police car arrived. An ambulance man knelt and put his hand on the little mangled bundle of blood and bones and fluffy pink clothes, while the police ushered the crowd away. The tiny girl opened her eyes and looked up at her mother. There was a childlike, slightly puzzled look on her little face. The look became more distant and the corner of her mouth twitched with a little smile as if she was thinking of somewhere far away. The little body gave a tremor and then just relaxed and was still, and the eyes did not see in this world anymore.

There was silence all around, apart from the mother, sobbing piteously now, and clutching the little lifeless body.

Dabber looked around for Cyril. He was crouching in a corner, snivelling and gasping. Dabber went over and put his hand on the young driver's shoulder. Neither of them spoke. Huge gasping breaths started to come from the crouching driver.

At first no words came, but as he slowly rose to his feet he stuttered, "I-I had no chance. I couldn't avoid her. She ran out. I didn't have no chance. She just ran out."

Dabber put his arm around him. "An ambulance is here, mate," he said. It was all he could think of to say. And then someone came over and said that the child had passed away. Immediately Cyril screamed, turned to the wall and started banging his head against it.

Dabber put his hand on his shoulder and pulled him back. "Don't do that, mate," he said. The young driver turned with a moan, his face wet with tears, and then he was running fast, racing away into the back streets, leaving his bus, the police and the whole nightmare behind him.

Senior managers from the bus company arrived, and one of them came over to Dabber and Rulebook. "Which is your bus?" he said.

Dabber indicated his number four.

"Where's the other driver? The one involved in the accident," said the manager.

"Gone. Ran away," said Dabber.

"Ran away. What? He just ran away and left his bus?"

"Yeah."

"Had he spoken to the police?"

"I don't think so," said Dabber.

The manager was silent and grim-faced for several seconds while he looked at the emergency service people who were efficiently going about their tasks, and then he turned to Dabber again. "You'd better take your bus away. Just stick to your normal schedule," he said. "There's nothing more you can do here."

That night demons came to Dabber's sleeping mind. He saw again the vision of the little girl the bus had killed. Her head was hanging loosely to one side. Her face, which should have been the serene and trusting face of a child, was now, in Dabber's nightmare, filled with horror. The eyes turned and stared straight at Dabber; the tiny face, filled with sadness, seemed to plead: *Please, make me be well again.*

Dabber wanted to reach out to the vision, to touch the little girl, to say, "Get up, my little darling – you've been asleep, don't worry. Everything is all right now." But even in his nightmare the words would not come and the vision of the girl disappeared.

A few weeks later Dabber was in the cab of a number nine. His conductor was a former driver nicknamed Hedgehog. Hedgehog had found the stress of being up in the cab all day, trying to deal with traffic, timekeeping and passenger bells, too much and the company had given him the chance to retrain. Now Hedgehog was enjoying a much more sedate life as a conductor.

With Dabber as the driver and Hedgehog as the conductor the pair ran up and down the number nine route through the late afternoon rush hour with darkness falling and the evening coal fires of the houses from Hanham to Ashton pouring out their dirty grey smoke.

In the early evening they switched to the sixes and ran north up the stretching Gloucester Road, through groaning Bishopston and tormented Horfield where despairing souls languished behind the high walls of the grim prison. They emerged at the end of the route into

Filton in the darkness of the city boundary. Here they swung round the church, parked the bus up and ran fast into the tea whack to tip two quick cups of hot belly-belter tea down their throats.

And then they rolled their bus more leisurely back down through the livening city, bright now and noisy at the height of the evening. They whined and roared through Bedminster and out along the lonely streets to the terminus on the isolated council outcrop of Hartcliffe. Then once again they burned back up the route with the great Gardner engine pounding and pulling so that at times Dabber had to rein it in lest they overran the stops.

And at that time every evening Bristol was wild and noisy and dirty and hell-bent on extracting every ounce of experience from life. There was a massive and uproarious exodus from the houses and the flats and the bedsitters of the suburbs, and a boisterous rush up to the city centre, and into the pubs and clubs and the theatres and picture houses. People shouted and clamoured, pushed and screamed and ran along the pavements shouting and drinking.

The Gloucester Road, which was the northern territory of the number six route, was part of the famous A38 which ran through Bristol and stretched grey and endlessly into the distance. If one went far enough to the north, one would encounter Tewkesbury, Worcester, Droitwich and Bromsgrove, then Birmingham and Burton. And to the south the wandering, winding road reached Bridgwater, Taunton, Exeter and Plymouth and ran on into the desolate, wild, dark lands of Cornwall.

Oh, how the poor prisoners lying on their bunks in Horfield Prison, so close to the road that they could doubtless hear the roar of the mighty engine of the bus as it swept past, must have wished that their feet could tread that road again. But the road and the sinful life of the city were not for them that night. They would have their nightmares and that is all, for it is like that in the nick. It is at night that the demons come to a man's mind.

And especially then, for in a few days' time they were going to hang a man in that prison. dangle him by the neck until he was dead. Down through the trap. Break his neck. Never again would the doomed soul see the sun rise and the stars shine, feel the soft mists of spring or the gentle rain of summer. Never again would he wander through the mellow banks of the Cornish lanes or smell the flowers or gaze at the fauna of that enchanting county. Never again would he hold those precious to him or taste the sweet lips of a beloved.

Well, at least he'd be out of this miserable world, Dabber, who had followed the case closely in the newspapers, thought. And the Cornish farmer whom the doomed young man had killed while trying to rob him, Dabber thought of him too. The farmer was gone to the grave, and soon his murderer would follow him. The pair of them would be out of this ridiculous, unfair world.

And often in his deep depressive periods, Dabber had thought about death and imagined himself dangling there, kicking and croaking, with his eyes bulging and his neck stretched. And in his black moods, Dabber thought about death and funerals and thought how peaceful a cortège always seemed to be as it made its slow and reverent way towards some poor soul's last resting place.

But it was sad that, before the final day came, so many troubled people lived troubled lives and sometimes Dabber thought that if he had been the Creator the first thing he would do would be to have a look at all the misery that was going on down here. What was it all about? And he'd also, as a priority, have a look at that poor sinner they were going to dangle at Horfield Prison in a few days' time. Have a look at his case. See if there was anything that could be done.

CHAPTER 33

A few nights later Melody was sitting curled up beside Dabber in the car. He had to click the wipers on every so often, for the night was damp and misty and miserable. But inside the Glen it was different; this was what he had promised her: a night out to forget all their troubles.

The sound beat at the two of them as they paid at the desk. And when they pushed open the swing doors of the dance hall, the blasting of the music, the heat from the clientele and the rat-a-tatting of the rapidly bopping feet on the wooden floor nearly knocked them back out again.

Well, one look at the crowd on the floor, whirling and twisting, arms and legs flying, elbows whacking, bodies crashing, was enough for Dabber. He headed to the bar and got a Double Diamond for himself and a vodka with a dash of lemonade for Melody. They sat at a table at the side of the dance floor watching the mad scene, but after two or three numbers she was tapping and swaying and he could see that she was really getting in the mood.

"You get up for a dance if you want," he said. "I'll sit here for a bit."

A young lad came up and asked her onto the floor. "Go on, go on, get going," Dabber encouraged her through the tumult of noise, and he sat there watching the pair of them kicking and jerking and whirling and swaying. The noise poured over everyone in huge thundering waves, as the band threw out everything it could.

The rhythms beat and fell and rushed out of the instruments, the notes flooded and fell over each other in a mad frenzy, the chords hammered, the vibrations ripped through the hall and the beat vanquished every bit of misery in the place.

Dabber sat happily sinking Double Diamonds and watching it all. Sweat poured off the drummer, his hands were a blur, his sticks rattling and rolling and beating and banging.

He swayed backwards and forwards in a frantic rhythm screaming, "Yeah, yeah, man, this is it." He looked like he was in his own world of freaked-out madness, mouth gaping, breath heaving, eyes staring, pupils dilated.

The eyes of the trumpeter were glazed and half-closed. He blew for all he was worth, arching backwards and blasting at the ceiling, then bending forwards like a hairpin and punching out the music with the trumpet between his legs. He looked like he was trying to blast God out of Heaven and the Devil out of Hell, such was the ferocity of his blowing. It was incredible, the whole scene.

And then the trombonist came to the front and ripped out a crazy, golden sound with his arm moving in and out so fast it was like a piston. Dabber had never felt so joyful. Melody came back and they sat there, leaning back, smoking and relaxing. Dabber gazed absently around the whole place. The dance hall, dancers, musicians and all the rest of the crazy scene seemed to be swaying back and forth.

His bleary, smoke-raddled eyes tried to focus on objects and human beings, but they all seemed to be drifting in and out of focus. He leaned back, pulled on his cigarette and tried to contemplate the meaning of it all. Every backside in the place seemed to be bumping and grinding and rotating at faster and faster speeds, until everyone on the floor seemed to be one heaving, pulsating mass.

Across the table, Melody's cigarette seemed to waver about as she tried to get it into her mouth. Joe, the drunken boxer, appeared and disappeared in the dim and smoky atmosphere. He seemed to have his arm around a dusky girl with a headscarf. Dabber groped for his drink and tried to get it to his mouth as he studied this strange phenomenon of Joe and the dusky girl. It couldn't be real, surely, this apparition of his enemy, the drunken boxer, with his arm around a dark-skinned girl. Dabber decided that it would pay to watch them very carefully. The pair reappeared as the mass separated. They grew larger and smaller, advanced and receded, pushed this way and that, but all the time somehow came closer. *Hell*, Dabber thought, *I must be hallucinating.*

Then Joe was looking straight at him and the girl was standing quietly beside him. The pair stood there gazing silently.

Melody noticed them for the first time and squealed, "Oh my God!"

Dabber put down his cigarette very slowly and studied Joe and the girl carefully. He couldn't figure out if they meant trouble or not.

"Hello, mate," said Joe.

Dabber was silent.

"Listen," Joe said, "listen. Pleased I found you 'ere. What I want to say is, mate, no hard feelings – about that fight, I mean. No hard feelings, I don't hold no grudges, mate."

Dabber picked up his cigarette again and studied the pair of them. "No hard feelings on my part," he said cautiously.

"The point is," said Joe, "it's thanks to you that I met this beautiful girl here, my Latifa. She's from Pakistan, mate. I was going round the pubs an' the cafés looking for you, to whack you, for revenge, and I met Latifa here."

Dabber was silent.

"That all right, then?"

"What?"

"There's no hard feelings?"

"Yeah. I just told you, there never was any hard feelings on my part," said Dabber.

He pulled up a chair for Latifa and she hesitatingly sat down. Melody was looking at her.

"Sit down, mate," Dabber said, and he pulled a chair over for Joe.

Joe and Latifa sat close together with their arms around each other. "Yeah, me and Latifa – we been together a few weeks now," Joe said.

"Four weeks," said Latifa shyly, sitting down and looking across the table at Melody.

Melody stared back at her, examining this girl who was now with her ex-boyfriend.

Dabber felt happy and relaxed. "Hey," he shouted, "let's get some more drinks in."

But Joe sprang up. "I'll get 'em," he insisted. "I'm in the money now – got a job on a building site. Big money."

After he had gone to the bar, a thin youth came up and asked Melody to dance.

"Off you go," Dabber said. "I don't mind."

Joe came back with the drinks. He held his glass up. "My first for a week," he said.

"He doesn't drink much now," Latifa said. "I won't let him. Too much is not good for him." She turned her face up and Joe pulled her to him and kissed her.

"Joe's going to start boxing again," Latifa said.

Joe said, "I was a top man. I could have gone on."

"I've heard he was the best in the gym," said Latifa.

"It was this." Joe raised his glass. "This was what done it. But I'll come back."

"I'll help you, Joe," said Latifa.

The band was still ripping it out. Another young man came up and asked Latifa to dance.

"Go ahead. Go ahead," Joe urged her.

When they had gone, Joe and Dabber sat at opposite sides of the table, both drinking slowly and gazing at the dancers.

"I'm not one for dancing," Joe said.

"Nor me," Dabber replied.

"Can't see no sense in it," Joe said. He looked at Dabber and then said, "Are you sure you're all right, mate? After that night, I mean?"

"Sure. I'm all right," said Dabber.

At that moment the trumpet hit a peak of sound that ripped and roared right through everyone. And then a saxophonist joined in, swaying backwards and forwards, blowing out his cheeks, sweating and trembling with the effort of it all.

The dancers were careering wildly around. *Bang! Bounce! Bop! Twirl! Thump!* Whirling and twisting, holding each other, letting go, with jackets open, skirts lifting, arms flying, legs kicking, breath heaving, sweat pouring.

Joe leaned forward. "Look at those two crazy tarts."

Melody and Latifa were whirling around with their slack-jawed, half-cut partners. The girls were dancing back to back, very close to each other. The floor was a fast-moving, heaving, sweating mass of young people who were all delighting in the noise and intensity of the evening. The band swayed and blasted. The sound speared the souls of everyone. The two girls were up there on the floor, kicking, prancing, twirling and whirling with all the concentration and madness of young spring hares. Their bums met, bumped each other and then met again. Each girl glanced round simultaneously to see who was behind her and then Melody, in one smooth movement and without pausing in her rhythm, edged backwards again and with her own shapely posterior gave Latifa's bottom a whack.

Latifa giggled shyly, and then you never saw such a display as was put on that night by those two girls. Without stopping their dancing for an instant, each girl in turn edged backwards, gave a swift glance to ascertain that the other girl was correctly placed, and then whacked backwards with her bum. *Jostle, swat, swipe*, the rears went in turn, and never did a more attractive, more entrancing pair of posteriors battle it out.

Breasts bouncing, eyes flashing, legs kicking, arms whirling, the girls danced like demons. The slim bottom of Latifa went to war with delicate thrusts and whacks against the plumper hindquarters of Melody, who responded one for one, with graceful, beautiful backward swipes.

And then when Dabber looked at their faces he realised that the girls were loving it.

Each girl was glancing round and then positioning her bum in precisely the right position for her rival to hit. Excitement was in their eyes and delight in their frenzied antics as they became more and more the centre of attention. The floor was slowly coming to a stop and dancers were crowding around and calling rude remarks.

Suddenly the girls were laughing and stumbling about at the absurdity of it all and their useless partners were standing blank-faced and ignored.

"They're crazy, that pair," Joe said.

Bump, bang, rubbery-whang; the bottoms battled again, ricocheting and cannoning off each other like two rubber footballs. And then the girls were laughing and flopping about so much that they turned and fell into each other's arms.

All at once a thought came to Dabber, and he shouted, "Melody's pregnant. She shouldn't be dancing like that."

He rushed over and brought the two girls off the floor and back to the table.

Joe was leaning back in his chair and looking at them with a big silly grin on his face.

"You pair of stupid tarts," he said, and then somehow the four of them were all chatting and laughing together like old friends. The two girls went to the toilet and came back arm in arm, giggling and whispering, as close and conspiratorial as anything.

Then the final tune was played; a slow, relaxed, almost mournful number that had Latifa pulling Joe onto the floor where they circled, clinging lovingly to each other.

Melody and Dabber just sat together silently, gazing at the dancers, happy to be part of such a joyful evening.

The dance hall was in an old quarry, and when the dance was over the fog hung everywhere like grey blancmange.

Joe and Latifa got in the back seat of Dabber's big black 1948 Austin 16, which was standing damp and heavy in its parking spot. They sat for a time in the freezing interior of the car with the engine running, watching the blurred grey shapes of couples clutching each other, leaving the hall and disappearing into the gloom almost immediately.

The fog had come down so thick that Dabber had to drive slowly with the window wound down so that he could follow the white line. The fog swirled around the car and the white line disappeared.

"Open your window," he said to Melody, "and see if you can see how far I am off the kerb."

She wound down her window and put her head out. "It's bloody cold out there," she complained. She pulled back in and closed the window.

Dabber looked in the interior mirror. Joe and Latifa were kissing on the back seat.

Going down Whiteladies Road the streetlights were like shrouded sentinels silently monitoring the progress of the car as it crawled along in their weak and glimmering phosphorescence.

Dabber said, "Open the window again, quick."

"Not again," grumbled Melody.

She wound down the window nevertheless and immediately the pounding and thrashing of a mighty diesel engine was heard, and out of the fog loomed a bus with its cab window open and crazy hullabaloos and shrieks coming from the driver. The bus aimed right for the car and then veered off at the last moment amid exultant yells of madness from the bus driver and crazy hooting of the horn.

"That was Lepiniere," said Dabber. "He must be having one of his bad spells, poor bastard."

There was silence then, and shock at the near miss. When they had all recovered Dabber said, "That wasn't a bad night up the Glen."

"Yeah, it was good," Joe said.

Melody leaned her head tenderly against Dabber. "I wish we could have more nights like this," she said.

"No more for us two for a bit," said Dabber. "There's gonna be three of us soon, remember."

"Yes, congratulations. Melody told me in the dance hall," said Latifa. "You must invite Joe and me to come to see the baby when it arrives."

"Sure will," said Dabber.

After Dabber had dropped Melody off at her Totterdown place he got back to his own bedsitter in high spirits and sat hunched and drinking in front of the gas fire. He was leaning back and putting the bottle to his lips again when he heard a sound at the door. There came a knock, a quiet little knock, and then another.

He edged across with his back to the wall, waited and listened. There wasn't a sound. He pulled open the door fast. Mrs Racks the landlady was there, Amy, in her nightgown, with bare feet, tipping sherry from a bottle of Emva Cream down her throat.

"I just wondered…" She was swaying about. "I just wondered,

Dabber, about your little girlfriend, Melody. I haven't heard her voice for some time. I haven't seen her. Is she all right?"

"She's all right," he said.

"Oh, that's good, she's all right!" Amy exclaimed, and then she had another swig of her sherry, straight from the bottle. "Well, I'm pleased about that. I'm very pleased. It's just, I haven't heard her voice or seen her, and she hasn't been popping down the stairs to see me, like she always used to do."

"She's pregnant," Dabber said. "That's why she hasn't been about very much."

"Pregnant? Oh, that's nice. That's very nice. Oh, she's a fine young girl, she is. We get on well, me and Melody. Yes, we get on well, we do. We have many a fine talk together, we do."

While she was saying all this she somehow stepped past Dabber into the room.

"A baby? Well now, that's nice. That's really nice for both of you," she said.

"Yeah," Dabber said, looking at her.

She clutched him by the arm. "That's really nice for you, Dabber. That surely is nice. A handsome young man like you."

Dabber took a drink from his bottle, closed the door and gazed at her. Amy was sitting on the bed. She took a long pull of sherry, lay back on the bed and rolled onto her side, gazing at Dabber. She pulled her legs up, and in a demure little movement brushed her dressing gown higher up her thighs.

Her dressing gown, partly open, revealed a well-shaped pair of legs and her firm middle-aged bosom. Her eyes were half-closed. Without looking she reached sideways and slid the sherry bottle onto the bedside cabinet. She rolled onto her back and reached up with both hands to slowly push her hair back while arching up so that her dressing gown fell fully open.

Dabber stood looking at her, then silently closed the door and walked towards the bed. He lay down beside her.

After a time she wanted another drink of sherry. He reached out in the darkness, found the bottle, passed it to her and she took a long, long draught. Dabber got up, knocked the top off another bottle of brown ale and drained three-quarters of it in one go; then he lay back down again beside his landlady. He felt utterly calm and tranquil.

And then he was slipping away into a strange, floating space. It seemed remote and vaporous, like a billowing, bliss-filled cloud, and he slipped deeper and deeper into it until he had no cares in the world anymore.

It was still dark when Dabber jerked awake. He remembered Mrs Racks and what had happened with her. He wrapped his arms round his head and lay there shaking. After a time he slowly reached his hand across in the darkness and felt the space beside him. It was empty.

The thought came to him that perhaps he had imagined Mrs Racks' visit. And the more he thought about it, the more certain he became that it had never happened. He rolled over onto his side and stared into the gloom. His eyes gradually made out a shape on the floor beside the bed. He reached out and touched it. It was an empty sherry bottle.

He lay silent and trembling in the darkness while he tried to think and to work it all out. It seemed that his brain was being stretched in all directions in the blackest of voids, terrifying beyond imagination. The room seemed to yawn into a dark and mysterious infinity. Every time he tried to think about Mrs Racks and the previous night his thoughts approached and receded, never becoming clear; they were always muzzy and cloudy. He lay in the deepest depression for a long time before he got up.

CHAPTER 34

A few days later Dabber and the elderly conductor nicknamed Hedgehog were crewing a number six bus together again. At the terminus at Filton the café was closed, the street dark and silent with not a soul moving. Dabber jumped from the cab of the bus and strolled round to the back. Hedgehog was sitting with his feet up on the seat, smoking a small cigar.

"You still like this conducting?" Dabber said.

"It's all right, mate. I'm better off without the sodding driving," Hedgehog said. "I was near a heart attack, man, with all the stress and that. No good denying it."

"You look okay now," Dabber said.

"Yeah, but I was nearly a goner, mate. In intensive care for a couple of days. They give me a lot of lectures and pills and all that stuff. I abide by most of it, but I still have a smoke now and again, and a pint. No good giving up all the pleasures of life, is it?"

They rolled gently back down the road with the lull of the evening around them. Hedgehog was fast on the bell and at the end of the shift they pulled the bus in early to hand over to the new crew. The pair went straight in the Queen's Head and sank most of their first pints of scrumpy in one go.

"Yes, it's hard work, the conducting," Hedgehog said after they had settled down. "Up and down them stairs all day. Hard work, but it keeps me fit and it's better than being stuck up in that cab all day with all the stress and stuff." He took a long, contemplative pull on his cigar and then continued, "You're young now, kid, you got it all to find out – how being up in that cab all day can give you a pot belly, shot nerves and a heart attack. Don't make the same mistake I made."

The only other customers in the pub were the two ragged old men who had shaken their heads sadly as they viewed Dabber and Greasy staggering along with their two girls a few weeks before. The old men were silently clutching their pints of scrumpy and gazing at nothing with rheumy, hope-abandoned eyes. Their battered tobacco tins were on the rough wooden table in front of them.

Hedgehog settled back comfortably. He patted his stomach. "Yes, up and down those stairs all day. I'll soon get rid of this belly."

"Still knocking the overtime in?" Dabber enquired.

"Overtime?" Hedgehog said. "Mug's game, mate. I was barmy, the way I used to carry on: grabbing overtime, hammering around like a maniac and getting all worked up about everything. Know why they gave me the nickname 'Hedgehog'? I was getting all worked up and prickly about everything. Stressed up all the bloody time. It's taken thirty years and a big pain in the chest to open my eyes to it all."

There was no music in that pub, no jukebox, no one-armed bandit, no pinball machine, no jollity. There was no noise save the shuffling and occasional mutterings and coughing of the old men and the clink of glasses on the wooden tables. Mrs Higgerty, the landlady, tolerated no fiddle-faffing around from any of the half-pissed knick-knacks who came through her door.

One of the ragged fellows went up to the counter and the other one looked around with squinty eyes.

The one at the counter muttered, "Pint of rough, missus."

Mrs Higgerty did not move.

The old fellow searched in every pocket of his torn and ancient overcoat and found some coins. The landlady examined them suspiciously and silently as they lay on the counter. Then she glared at the customer, who looked away and looked at the floor and then looked back at her. When Mrs Higgerty had completed her silent scrutiny of him she took the money. As she pulled on the pump she examined the ragged customer again, glared at his companion and scowled in the direction of the two busmen. No customer remained unobserved for long in Mrs Higgerty's establishment.

Hedgehog sat back comfortably. "You're a young bloke," he remarked to Dabber. "Don't make the mistake I made. I came on the job when I was about your age, mate. I just wanted to grab as much money as I could. I thought that overtime was what it was all about. But it wasn't doing me any good, man. I was getting in a right old state. I was looking at the passengers as enemies, them ringing the bell and being slow to get on and off. It drove me barmy."

He blew some smoke out and glanced around, then he continued, "Overtime is the curse of the working man, mate. The working man is forced to grab overtime because we don't get enough wages in the first place. In the end, though, overtime is a dead weight. It drags a bloke down and then after years of it, his health starts to go. He gets bitter and unsociable and his home life ends up a mess." He leaned back, smoking happily. "Yeah," he mused, "this job can send you barmy if you don't watch out. Many a man has cracked up on this job."

He paused and glanced at Mrs Higgerty. "Look at that cow," he said.

Mrs Higgerty had fixed her eyes on the two old men.

"What?" said Dabber.

"Look how scornful she's looking at them two."

"Yeah, like she's got contempt for them," said Dabber.

The old men, with their stubbles of beards and watery eyes, wheezed, clutched thin cigarettes and huddled in their ragged clothing.

"Blokes like that is lonely, lonely in their hearts," said Hedgehog.

"She should respect them," Dabber said. "They're customers. They ain't causing any trouble and their money's as good as anyone else's."

"Yeah, blokes like them probably had hard lives," Hedgehog said. "Now life's got on top of them. They've probably been kicked in the bollocks so many times they've lost count. In their brains is all the stuff from forty, maybe fifty years – all the times they been treated like crap and pissed on. Maybe they had the hell knocked out of 'em when they were little, maybe brought up by all kinds of nasty bastards. Now they're probably living rough – no effing hope."

"Yeah, and after all, they're still human beings," said Dabber. "They deserve to be treated with respect."

Mrs Higgerty was still staring at the two old men.

"They'll probably add that cow to all the bastards that have messed them about in the past," said Hedgehog. "Deep down they probably don't want to be reminded of the past, but it keeps clawing at their brains. They probably want to forget, but they can't help thinking about it, they can't blot it out."

"I expect alcohol helps them," said Dabber.

"Yeah, alcohol is their solace. It gives them a way to escape."

There was silence in the pub for several minutes and then Dabber got up. "I think I'll buy those two another pint each," he said, and he went up to the bar.

CHAPTER 35

It was the evening of the 'togetherness' party. The yellow streetlights of old Clifton flickered and slow-moving headlights of cars thrust thin streams of light through the flopping, wet leaves, and far up above, lonely stars slid silently.

Along the pavement came the busmen and women pushing through the streets, attracted by the idea of a free booze-up and a bit of grub, and wondering if there was any catch to it as they glanced here and there and trod suspiciously through the cold and wet to the venue.

Yes, some of them trod the streets warily, for the suburb of Clifton, on the edge of the great gorge of the River Avon, high up above the rest of the city, still tried to think of itself as a posh area where only the elite were welcome and the common man had no place. One or two of the busmen had had a jar or two already and as they stumbled and staggered along their eyes swivelled constantly from side to side, here and there, forwards, backwards, this way and that, for you never knew if some bigoted old blimp, screaming abuse, was going to spring out, grab you by the throat, dish out a beating and kick you back down Park Street.

Yes, this was a posh area and anything could happen to a pleb, or so their fevered imaginations told them. The only busman living up here was Dabber, and he only earned a measly ten quid a week and lived in a cheap cold-water bedsitter.

However, Rulebook had chosen the venue and Rulebook doubtless knew what he was doing, for he had never been known to get anything wrong, and on that evening bus workers, mostly white men and women, but also one or two Indians, some Pakistanis and some joyous-faced

West Indians, tremulously trod the quiet and gracious streets and into a tree-lined Georgian terrace. But here at last was the venue.

As they arrived some of the busmen paused outside and gazed up at the magnificence of the ancient building. Abdul, a big Indian driver, grave and turbaned, tipped back his head and drank deep from his bottle of Indian beer and wondered again if they had the right place, but Rulebook was there in the doorway ushering them in, and hell's bells, if Rulebook said it was the right place, it must be.

Rulebook was standing there on the door, dressed in his full conductor's uniform, all neatly pressed, his hands and nails clean, his face shining, drawn up like a guardsman on parade.

"*Bonsoir, messieurs et mesdames.* Your names, *s'il vous plaît,*" he said, holding the door open as Dabber and Greasy and Abdul and Old Sam and Diamond Lil and other assorted bus workers approached.

"You're heading for a smack round the head if you comes much more of that stuff," said Diamond Lil.

"Ah, yes, I recognise you now, madam," said Rulebook hastily. "And you, sirs," he added. "I recognise you also. Can't take any chances. Villains and rogues prowl these streets. The party is in this ancient and majestic building, personally chosen by myself, *messieurs et mesdames,* but before you enter, may I beseech you to glance up at the magnificent architecture of this building: observe the majestic Grecian balconies, marvel at the pedimented lattice panels, the unique cobweb spandrels and the imposing arrow braces."

"Shut your gibberish, Rulebook," said Diamond Lil. "Just tell us where the sodding alcohol is."

"Ah yes, straight up the stairs ahead of you, *messieurs et mesdames,*" replied Rulebook hastily, bowing low and gesturing them in.

And as the bus workers trod the scruffy scrap of carpet on the stairs they saw it was all a sham, this posh Clifton with all its la-de-dah stuff. The magnificent exterior they had all gaped at was a façade, for inside the ceilings were discoloured, the walls cracked, the carpets worn and the whole place had an air of neglect.

"Take care, sirs," shouted Rulebook after them. "Rented for one night only, the upper floor. Owner away. Responsibility ours. Everyone to have a good time, nevertheless not forgetting that we are representatives of a respectable and honourable organisation, the Bristol Omnibus Company."

And then out of a door on the ground floor popped the head of a posh, pot-bellied character, *Times* newspaper in hand. His spectacles hung from around his neck by a little chain, and his semi-bald head gleamed with perspiration as he gazed after the group going up the stairs.

He immediately hurried back inside and said to his wife, "Felicity, there are common people – common people in the house!"

And wifey responded, "It really is too bad. If they make the slightest noise, you must tell them, Harold, really, you must."

Upstairs in a dismal room were about twenty chairs and a table laden with bottles of beer, and there was a great whoop from the busmen and women when they saw the layout. But as they rushed forward Rulebook leaped ahead of them and halted them with his arms spread out just short of the beer. And then, as everyone was wondering what was going on, Rulebook hopped up on a chair and launched into a speech.

"Ladies and gentlemen," he called, as if his audience were a hundred yards away instead of just two yards. "Ladies and gentlemen, we are here tonight to have a good drink, a good drink, certainly, but what we are really here for tonight is to welcome our West Indian and Asian friends who have joined us in recent days and months to man the buses in this famous old city of Bristol.

"We must remember that our brave immigrant friends who work so hard and so tirelessly, must nevertheless feel many times that their poor hearts are nigh to bursting with grief and untold sorrow, alas, at thinking of their loved ones so far away across the oceans.

"As they neared this great land of ours, did our dear friends with tearful eyes..." Rulebook paused, and seemed to sob and wipe a tear from his eye. "Did our dear friends, with tearful eyes, glimpse the shores of this, their mother country, with hearts filled with hope, or did cold eyes regard them with cunning hostility, alas and alack? Sadly, my friends, it was often the cold eye and the cunning hostility which greeted them. And did the hearts of our dear immigrant friends fall, when they saw 'No blacks, No coloureds', and heard, 'Get back where you came from, go home, we don't want you here'?"

And then Rulebook went into a great spate of moaning and groaning and swaying about with pretended grief, and the men and women watching him were too amazed at his performance to say anything or to shout any ribaldry.

But Rulebook soon roused himself and took off with his speech again. "Our poor Asian and Caribbean brothers, arriving here on our shores, feeling all friendless and forsaken by the world, alas." And then Rulebook fell to moaning and groaning again and clutching his head as if he had the most bastard of all headaches, before he went on, "Were our dear black and Asian friends, our cousins, our comrades, turned away even by our very own employers, the Bristol Omnibus Company, alas and alack? Yes, indeed, our dear immigrant friends must often have wandered the mean streets of our city homeless and friendless, turned away nigh everywhere for jobs and lodgings—"

"'Ow much longer, Rulebook? 'Ow much longer you going to rabbit on?" somebody shouted. "We've 'ad enough alacks and alases – what we want now is to get at the beer on that table."

But Rulebook, ignoring the interruption, went on. "After their long and arduous journeys across the seas, were they shamefacedly turned away? Were there no vacancies wherever they turned? Were they victims of cruel deceit and cunning duplicity? Yes, indeed they were, alas. But thankfully all is now changed, all is now forgiven. We welcome them here now, our dear brothers, with all our hearts. We have received and revitalised their worn-out spirits, mended their broken hearts. We are strangers no more to each other and—"

"Give over, Rulebook, shut up," men started shouting. "Them blacks and Asians suffered heartbreak, we all know. We all got sympathy with 'em, but it's breaking our 'earts seeing all that booze there on that table and you blocking the way."

And then a West Indian man stood up and called, "Yes, that is right, man. We don't want to be reminded of all that stuff now. We want to forget all that stuff for tonight. White man has suffering too. Everyone has suffering. We have been welcomed here. We are all brothers here. Let us just drink and forget and be happy for this one night at least."

Rulebook then, sizing up the situation fast with his usual acumen, hastily finished with, "Yes, yes indeed. That is the very point I was coming to. That is the crux of the—"

But then there was such a great rush of busmen and women that Rulebook was swept aside, and there were whoops and yells as Greasy, Dabber, Barhanger, Poody, Lepiniere, Diamond Lil and other white crews rushed for the bottles, but there was a more sedate approach by the Indian, Pakistani and West Indian busmen, for they preferred a more statesmanlike and unhurried approach.

And there were old busmen there already, with big bellies from countless years sitting behind the wheel and know-all fat faces and big meaty hands clutching bottles, and the old geezers' bald heads were nodding and they were saying, "Yeah, them old days, they was the best. I remember on the trams, yeah, them was the days, much better'n now – these young 'uns don't know what it's all about, don't know they is born."

"What's happened to the music?" somebody shouted. "Ain't there no music?"

And Solomon, a jovial West Indian driver with a big round belly, was saying, "I hope there is food tonight, man. I dream of spicy chicken, vegetable kebabs and big juicy prawns to remind me of home."

"And dancing," said Marti, a West Indian conductress. "We got to have dancing. I just want to dance with a handsome man and forget all de troubles we had since we got here."

Everyone was gazing round and wondering what was going to happen next, and then up popped Rulebook and shouted, "Ladies and gentlemen!" He raised his hand and waited for silence before he began again. "Ladies and gentlemen, it is indeed good to see such a marvellous gathering here. Now some of you may have thought of me in the past as a rather staid person, a stickler for the rules, a man who does not know how to relax and who frowns disapprovingly towards any untoward activity. You may have thought of me as miserable and boring—"

"That's because you are a miserable and boring bugger," somebody shouted.

Rulebook held up his hand again. "What I want to say is yes, I know that some of you have an adverse opinion of me and to a certain extent I do not quibble with that, no, indeed, I do not quibble for we are all different, are we not, but in the end we are all the same, and what I want to say is—"

"Where's the music?" someone shouted.

"Yeah, where's the sodding music?" came another shout. "Whoever 'eard of a party with no music? And what you want to drag us all the way up here to this posh area for? We'd 'ave been a lot more comfy in one of them boozers down Old Market or the Centre."

"Ah, now indeed we get to the crux of the matter," went on Rulebook. "This area, Clifton, has for too long thought of itself as an elite suburb, a wealthy, snobbish place where working men and women such as ourselves are not welcome. I have heard it said that poor people would never have a right to walk the streets here."

Rulebook paused and then, when he saw that he had everyone's quiet attention, he continued. "There is absolutely no reason why these tree-lined streets, the gardens, the sanctuaries of peace and calm to be found in the quiet squares should be reserved for one class only – for the moneyed classes who attempt to lord it over those they consider their inferiors." He paused again and then shot his arm into the air and shouted, "And that is another reason why we are here this evening – to strike a blow for humanity and equality, to blow a few breaths of fresh air into this outdated Victorian pomposity.

"And the band will be arriving at any moment for your entertainment, *messieurs et mesdames*. In the meantime, please feel free to avail yourselves of a little more alcoholic beverage if you so wish."

As he finished speaking a great cheer went up and there was another rush for the beer. In their haste most of the men failed to notice a quartet of men and women, dressed in loose-fitting Indian clothing and carrying musical cases, entering and setting up their equipment, and then Rulebook was announcing, "Ladies and gentlemen, we have managed to obtain, for one hour only, some friends from the East, who are going to entertain us with their musical acumen."

And then the foursome began to play: sitar and tabla, violin and cello, and the assembled bus workers were stunned into silence by the beauty of this strange, exotic music.

The players began to chant then, soft, mantric chants and sacred tunes which soothed the listeners and filled them with haunting beauty and soulful expression.

"God, that's marvellous," breathed Greasy. "I never knew them Indians 'ad music like that."

"Yes," whispered Rulebook, "there is nothing like music, my friends, for building bridges and promoting friendship. We may be from different lands and have different cultures, but we are all human beings, are we not? We are all part of the great community of different peoples who have come together—"

"Shut the hell up," hissed Greasy. "I want to listen to the music."

The big Indian driver, Abdul, was weeping openly. "Ah, my friends, you must forgive me," he sobbed between his tears. "When I hear the sitar I am so sad. It reminds me of…I do not know exactly. What does it remind me of? I cannot think, but I know it is something which makes me extremely sad. Perhaps it is the memory of my dear wife Selvi whom I left behind and have not seen for three years now." He paused and wiped a tear from his eye with the corner of a large colourful handkerchief. "I cannot speak how much I miss her. How do I survive a single hour, a single minute, without my beloved Selvi?" He took a long drink and nibbled on an Indian delicacy. "Yes, for three years now I have not seen her beautiful face, I have not heard her sweet voice. How I long to have her in my arms again and to feel the caress of her tender lips. Oh, it is unbearable." He tilted his bottle up and took another long draught. He paused and looked thoughtful. "I think I will stay in this country five years more," he said.

And just when the whole room was most entranced by the music the hour was up, and the quartet stopped playing and began to pack away their instruments.

"I must thank you on behalf of the assemblage," Rulebook told them. "Your music was a most uplifting experience. I only wish that our funds could have enabled you to play for a little longer."

The quartet came over and sat talking to Abdul and an Indian conductor, and what a joyful babble and wild laughter took place between them all. No one knew what they were talking about, but it sure was a happy conversation and most of the other busmen reckoned that Abdul was probably telling them all about his dear wife, whom he missed so much.

But the drinkers were getting impatient, drinking, looking round and shouting, "Where's the rest of the entertainment?"

Then Lepiniere lumbered up from his seat and stumbled around at the front of the room while doing strange things with his foot. He had a bottle in one hand, taking swigs from it every now and again. His other hand was against the wall for balance, but everyone was fascinated by his right foot, which was contorting this way and that. His foot was dragging an upturned beer crate about until eventually he got it into the position he wanted and, still holding the wall with one hand and clutching the bottle with the other, he got up precariously onto the crate and began to sing. He sang a slow, sad ballad full of raw feeling and heartbreaking emotion.

The busmen and women sat spellbound and gobsmacked at the unexpected beauty of his voice, and someone murmured, "Eff me, Lepiniere can sing." And then Lepiniere wobbled about dangerously on his box and stumbled and fell into a seat, still clutching his bottle.

Everyone was shouting, "Give us more, Leppy, give us some more," but Lepiniere was just sitting there blankly, staring at nothing until someone rushed up, took the empty bottle from his hand and stuck a full one into it. Lepiniere gazed at the new bottle in wonder and immediately took a mighty swig from it.

Blokes started pulling him and pushing him and saying, "Come on, Lep, give us another song, man."

And Diamond Lil left off from snogging Old Sam for a second and shouted, "Yeah, come on, Leppy. That was a beautiful song what you sang. Don't stop now."

And then Lepiniere was on his feet again, only just, wobbling about and all disorientated, but they shoved him up to the beer crate again and supported him as he got up onto it. He blinked, opened his eyes wide and gazed around as if he'd never seen the room or any of the people in it before. He looked panic-stricken, but when he saw the bottle was still there in his left hand he was reassured, took a long pull and gazed around with wondering eyes once more.

He started to sing; another ballad, soft and gentle, but full of great, searing lamentations, and once again the assembled busmen and women were hushed into a reverent silence under the spellbinding quality of Lepiniere's voice. He sang a bleak tale of agony and loneliness and madness which laid his soul so bare that the listeners almost beat their heads at the thought of what he must have encountered on his sad journey through life. But no one would ask him, for on the buses you did not ask after a man's background, you did not try to reach into his soul, but everyone there, when they heard that song, knew that Lepiniere was lost, and that he himself knew that he was lost, and the sound was enough to rip anyone's heart to shreds.

And then in the midst of the profound and respectful silence as he sang, the doorbell rang as some latecomers arrived, and as soon as he heard the ring, Lepiniere let out a great wail – "Aaaaghh!" – and the men around fought to steady him and keep him on the beer crate. Everyone was urging him to keep singing, but when he tried to pick up his song from where he had left off, his voice was an awful, tortured sound, and then the doorbell rang again and Lepiniere was on the floor, clutching his bottle and screaming, "They're 'ere, the bastards, the passengers. They've followed me with their bastard bells." And he drained his bottle fast with one huge, desperate swallow and glared around with bulging eyes.

People stood gazing at him. Someone muttered, "'E might be a nutter, but I tell you what, he's a hell of a singer, ain't he?"

All at once Rulebook strode forward brandishing a key and announced, "Ladies and gentlemen…" With an air of great importance he unlocked a side door and gestured inside at a long table on which were plates of sandwiches. There was a rush, everyone waving bottles and drinking and crowding into the room to see what was on offer.

"Ham sandwiches, my favourite!" somebody exclaimed.

"They're all sodding ham," grumbled Barhanger.

"Surely this is not true," said Smiler, the Pakistani conductor, peering into sandwiches with a look approaching horror on his usually smiling face. "I am afraid, then, that I cannot eat. If it is pig, I cannot eat."

"Just get it down you, it won't kill you," shouted Diamond Lil. "Nothing like a bit of ham, although I'd 'ave preferred a few nice rashers of lovely crispy bacon instead."

"It is pig. Dead pig is in sandwiches. It is unclean," said Smiler, struggling vainly to resume his normal cheery countenance.

"Oh my goodness, yes, yes, of course. This is my fault, my fault entirely. I do apologise," said Rulebook.

"I cannot eat these sandwiches," said Smiler. "They have the flesh of swine. It is forbidden by our glorious Qur'an."

Rulebook stood up and held his hands up again. "Oh, *frères humains*, dear friends, I am afraid I have made a grave miscalculation. I have omitted to cater in a correct manner for our Pakistani friends. I should indeed have ordered a greater variety of foodstuffs and for that omission I do most sincerely apologise."

"It is unacceptable," Smiler cried. "It is *haram*."

"You're in England now, you foreign lot," shouted Diamond Lil. "We've welcomed you 'ere. Get some good English grub down you and stop moaning."

Everyone stopped eating and drinking and talking. The Pakistanis and Indians and West Indians glanced at each other, and then everyone stared at Diamond Lil. Blokes put down their pints and waited.

But after a threatening silence, during which nobody moved, Smiler said quietly, "My friends, there is no problem. It is a mistake, a genuine mistake. I do not wish to cause upset with my English friends. We are indeed all brothers here. I am not really hungry..."

But immediately Rulebook jumped up and said, "No, no, no, Smiler, my friend, you must not apologise for what was a mistake, a dreadful mistake on my part. You have been a good and amiable workmate and friend to all of us. Sit down and make yourself comfortable and I will go for fish and chips for you. It is the least I can do."

"Please do not bother, my friend," replied Smiler. "Every person on the buses has been very friendly to me. Never once have I felt unwanted. Never would I wish to seem ungrateful. The matter of the sandwiches is already forgotten."

But Rulebook was already going out of the door for the fish and chips and at that the party was on again. Blokes were grabbing more beer and plates of sandwiches and hurrying back to their seats.

"What about you, Abdul, and your Indian mate?" enquired Greasy. "Can the pair of you eat ham?"

"I am a Sikh," announced Abdul, drawing himself up proudly and adjusting the turban on his head. "For me the cow is revered. About the pig I give little thought. Nevertheless, I would have preferred it, Rulebook, my friend, if there had been some biryani, some delicious special biryani. Yes, chicken and lamb tikka, king prawn with nice omelette. That would have greatly pleased me and my fellow Indian friend."

Everyone was gaping at him, and then Abdul added, "Yes, we are indeed guests here. I do not normally drink alcohol but tonight, you will observe, I have been drinking. We are all together now in this country and must respect each other's customs. Tonight, I think we are all brothers and – what the hell – give me another bottle." And he too grabbed another bottle from the table.

And Jermaine, with a faraway look in his eyes, said, "Every day, every night, I dream of ackee and saltfish, I dream of jerk chicken nicely cooked and served to me by a pretty young lady. Ah, yes, that is what I yearn for."

And then music filled the room and everyone stared, for there on the piano stool, playing like an expert, was a young West Indian, who was now a conductor. Who would have guessed that this new busman had such a great talent?

The young pianist played with speed and energy, swaying this way and that, his fingers flying over the keys, hitting out one of the most popular tunes of the day, and Rulebook shouted, "Yes, yes, music, it is good. It cuts through all the differences. When we listen to music, we are all equal, we are all the same."

"Shut the hell up, Rulebook," shouted Diamond Lil. "No more speeches. Clear the floor. Me an' my Sam 'ere, we're going to have a dance." And she dragged Sam to his feet.

He was still clutching a bottle and protesting, "But I don't wanna dance. I just wants to sit and drink."

But Lil was clutching him tightly as she danced and was whispering into his ear how much she loved him and other sweet things, but Old Sam had served right through the Second World War and had seen men lose limbs and eyes and bits of brains. He knew he was being served a bit of ropey love and was not fooled by any of it. He just wished that he could sit back down again and quietly enjoy his beer, but Diamond Lil had him in a smoochy, romantic hug and had no intention of letting him loose while any of the other man-eating women were prowling round.

And then up bopped Marti, the West Indian conductress. She grabbed a driver and had him on his feet and waltzing round the floor in no time.

There were only a few women there, but most of them were conductresses. Every day they had to deal with the dregs and dross of human society on their buses and they were not frightened of anybody. Most of the men, when they saw the women pacing the floor, were trying to shrink back and hide themselves, but the women weren't having that. They prowled round, grabbing men at random and yanking them onto the floor.

Smiler was sitting quietly at the side, happily eating his fish and chips. Dion and Jermaine were just gazing with wide eyes at the dancers, and then a brassy blonde conductress with a figure like a sack of turnips grabbed Dion, clutched him tight and screamed, "Oh my God, this is what I've always wanted, this is what I've dreamed of – to have a big handsome black man in my arms," and then she was running her hands all over his body. "Kiss me, kiss me," she breathed, turning her face up to him. "Oh, dear God, how strong you are, what big muscles," she cried, pinioning him in a tight embrace. She pushed him down into a chair and fell on top of him. "You gorgeous, gorgeous man. Oh, let me get my fill of you."

She was running her hands all over his body and trying to unbutton his shirt, and Dion screamed, "This is it, man, this what I come to old England for – to meet beautiful English rose. Why she take so long to find me? This is de life I been dreaming of." And then the brassy blonde conductress was smacking big kisses onto his mouth and trying to get her hand down his trousers.

Jermaine was gazing, amazed, at his compatriot, and then he just chortled, turned away and helped himself to another bottle of beer from the table.

But there was someone whom no one disturbed. Who was it, tucked away in that dark corner? Why, it was none other than Amaryllis. She had shed her 'warrior woman' appearance and was looking seductive and beautiful in a clinging blouse which accentuated her delicate curves. Her skirt was split to the thigh to show off her gorgeous nylon-clad legs. Yes, for this important occasion Amaryllis had joined the busmen and women, and especially the Caribbean and Asian recruits on whose behalf she strode so stridently at the head of several marches.

And who was Amaryllis cuddling and kissing in her dark corner? It was none other than Zorbo, her faithful campaigning lieutenant. The two were whispering sweet nothings to each other and their lips were in almost continuous loving contact. Amaryllis was discovering that clinging close to Zorbo, feeling his warm body and receiving his tender kisses, was infinitely more satisfying than being in some of those lectures back at the uni. Zorbo, on the other hand, was amazed at how easily, in the last few weeks, he had crumbled and capitulated so eagerly to the heady charms of Amaryllis. He felt sure now that he had discovered, in his love for her, a new passion, a new cause which was far more satisfying than all the various causes that had in the past beguiled him.

Amaryllis and Zorbo were guests of honour at the bus crews' party. They had a constant supply of drinks brought to them and had heard whispers that in all probability they would never have to pay for meals again in any West Indian or Asian restaurant in the city. And on any bus with an Asian or West Indian crew, the ride would be free.

Tucked away in another corner, quietly enjoying the evening and engrossed in each other's company, were Dabber and Melody. On Melody's finger gleamed an engagement ring and beside them in a pushchair, fast asleep, without a care in the world and no doubt dreaming sweet baby dreams, was a little boy, barely a month old. A short distance away, their special guests, Joe and Latifa, were also quietly and happily drinking and gazing around in wonder at the assortment of guests from across the world.

Amos was there, quietly sipping a bottle of strong West Indian beer and feeling so happy that white people and black people were now mixing so well together.

Only Cyril – the young, boastful driver who had had the accident where the little girl was killed – looked unhappy. He was crouching alone on the floor in a corner, drunk, minus his red driver's badge. He now only had a green conductor's badge in his lapel.

The piano player, meanwhile, was now jazzing it up, hitting the keys like a wild thing, his fingers flying over the keyboard, and then his face for some reason started to look perplexed as he tried a torrent of syncopation. He looked increasingly exasperated as he switched from one tune to another while the dancers whirled faster and faster and wondered what on earth was going on.

Diamond Lil had Sam in a clinch and was dragging him round, thrusting her considerable bosom against him and pulling his head down so that his face was stuck in her cleavage. He was stumbling about without a clue which part of the room he was in. And then all of a sudden the notes flying out of the piano were hurtling about as if they too had been hitting the booze. The notes staggered and stumbled out of the piano, wobbled about, bounced around the room, crashed into people, hit the walls, ricocheted off and shattered into pieces.

The music stopped. The piano player swivelled round on his piano stool and declared, "This piano, it is no use."

"What's up with it?" someone shouted.

"I am afraid that this piano is not of the quality I am used to. I hit a note and another note flies out. The graduations of pitch are uneven. When I try to syncopate rhythm in the melody it is hopeless. I am very much afraid that I cannot continue."

"The pianner sounded all right to me, mate," Greasy shouted. "When you syncopated that whatsit, I didn't notice nothing wrong."

"No, it is out of the question that I continue," the young West Indian said. "I absolutely refuse to have my talents debased by this monstrosity. It is beneath my dignity to persevere with such an abomination." And he stalked over to the far side of the room, turned his back on the gathering and sat drinking gloomily.

"Well, now we're knackered," someone said. "No music."

And Rulebook said, "Yes, no music. But my sympathies are entirely with the pianist. I too am a piano player of some renown and as soon as he commenced to play I recognised that something was not right. What are we to do? There is nothing like music, my friends, for building bridges and promoting friendship, and here we are without any."

There was a long silence while everyone drank furiously and tried to think, and then Barhanger shouted, "I sees a geezer in a pub once, he played the spoons. Two spoons 'e had in each hand and clattered and clacked them together brilliant. Where's the kitchen in this place? We'll soon have a bit of music going."

Before anyone could say 'booze-up' Barhanger had a pair of spoons and was prancing around rapping them together fast. Greasy grabbed a washboard and was sliding the back of an old scrubbing brush up and down it. The pianist had regained his good mood and was belting a tune out of an upturned soup pan with a meat tenderiser. Someone had two frying pans and was banging them together with almighty clashes. Abdul had a metal washing-up bowl upside down on his knees and was hammering out a rhythm with pudding spoons. Someone else had two pans, which they were hammering on the floor in a staccato tune. Amos was leaning back, clutching a drink and grinning with delight at the whole scene.

And then the whole tumultuous racket came together; deafening, but infectious and entrancing in such a way that few of those present could remain sitting down.

"Ah, yes!" Greasy screamed. "Music! It is the greatest thing!"

The women were singing in shrill voices and men were belting out discordant, raucous vocals that somehow blended and harmonised with the overall cacophony. Nobody could sit still with that racket going on. A few dancers were still careering madly around and it was dangerous to get in the way of any of them for fear of being sent staggering.

"Yes, yes!" screamed Abdul. "We all together now. We make the music together and sing, black and white together. We all brothers now, and sisters. Everyone the same. It make no difference."

And in the midst of all the amazing brotherly and sisterly scenes came a loud and angry hammering at the door, and everyone stopped and stared and then the door banged open and the posh bloke from downstairs was saying, "Really. It really is too much, this noise. Really, it is."

A big West Indian driver went over and said, "Go away, man. We enjoy ourselves. Can't you see? We not all stuffy and miserable like you rich whitey people."

"I really must ask you to desist from your unbearable cacophony," said the man, "and I insist that you leave the premises altogether, you and all your abominable friends."

Then Rulebook stepped forward with all the dignity and gravity he could muster as the organiser of the party and said, "I am very much afraid, my good man, that we have hired this room for the duration of the evening and we have every right to indulge ourselves with a little music. If you do not like it, then may I suggest that you take your petty objections elsewhere?"

"Yes, clear off before I smacks you round the 'ead," shouted Diamond Lil.

And everyone in the room – conductors and drivers, men and women, white and black – was shouting, "Yes, yes, clear off, you old fogey. We are all together here. We have paid the money for the room. We are having a good time. Clear off, clear off."

The posh bloke went red in the face and stuttered and stammered and looked on the verge of a heart attack, but he knew he was beaten. He turned and went back down the stairs with the great laughter of everyone at the party following him.

But Rulebook was considerate, and a stickler for fair play. He held up his hands for silence and announced, "Perhaps, after all, it is time to end the party. We have all had a good time. We are friends now, all together. The beer is finished. The sandwiches are gone. It is late, very late. Let us make a move."

Everyone threw their musical utensils down, grabbed their belongings and started to pile down the stairs in one big hurry. The posh geezer was standing at his door going, "Absolutely unacceptable. Working-class rabble."

But by then the busmen and women were rolling and shouting

on the dark, watchful street: the young drivers and conductors, white and black, whooping and yelling, jumping around, wrestling with each other in mad, beery fun and the whole night throbbing and pulsating with joy and vitality.

The older drivers had all had a bellyful also, but they were staid and scornful. "These young 'uns, they can't handle it. A couple of bottles and they're rolling around stupid."

Diamond Lil was still clutching Old Sam tightly, and Sam was moaning, "Oh, oh, I think I've dislocated something."

She cuddled him tenderly and said, "Don't be silly, Sam. If your body is sore I'll give you a lovely massage tonight." And she fastened her gaudy red lips onto his mouth in a huge, sucking kiss.

"But I just wants to go home," complained Sam, but Diamond Lil just pulled him tighter to her and said, "You ain't going nowhere, Sam, you naughty, naughty man. You're coming home with little me." And she pulled his head down and glued another big squelching kiss onto his mouth.

Sam protested, "I just wants to sleep," but she tightened her grip on him and said, "No, first we got to go bonky-bonky-bonky, you and me, lover boy."

Old Sam moaned, "I don't want to go bonky-bonky-bonky," but Diamond Lil, sizzling with lust, said, "You'll like it, Sam, you really will, you little sexy devil, you."

Greasy quit jumping around, threw his head back and shouted up into the deep, continuous reaches of cold infinity, "Whoa, whoa, man. What a night. We stick together, us busmen. Black and white. We all stick together. Whey-hey."

And Abdul also turned his brown face to the huge dark sky, punched the air and screamed, "Yes, yes, what a night! The mystery unfolds. The eighth chakra of the sacred universe: it is here. It enfolds us now in the great collective universe of mankind."

Greasy stopped dead, stared at him and said, "What the eff you on about, Abdul? You've had a bit too much of that Indian beer, mate."

Abdul placed his arm around Greasy, hugged him like a brother and screamed, "Yes, yes, we need more beer! More beer will transport us beyond the new dimensions of brotherhood which we have this night discovered." He turned his turbaned head up again, spread his arms wide and yelled, "Thank you, oh master of the huge, wide emptiness of the sky. I feel a tremendous bursting and explosion of joy within me, and within all us busmen of the world here tonight."

Trailing along behind them like a neglected toddler was Lepiniere with his paranoia-raddled brain, stumbling and wailing and drinking from a bottle, trying to keep up with the rest of the busmen.

"The noise he's making, you'd think he was going into hell," Barhanger said. "You'd think the devils were prodding him with their pitchforks to get 'im inside."

"If that's what it is, he sure looks like he don't want to go," somebody else said.

And then everyone forgot about Lepiniere and was shouting, jumping about and embracing each other.

Greasy grabbed a passing pompous, pot-bellied citizen by the arms and waltzed around with him, singing, "Frolic, frolic, oh, how we love to frolic."

The pompous old geezer tried to whack Greasy with his walking stick and blustered, "Damn working-class rabble."

The other posh citizens passing by pretended not to notice in case they themselves were grabbed; they just stood silent and disapproving as they gazed after the crazy, rolling busmen.

CHAPTER 36

The black and Asian workers settled in well, and after a few misunderstandings were well accepted by the white workers. After a time it was as if ethnic drivers and conductors had always been there. They learned the busmen's lingo and how to work the little flankers that made the job a bit more enjoyable: they ran late, ran sharp, dipped a few times, faced the usual complaints from passengers, but for the most part did the job conscientiously and were proud to provide good livings for themselves and their families.

But slowly and surely the job was changing, and one day Greasy came into the Spring Chicken, where a small group of busmen and women were drinking tea. There was a long pause while he gazed around as if he didn't know what to say, and then he said, "I'm packing the job in. I've had enough."

"Packing it in?" Dabber exclaimed. "What for?"

"The job's finished, mate," Greasy went on. "It ain't the same. They're bringing in buses with doors on, so there'll be no hanging off the back whistling at the birds. There's even going to be buses with no conductors whatsoever, just a driver. And the Hart is closing down – going to be demolished to make way for an underpass and escalators, and God knows what. And 'ave you heard about the breath tests that's coming, mate? They're going to be able to test our breath – see if we've been drinking. We won't even be able to have a bevvy on the job in the future." He paused. "The whole situation is finished, mate, up the creek. Everybody's going barmy. Lepiniere's in a nuthouse."

"Yeah, well, he had problems, poor bastard, didn't he? Hopefully he'll get a bit of treatment in there," said Dabber.

"Ratso and Skully have left, just cleared off – said they weren't going to work with black staff," said Greasy.

"Yeah, well, good riddance – nobody'll miss those two idiots," said Dabber.

"Diamond Lil's in the clink," Greasy went on. "A copper asked her to mind her language, so she whacked him. Got twelve months. She's finished on this job. Old Sam's been jumping around happy as a spring lamb. Luella's pissed off, shacking up with a wealthy bastard – good luck to him. Everything else is knackered, though. The old life, forget it, mate, it's gone."

"What you gonna do when you pack it in?" Dabber said.

Greasy stood for a minute, suddenly shy, embarrassed. "I thought I would go to college, man."

"College?" somebody exclaimed. "What the hell you gonna do there?"

"I dunno," Greasy said. "Study something, learn stuff, get some kind of a decent job. It's gotta be better than being on the back of a bus trying to chat up birds."

There was a sudden sadness among the group. They stood there in the Spring Chicken, not knowing what to say to each other.

So Greasy left to better himself, but Dabber and many of his friends stayed on and the job did truly change.

But always, whatever the fortune and fates that hit and befall the people of Bristol, through every district and suburb, in all weathers, the buses run non-stop, for life goes on, and while there is life on the streets the buses must keep rolling, never stopping for long in one place, for the passengers have places to go and they don't want delay, so on they roar through the city. On each bus the driver and conductor see it all, observing everything, thinking, pondering, talking, for always the people of Bristol have an overwhelming desire to be with it; they want to dive in, to live, scream, experience everything, dig every crazy happening, rush here and there with incredible energy, not caring what the future might bring.

The crews of the buses see it all: students, down-and-outs, rich people, tourists, ambulances, fire engines, people of all colours gazing in amazement, drunks, squabbles, romances, lovemaking, traffic accidents, hold-ups, cop cars, excited faces, sad faces, lonely faces; yes, truly no one knows more about what happens on the streets of Bristol than the bus crews, for there is not one corner of the city where the buses do not run.

REFERENCES

BBC History Magazine, various articles

Black and White on the Buses: Madge Dresser

Blue Stockings (a play): Bristol Old Vic Theatre School

Bristol & Transatlantic Slavery: Bristol Museums and Art Gallery

Bristol Art Gallery 1905–1980: Karin Walton, Collections Officer, Applied Art, Bristol Museum & Art Gallery

Bristol, a Darker History: Derek Robinson, Countryside Books, 2005

Bristol: Pevsner Architectural Guides: Andrew Foyle

Memoirs of a Black Englishman: Paul Stephenson OBE and Lilleith Morrison

M-shed, Bristol Museums: various exhibitions and events

No Borders? – An Art Show: Bristol City Museum & Art Gallery

On the Road: Jack Kerouac

Presidential address to the Constituent Assembly of Pakistan, August 11 1947: Muhammad Ali Jinnah

Slave Trade Trail Around Central Bristol: Bristol Museums, Galleries and Archives.

Speech on the Granting of Indian Independence, August 14 1947: Jawaharlal Nehru.

Suffragette: Emmeline Pankhurst.

The Bristol Heritage Walk: Bristol Junior Chamber and Bristol Tourist Information Centre

The Bristol Suffragettes: Lucienne Boyce

The Building: Bristol City Museum & Art Gallery: information leaflet.

Bristol Post, various articles and readers' letters

The Watchtower: 'Prejudice and Discrimination': date uncertain.
http://discoveringbchapterristol.org.uk/browse/slavery.
Wikipedia, various articles

Lightning Source UK Ltd.
Milton Keynes UK
UKOW01f0216310317

297972UK00001B/47/P